For April, who has kindly listened to my rantings about my writing for years, and this series for the past year.

This is the origin story of Hadhira Dawson, Haddie. Events in this book happen just a short time before Book One of the AngelSong Series.

SHATTERED BLOOD

THE ORIGIN STORY FOR THE ANGELSONG SERIES

KEVIN A. DAVIS

Inkd
Publishing

SHATTERED BLOOD

PART 1

*I hope this correspondence finds you well and you do not find
my method of introduction too alarming.*

CHAPTER 1

A GROTESQUE, blackened corpse froze in a terrified pose. Charcoal fingers splayed out in a defensive posture toward the screen, framed inside a scorched car window as if pleading with the camera. White teeth shone through charred lips that pulled back across the black mouth partly open, like a scream cut dead. The background, the burned-out interior of a sedan, fuzzed out of focus.

Haddie grimaced at her monitor, her hand rising off the mouse as if she had touched the corpse. "Ugh."

She'd been scrolling through the newspaper's online images, already gruesome enough. Horrifying pictures of discarded mangled pets from an article on a dogfighting ring. Dobermans left in hillside brush outside of Eugene, a pit-bull torn open on the side of a road, and one dog so badly mutilated and decomposed that she could only guess it had been a German Shepherd. She wanted to kill someone who would do that to animals. From there, she'd mistakenly moved into another news article that involved a car fire.

Terry, her lanky friend, hunched over his laptop beside

her. He'd squeezed in at the edge of her desk. A tech major at the same school she went to, he was the only one savvy enough to help her stop the dog fights. He hadn't seen the car fire, but he looked up as she scrolled back through the dogs.

"You're obsessed — I mean — don't get me wrong, we're doing the right thing." He had light brown skin like her and straggly black hair that hung in his eyes.

Terry hadn't been the first one to mention that to her, but Haddie considered herself passionate, not obsessive. Who couldn't be, especially when it came to the brutality of dog fights? She clicked back one picture and saved another of the horrific pictures of a dog, barely recognizable as a Doberman. Her target had bought the one-year-old six weeks ago; she and Terry had tracked it down. Its tan and black markings were distinct.

If anything, Terry was right in that the timing was bad. *I don't have the time.* She had a paper due, finals were only four weeks away, and the internship took more of her life than she'd imagined. Terry had been a gem working around his tech classes, but he breezed through those.

He looked up at her with a red straw between his lips. He loved those citrus-smelling drinks from gallon-sized convenience store cups. Offering an apologetic smile, he turned back to his keyboard. "It's just that you obsess until everything else in your life falls to the side. You've got a new job and you're barely sleeping. You missed a class last night and you've got a paper due."

Haddie sat up, tugging her hair from being stuck between the chair and the base of her back. She smoothed it in her hands and absently twirled it into a black ball around her fist. "It'll be over tonight, I'd imagine."

They shared her desk, having moved some of her piles

behind her monitor or stacked on the floor with her yoga pants and sweatshirt from a few nights ago, maybe last week. After seeing the off-white laminate desktop again, she'd remembered assembling it with Dad, probably three years ago, before things had gotten weird with him. It stretched out six feet, with drawers at each end that had collected random assortments of junk over the years. She'd gotten it specifically so she could have a big enough desk that she could keep organized. Somewhere, under the piles, lay a wire mesh inbox and a black organizational tray with little cubbies.

The white takeout box hung over the back corner. As part of the deal, she'd bought dinner with Dad's card. Thai curry, not too hot.

Rock, her black pit bull with a white giraffe on his chest, had found a space at her feet, his back pressed against one of the piles of manila folders and binder-clipped papers.

Terry flipped to a bulletin board, where the same gruesome picture of a burnt body joined photos of a slightly charred gray Ford Fusion. He must have seen it on her screen. He grunted. "Back to spontaneous combustion."

Haddie raised her eyebrows. "What?"

"This charred guy in the car the other night. On the news." Terry gestured to the screen. "Supposedly no accelerant, so the board's been all about spontaneous human combustion. The big argument is some troll going on about amino acids being the cause, while the rest are going with the tried-and-true alcohol or wick theory."

"Gross." Haddie focused back on her screen. The chat where she'd posted Rock's photo as bait still had no response. Surely this scumbag didn't go to bed early.

"Yaass." Terry typed a comment. "Now we're on to

Armageddon, aliens, fallen angels, and government implants. This is awesome."

"You are strange, Terry."

"Exquisitely so."

She'd met Terry when he'd been a freshman. Haddie had been swearing at a library monitor when he'd been passing by with an armload of books. After dropping a stack of tech tomes on the desk — each as thick as any of her legal books — he got her on track with an obstinate program and out from under the glare of the librarian. They'd hit it off. He could be as irreverent as she and didn't seem intimidated by her height. Besides, he'd been willing to play a cleric at her local game. Presently, he was the group's wizard.

He'd rescheduled a date with a med student to help Haddie. She hadn't wanted him to, but he thought she might get into trouble.

Rock's chin slid onto Haddie's thigh, his dark whiskers sprayed over her red jeans. Dark eyes mooned up and blinked.

Haddie rubbed behind his black ears. "Hey, Boy. Momma's gonna kick his butt, don't worry."

Her phone chimed, and she picked it up. Dad. Again. He'd gotten insistent the past few days. She'd sent a noncommittal reply once and ignored the rest. She closed the screen. At the moment, she couldn't deal with their issues. He wouldn't explain, not everything, and she couldn't wrap her head around what she did know. She flipped the phone over.

Her monitor flickered, a message appearing in the chat.

"He bit." Her heart raced as she poised fingers over the keyboard. *Not too eager.*

She'd set up a profile in the chat room where "Maxmillian" had purchased two dogs so far; both had turned up dead from dogfighting. She had Rock posted as needing an adoption, with a story that she had to move into an apartment that wouldn't take dogs. Haddie knew she would live in her RAV4 before that happened.

"He's a purebred," she wrote. "150 firm."

Maxmillian took a few moments. Haddie turned to Terry, who had a finger wedged between his teeth but still managed a goofy smile.

Maximillian responded, "Agreed. Cash. When can we meet? Amazon Park by the dog walk."

Now for the tough part. "Tomorrow morning. I'm out of work, so I can do any time, you pick. I'm dead on empty though. You'll have to send me $10. The rest in cash."

Terry leaned back and watched her screen. He pressed his short hair back with both hands as if trying to force it into place and out of his eyes. He paused, both hands at the back of his neck and his eyes somewhat bulged as the skin pulled taut.

He bit his lip. "Still gotta warn you again, Haddie. As easily as I, or the police, can find this guy's identity with these money apps, they can find yours."

"He'll be in jail."

"This could be the mob or something."

Haddie raised her eyebrows. "Drama much?" She shook her head. "Don't worry. This is just some local scumbag. Wasn't even on the police radar until we brought it to them."

As much as she dismissed it with Terry, the thought had been disconcerting. She couldn't think of another way to get to these people. The dogfighting had to stop, and the police seemed disinterested. If their buyer flipped, perhaps the whole ring would go down.

Jisoo, her calico, called out from the kitchen.

Haddie leaned her head back. "Just 'cause I'm up doesn't mean you get fed."

Maxmillian responded. "Venmo?"

Terry whooped. "You did it, Haddie." He pointed a finger at her, thumb extended up. "Now you can get back to learning how to be a lawyer — if you haven't flunked out from all this." He gave her a friendly smirk; he'd bust her chops, but he was always there when she needed help.

After sending her information, she waited for the confirmation before she agreed to a time later in the morning when they were to meet. She'd send the detective the details, and hopefully with all the other evidence she'd sent the police would meet this creep. Her part was over — unless the police failed to shut down the ring. Then, she'd have to think of something else.

Terry started closing down his laptop. "Fun time, Buckaroo."

Her phone buzzed and she glanced down, thinking it might be another Venmo alert. Another text. *I'll end up blocking Dad.* It wasn't Dad. Andrea, defense attorney and Haddie's new boss, sent a single line: "New client 8am."

Haddie groaned, glancing at the time — 2:11, less than six hours from now. She typed a cheerful reply and placed the phone beside her keyboard.

CHAPTER 2

HE TOOK A DEEP BREATH, trying to calm himself. Sarah hadn't stopped trying to scream, despite the gag. *I should have taken this back to my house.* There, noise wouldn't have been a problem. However, the money had to be here, in the Colmans' house.

Sarah had denied knowing anything about the theft. How was that possible? He'd known the couple for years, and Sarah had been a part of every deal. The idea that her husband would steal that kind of money and not involve her made no sense. *I hate thieves.* It had to be here in the house. He had tracked every banking activity Mark had made, and they all led to cash.

A middle-aged woman, Sarah had short brown hair styled into wavy curls above her shoulders. She'd been packing to leave. They'd gone through her luggage. She wore a jacket and skirt, dressed for a trip, not bed. She would have been gone by morning. He couldn't let that happen.

His men had tied her to a cushioned wooden chair, but

it was too light. It rocked and threatened to fall over as she struggled. Everything about the situation annoyed him.

Pulling the jacket off her shoulders with her elbows tied to the armrests proved difficult. "I don't want to do this, Sarah, but I won't have people steal from me." He managed to expose the white button-down shirt beneath, at least enough to get to her collarbones. He'd found them an area particularly painful when burned.

Her screams turned to sobs as he unbuttoned the first few buttons and pulled the collar aside to expose the skin around the neck. She would be dead when he was done tonight. He intended to leave with his money.

Smiling, he held the gag at each side of her mouth. "I think I've made my resolve clear. This will be your last chance to tell me, unharmed." He pulled down the gag.

"I don't know. I don't know." Sarah spoke quickly, breaking into sobs, then her eyes focused on him. She drew in a deep breath, likely planning on screaming again.

"Bollocks." He yanked up the gag and shoved it into her mouth.

Jaw clenched, he placed both hands on her collarbone and smiled. Carefully, so the entire body wouldn't ignite, he hummed.

A high tone filled the air around him. The light from his hands lit the room, and a long shadow from her head cast up the oil painting behind her and to the ceiling.

He barely felt the heat; however, her skin crackled and the stench of burnt flesh filled the air.

A different pain raced up his arms and neck. His own skin felt as though it peeled off. Teeth grinding, his joints throbbed, aching worse than ever.

The visions came, sweeping him into a bright day. Angry soldiers, peasants with staffs sharpened to spears pressed in through a broken gate. The splintered wood groaned and snapped under their feet. He growled, and his light bathed the score of attackers. Clothes, weapons, and the wood from the gate ignited; flesh blackened and stank.

Next, he found himself over a terrified woman with ripped clothes and bruised cheeks. His hands rested on each side of her head as he sang. The light and heat poured out her open mouth and burnt through her eyes. This had been a lover, someone who had betrayed him.

He sagged back to the present. Smoke trailed off the blackened edges of Sarah's shirt.

Those were not his memories, but he learned from them. The eyes he saw through had more skill and control than he did. They had lived thousands of years ago, but he learned more each time he used his skill. He would master it.

Sarah shook, red and black skin spread across her neck and collarbones. She managed to mouth past the gag and screamed. Shrill and loud, it rang throughout her living room.

The neighbors had likely heard that one. *Daft woman.* This hurt him nearly as much as it hurt her. She would ruin everything. Thief.

"Shut up!" he yelled.

The tone rang. Light rippled from his hands, still at her neck, then fire burst from her clothing. Sarah Colman ignited. Flesh along her jaw charred instantly, cracking.

This only happened when he lost control.

Pain staggered him backward and he dropped to a knee. Sarah faded as the visions took him.

He saw an army this time. Others of his kind, people he knew fought beside him. Their soldiers clashed against a wave of the enemy, the man beside him whipping their troops into an unstoppable fury. He raised his hands and sang. His fine-tuned skill seared a section of the enemy and left bodies smoking.

The next vision proved disappointingly mundane as he left a family of corpses inside a mud-daub hovel.

He felt hands under his arms as he returned to the present. One of his men, Burke, lifted him and pulled him away from the fire.

Flames from Sarah's corpse engulfed the painting above, and the crown molding had begun to burn.

He would never find the money now. Better that it burn in the Colmans' house then.

I hate thieves.

CHAPTER 3

HADDIE SAT in the corner with a yellow pad and pen trying to look inconspicuous, which was difficult when she measured nearly six feet tall and sat higher than anyone else in the room, especially their newest client, a hunched-over murder suspect.

Nearest to Haddie, Andrea, attorney and owner of Andrea Simmons Law Firm, sat at the end of the oval mahogany conference table. "Ms. Schaffer, why don't we start with your relationship with the deceased, Mark Colman." Andrea wore a navy suit, awkwardly similar to Haddie's — like they'd coordinated or followed some corporate uniform rules. Though she was over fifty years old, the woman dyed her hair a bright red, then twisted it tightly into a bun that she stabbed in place with two black and gold hair sticks fashioned at the end into painted lily flowers.

Haddie sat just behind and to the left of her boss, wearing her own long black hair in a loose ponytail, having resisted the urge to put it in a bun after she started working for Andrea. Her pen brushed on the pad silently while she inhaled Andrea's overwhelming perfume — a floral scent that bordered on sweet.

The client, Mel Schaffer, was dressed professionally in a blue pinstriped blouse with a knee-length gray skirt and black pumps, but her red, swollen eyes looked ready to cry at Andrea's comment. From the look of her roots, she dyed her hair blonde; it was cut into a fashionable bob, but today it could use a brush. She'd been near falling apart, refusing coffee or soda, since they'd tucked her in the conference room. She remained, timidly trying to curl in on herself, where they'd placed her at the first chair of the sweeping table.

She wrung her hands just under the scroll-worked edge of the table, so that her knuckles and thumbs popped up on occasion. "Mark? Our relationship?" Mel asked.

Andrea nodded. "Yes. When did you start seeing him?"

"March, last year." The woman silently began crying and frantically wiped tears with both hands.

Haddie scribbled down the date.

Their client hardly seemed the murderous type, more of an emotional wreck. She'd barely touched her face with makeup, and her white skin highlighted the red rims around her eyes. Tracks and smears from her tears glistened on her cheeks.

"And where did you meet him?" Andrea flicked a hand toward the shelving and cabinet behind her, toward a box of tissues.

Haddie jumped up and set the pad and pen on her seat. Behind, the wall unit stretched the entire width of the room. Glass displays held random African or Asian statues that were decorative rather than memorabilia. The center bookshelf held a blue-spined series of Oregon law, while the display cubbies on each side held acrylic awards, a lavender box of tissues, and a bowl of fake fruit.

Haddie proffered the box to Mel, who took one and said, "Thank you."

Haddie left the box on the table in front of her.

"The Sailing Inn. They had an Irish party of some sort. I went with Beth." She sobbed, choking. "He sat with us. He was very nice."

This was no murderer. Haddie scribbled down the woman's response. Drained from the stress of trapping the dog buyer and staying up into the morning hours, she'd been dragging all morning, but now she perked up. This is why she wanted to be an attorney. The district attorney's office had a horrible case, based on perceivable motive rather than evidence.

Andrea swallowed and touched her bun, fingers probing the tightness of it. "And, at this time, did Mark Colman explain to you that he was married?"

Mel groaned in her sobs. "Yes."

"There will be uncomfortable questions that come up surrounding this, but we can prepare for that later. Let's move to the night of the incident."

Haddie imagined the blackened body, twisted in the front seat of the burned car. She'd first seen the pictures with Terry the night before. After a reflexive grimace, she controlled her expression and glanced up to see if either Mel or Andrea had noticed the inappropriately timed grin.

Mel's eyes were down. She blew her nose with a mumbled apology and then kept the wadded tissue in her hand.

"Where were you the night of Mark Colman's murder?" Andrea asked.

"In my apartment — we were supposed to meet at his

office, but we'd had a fight and he canceled." Mel spoke the latter part almost frantically, as if still regretting the fight.

Haddie mentally ticked through the follow-up questions Andrea would ask. When was the planned meetup? What was the fight about? Did Mark give a reason for the cancellation?

Instead, Andrea remained on topic. "What did you have for dinner?"

Haddie tilted her head in a light twitch. Of course. Keep on the alibi. A delivery could be perfect.

Mel blinked. "Frozen cheesecake. And some whip cream."

Haddie winced. Must have been a nasty argument. Hastily, she scribbled down the question and response. She could easily forget her job, trying to outguess Andrea's next round of questioning.

Andrea nodded. "What did you watch? Did you pay for any movies?"

Yes. Service-provider logins had been used successfully, even if you didn't order something. IP addresses and times were all logged. Haddie twisted her lips. She'd been more invested in the circumstantial evidence and motive, while Andrea went straight for the alibi. Prove that, and little else mattered.

Sniffling, Mel reached for a fresh tissue, the previous wad tucked in her palm. "Nothing. I drove to the park by the courthouse, sat there a while — I don't know how long — and went back home. I told the police, I don't remember the times."

Haddie groaned inside. Four or five blocks from the murder. No wonder the DA had moved against Mel. She had the worst alibi possible, but Andrea would likely check the wife's, also.

"Did you buy anything? Coffee, gas?"

Mel shook her head.

"Make any calls? Texts? Check social media?"

Breaking into a sob, Mel put her elbows on the table and buried her face in her hands. "I just — waited to see if he — would text me."

Haddie put her pad down to her lap, fighting her own rising emotions. Unless Andrea found something exceptional for an alibi, Mel's only chance would be for someone to find the real killer. The police wouldn't bother, and Andrea had limited resources — Josh and Haddie, a stoner and a college student. Andrea might suggest that Mel hire a private investigator. She hadn't done so with any of her previous clients that Haddie had seen, but how many murder defense cases had the firm had?

Andrea picked up her pen and took a moment to write "park cameras" at the top of her pad.

Haddie thought of the other security cameras, those near the victim's car. She still focused on finding the killer, while Andrea aimed for the alibi. Haddie sniffed and tried to see her boss's expression. The actual attorney in the room might have it right. This job would be good, in the long run, to give her some needed perspective.

After an hour, Andrea did get around to some of Haddie's questions, which included the cause for the cancellation of the lovers' meetup. Mark had claimed to have a late client.

As Toby, the firm's secretary, escorted Mel out, Andrea went through Haddie's notes and added comments.

"Some of this will get cleared up as Grace goes through the police reports; they still haven't gotten all their interviews to us. I suspect the DA knows how weak of a case they have." Andrea added a sentence to one of Mel's responses, squeezing her nearly illegible writing between Haddie's best attempt at legible. "How long are you here this morning?"

"One this afternoon."

Andrea nodded. "Good. Type this up and get me something to proof. Then, put a call in to Mark Colman's mortgage company, see if the secretary is answering. I need you to do an interview with her. We'll get around to a deposition if it proves necessary. Get everything for the day and anything unusual for the past month, but most important is this late client."

Haddie wanted to dig, to ask questions designed more to suggest that they go after the killer than follow Andrea's focus. The murder had been brutal, more brutal than she could imagine Mel being able to follow through with. From Terry's comments last night, it also seemed highly unusual. The police should be looking at someone other than a meek insurance adjuster. Instead, she clamped her teeth and waited until her boss handed back her marked-up notes.

CHAPTER 4

HADDIE PULLED her Softail Fat Boy into the last parking space beside a white Durango. Her engine echoed in the alley after she turned it off. She'd slammed through the notes and gotten them off to Andrea with plenty of time to catch Mark's secretary, Jasmine, before she closed for lunch. Haddie's class didn't start until 2:15.

She'd parked behind Mark's office, a one-story brick structure on a downtown corner. Two alleys and four buildings divided the block into quarters. Half a block from where the victim's car had burned, a three-story brick building stood across the alley behind the victim's office. A brick and concrete parking garage rose equally as high beside it, catty-corner to the mortgage company's parking lot. Taking her helmet off, she faced the fading and peeling one-story repair shop beside Mark's office. The smell of grease and petroleum competed with urine and garbage from the alley.

She tucked her helmet, leather gloves, and jacket into a saddlebag and took out her pad of paper. Pulling out her hair tie, she smoothed her hair from the ride and tied it again. It needed a good brushing, but she didn't have time. Haddie tried to smooth out some of the wrinkles in her suit jacket. She would have driven the RAV4 if she'd known she'd be going out on an interview.

Clutching her yellow pad and pen, Haddie stepped over a curb into the concrete alley. The east section had been barricaded with two cones at her end, and orange barriers and tape guarded a blackened splotch at the exit to the next street. To the left of the singed ground, the second to last concrete pillar of the parking garage had black smoke trails sprayed across it. Paint peeled off the blue and white repair shop to the right, but its walls showed no sign of fire.

A one-way alley. She would check it out after the interview. She gave a cursory search for cameras and noted that the closest was at the drive-through, but that only covered the mortgage company parking lot.

The building housed a credit union and offices tucked inside, including Mark Colman Mortgage Company, clearly labeled on the glass door along with two others. Inside smelled of mold, like the carpet had gotten wet at some point. The second door on the left had the victim's company name lettered in gold and silver. How long would it stay open after the owner had died? The door, unlocked, squeaked when she opened it to reveal walls of dark green, like the color of a frog. The office air smelled of light perfume and some breakfast sausage.

Jasmine looked up from her phone, her dark brown face smoothing into a pleasant smile. "Are you Hadhira?"

"I am, thank you for taking some time to meet with me, Jasmine." Haddie raised her eyebrows and pointed to one of the chairs opposite the gray desk.

The room had little space for even the office equipment and two guests. The monitor and keyboard occupied most of the four feet of desk space. Behind the secretary, two short black file cabinets held a printer, an empty coffee pot, assorted sugar packets, and cheap creamer. An open door beside the cabinets led to a windowed office where the natural light helped fight the gloom of the dark room. How did Jasmine sit in here all day?

Jasmine had a round face and black hair that curled out in a thick frame. She wore a light blue blouse, unbuttoned over a darker blue tank nearly the color of her jeans. "You're going to help Mel?" The tone was helpful, cheerful.

Haddie nodded. "The firm is representing her."

"Good. I mean, don't get me wrong. I don't think he was right, sneaking around on his wife, and the woman should've known better, but she's a sweet thing. Don't deserve the police running over her like that." Jasmine lightly touched her hair, testing springy curls. Even over the phone, there had been no sense of condemnation of the victim's girlfriend.

Haddie had expected the affair to be more inconspicuous. "Did Mel often come here, to the office?"

Jasmine shook her head. "Nah, a few times. Mr. Colman tried to keep it a secret. He'd get all flustered and tell me some story about how she was running over papers from another company. He don't know we sat nearly two hours one afternoon when he run late getting back to the office. I dug it all out of her."

"Did he often work late?" Might as well get right to the point of it.

"Not usually. Some days, he'd dip out at lunch and never come back. I deal with everybody, few that there is.

'Til four if he don't show. Sometimes I work 'til six if some-one's coming in. I'll take the overtime. Normally four though. This week's been 'til four on the dot. Lunch at noon." Jasmine checked her phone, possibly for the time.

"The night that Mr. Colman died, did you stay late?"

"Nope. Got home on time. And Mel didn't show nor call — that I know of — that day." She smiled, white teeth framed in red lipstick. "Sorry. Same questions the police asked."

So, if Mark Colman had any late-night clients the night of his murder, he didn't include Jasmine. Possibly, he just made up the excuse to keep from seeing Mel. The fight hadn't seemed that bad. Mel had been a bit dramatic about it, but it could have been little more than a spat. Maybe the client had been the killer. "Anybody else show up that day that you didn't expect? Mrs. Colman?"

"She come by the day after — I'd just found out about — the death. First time I'd ever met her. She just took some papers, told me her son was coming in from the east to run the business, and left. I didn't get that she liked me, so I've been running my résumé around." Jasmine leaned on the desk with one elbow. "Your firm hiring?"

"I don't think so, but don't let that stop you." Haddie smiled. "I'd recommend you."

Haddie's phone vibrated in her jacket pocket. She pulled it out, and her friend Liz's text flashed at the top. "HELP!" All caps and an exclamation point — really? It could be anything from needing a pen to needing a ride.

Jasmine leaned back and pulled open a drawer, then slid a three-page résumé across the table. "Tell your boss I show up, rain or shine."

Haddie spent until 11:45 going through her questions

with Jasmine. There didn't seem to be anything unusual going on, except an affair and murder. The business didn't look too busy, and Jasmine did a lot of the actual work. Whoever the mystery client was, maybe they'd show up on the drive-through camera. It could have been Mr. Colman's way of blowing off Mel.

Getting up to walk out, Haddie noticed the alarm pad flashing an error. "Problems?" she asked, pointing to the display.

"Been like that. Mr. Colman usually gets his guy out here to fix it, but Mrs. Colman said not to worry about it. Her son would deal with it." Jasmine pulled her lipstick from her purse.

"When did this start?"

"It was like that the morning after Mr. Colman died. Happens every now and then. Some sort of short in the wiring." Jasmine used the camera in her phone as a mirror. "Nothing much here anyone would want."

"Good luck, Jasmine."

The woman paused, offering a wide smile, and pointed toward the résumé tucked in Haddie's pad. "Rain or shine!"

Once in the hall, Haddie started to dial Liz and wrinkled her nose at the odor. There had been water damage somewhere. They should check for mold.

A sharp-dressed man in a black business suit stepped from the door ahead. Short, almost military cut, light brown hair and slight stubble along a solid jaw made him look somewhat handsome in a blue-eyed, thirtyish way. "Good day." He motioned her ahead of him in the hall. "Please." The polite British accent rolled out and he became dashing in an instant.

Haddie hung up on Liz mid-ring. "Thank you." She

took a deep breath, having forgotten the mold. She paused just ahead of him, before she spun. "Is this your office?"

He was about to lock the door. With a charming smile, he held up his keys. "It is. Can I help you?" Purplish blotches covered the back of his hands, between fingers and even on fingertips.

Haddie raised her eyebrows. "Actually — yes. I was wondering if you knew the deceased, Mark Colman?" The sign on the door said, "Kupatal Imports."

He turned and continued locking the door. There was even a reddish-purple blotch at the back of his neck by the white collar. "In passing. Bad bit of news, that is." He finished, dropped his keys in his jacket pocket, and left his hand tucked out of view. Maybe embarrassed. "I'm Harold Holmes, and you are?"

"Hadhira Dawson. I'm working with the Andrea Simmons Law Firm." She took in another deep breath of the foul corridor and wished she'd waited until she was outside to corner him. There seemed only one way out of the building.

"I do wish I could help. We talked no more than you and I have, and on rare occasion at that. He seemed a sound fellow." Harold Holmes dropped his eyebrows down, darkening his eyes and smiling deeper. Despite being an inch or two shorter, he gave no sense that he'd been intimidated by her height. "I'm sure you'll do the miss good."

Miss? Did he know of Mel?

Haddie's phone rang. Liz. She hit ignore. "Did you know a Mel Schaffer?"

"Blondie? Is that her name?" He made a sly smile and shrugged. "I didn't ask about their business, or her name, but she seemed polite. Not as confident as yourself."

Perhaps too much of a charmer. So, he wasn't assuming

she worked for Mel. Who did he think the firm represented? Harold's information added little to Jasmine's interview, but the affair certainly didn't seem to be much of a secret. The police had probably gathered as much. Sarah Colman likely had known.

Liz rang again. Haddie moved to answer, but asked one last question. "When was the last time you saw Ms. Schaffer here?"

He looked up toward the ceiling and pouted. "A couple weeks, can't say exactly."

Haddie hit answer and nodded. "Thank you, Mr. Holmes." She opened the door to the parking lot and the less obnoxious city air.

Background noise filled the phone. "Haddie, thank the heavens, can you help?" Liz asked.

Two hours until class. "What's up?"

Mr. Holmes passed with a nod, making for a red Porsche Cayman that had not been in the parking lot when she'd arrived. His business seemed to be doing better than poor Mr. Colman's.

"Damn car. I got off I-5 at Franklin, and it died before I got off the ramp. I was getting ready to walk." Liz sounded stressed. She held it well, but they'd known each other for three years.

Haddie stood near the building, phone to her ear, when the door to the building opened again. "Don't walk. I'm close."

A tall man, possibly in his thirties, walked out of the building. His bright, dark eyes glanced over in surprise, then he offered a broad smile and nod as he passed. Thin and clean-shaven, he wore a light-blue polo shirt that fit tight across the chest and arms.

"Liz, wait a sec." Haddie swallowed, calling after the man. "Excuse me, do you work here?"

He paused and turned just a step away from her. He furrowed his eyebrows in a pleasant, questioning expression. He might have been an inch taller than she.

"My name's Hadhira Dawson. I work for the Andrea Simmons Law Firm. Did you by any chance know the deceased, Mark Colman?"

He shook his head. "David Crowley. I've got a client here. I hadn't realized someone died." His smile lessened, and he tilted his head slightly.

She hadn't meant to concern him. "No, not here. Down the alley." She gestured in the general direction. Close by, but not here. *Nice, Haddie.*

David nodded and smiled. "Sorry, I didn't know him."

"Thanks." Haddie returned the smile, and he continued to his car, a white Toyota Camry Hybrid. A solid sedan.

Haddie strode toward her bike, clipping her pen to her pad. Liz drove a 2008 Avenger that seemed intent on dying this year. This was the third time it had come up with something odd.

She unlocked her saddlebag, peeking down the alley. Her curiosity would have to wait. "You've got plenty of gas?"

"Engine-challenged, not engine-idiot. I know which gauge that is." A car roared in the background past Liz, muffling anything she said afterward.

"Is it getting fuel?"

"I tried to find out. I stared at the hood. Really mean-like."

Haddie slipped on her helmet, smiling. "Okay, I'll be there in ten." Westbound, she'd have to go to Glenwood. "Fifteen."

Liz paused for a moment. "Take your time. A nice axe-murderer, in what used to be a white pickup, just pulled up to help. Remember, I want to be cremated."

"Ten, dammit." Haddie fired up her Fat Boy.

HADDIE PULLED her Fat Boy behind the pickup, a beat-up Ford from the last century, absently reading the plate number.

A black-haired young man looked around the faded hood of Liz's Avenger, then watched as Haddie began strolling around his truck toward the passenger side where Liz waited, pacing in the grass. He wiped his hands on his pants, then across wind-blown hair. It had been nice of him to stop. However, two women were better on the side of the road, especially since she neared six feet and had a black belt in Taekwondo. And she'd probably learned more about engines in Dad's garage by sixth grade than this guy knew now.

Liz, her shoulder-length brown hair mangled by the wind, wore sunglasses, a white button-down blouse, and gray slacks. She jumped as she spotted Haddie during her last lap.

"Haddie, thank you." Her tone came across conversational, but desperation hung in it. She'd likely be late for teaching her class at the university, and Nice Boy hadn't been much help.

Haddie smiled and then focused on the young man extending a hand; she cleared three inches over him. "Haddie."

"Dan. You must be her mechanic she mentioned. I think it's her battery."

For a stall? Dan the man. "Could be. I'm not a mechanic anymore, I'm a law student." Haddie jumped in the passenger side, threw a leg over to reach the gas and turned the key. She hoped Dan didn't lean his knuckles into the fan. The engine wasn't getting any gas. Third of a tank. Filter, pump, or carb. Liz would need a tow.

That meant calling Biff, and he could be with Dad. Haddie sighed and pulled out her phone. She scrolled through her contacts until she came to "Jerk" and stabbed the call icon after a deep breath.

Wincing and holding one side of her hair calm while the other flailed like a hooked fish, Liz leaned in at the open door.

"Biff. Can you get out here on Franklin, westbound, just off I-5? Liz needs her car towed to your friend." Haddie looked toward her friend as she said the last sentence.

"Hi. Haddie." Biff paused.

Haddie closed her eyes. *Damn, Jerk was with Dad.*

Biff continued slowly. "I could make it out there in twenty. Need tools?"

And bring Dad as well? No, thanks. "Nope. Your friend out there, he'll have to figure out why it's not getting fuel. I don't have time. I'll trade him some legal advice; he always needs it."

"Benny? Sure. But we could save some time . . ."

Jerk. "Nope. I'd imagine we don't have time, and Liz and I are standing on the off-ramp." She avoided mentioning Dan the man, which would surely bring Dad out. "Just a tow."

"That's the hot professor with the beater Dodge."

"Yes, the one that works in the police department for her day job."

Biff paused. At first, Haddie thought it was her reminder of Liz's profession, then she heard muffled voices. *There's a mute button, Jerk.*

"You sure you don't need tools?"

"Tell Dad no."

"She says to take a hike, Old Man." Her father swore in the background, and Biff clicked his tongue. She could see his goofy grin. "Help's on the way, Haddie."

The connection dropped.

Haddie sighed. She'd have to face her dad soon. He'd gotten insistent, but she needed answers that he hadn't been willing to give. At least she'd make class on time. She itched to dig up some more information about Mark Colman; he had to have some other secrets besides Mel.

"I heard," Liz said. "How bad?" She leaned in deeper to get the wind off her hair.

Haddie pressed her phone to her chest. "It's not getting fuel. Biff will tow it and have his friend Benny look at it. Might be a couple days. I'll give you what rides I can. I've told you before —"

"I'm already upside-down in it. I can't afford to trade it in." Liz glanced back toward the front where Dan waited, and she squatted beside the passenger seat. "Can you give me a ride? I've got class in twenty."

"Of course." Haddie leaned over and pulled the key out, then off the ring. "You want me to break the news to your new friend?"

Liz rolled her eyes and nodded.

Haddie dropped the key under the mat where Biff would look. "I don't have a second helmet with me." She handed over the remaining keys and stepped out as Liz moved out of the way. Haddie strolled to the front of the beater.

Dan shuffled back and leaned his hand atop the open hood. "So, it's the battery, right?"

Liz dug in the car to find the tan leather satchel she usually carried for class. The black car leaned from her movement, startling Dan.

Haddie put the cap back on the washer fluid. "Fuel flow. I've got a tow coming."

He frowned and shook his head. "I checked the gauge, she's got plenty."

Haddie needed to close the hood and go. "Why don't you check the fuel filter, just in case."

Dan climbed under the car, on the wrong side, then fumbled in his jeans for his phone. He'd need more than a flashlight.

Liz closed the passenger door and settled her bag and purse over her shoulders. Hopefully, there was a brush in one of them.

Haddie's own hair pulled at the collar, trying to get free from under her jacket. She slammed down the hood, smiling as Dan's work boots kicked in surprise. "We've got to go, Dan. Professor here needs to educate."

Dan scrambled out, wiping flecks of rust off his cheek. "The fuel filter seems fine."

Dan the Man had X-ray vision. No. He had been nice enough; she should cut him some slack. She should have warned him that she was closing the hood.

"Thanks for your help, Dan. Biff will take care of this

heap. He'll be by to pick it up in about four minutes; we're not waiting."

Dan looked over to Liz. "You need a ride?" He sounded too hopeful.

He was Haddie's age, early twenties, maybe younger. Liz — early thirties. Haddie turned to look at Liz. Who was she to judge?

Liz shook her head, adjusting tilted sunglasses. "I can ride with Haddie, thank you, Dan."

Haddie tilted her head as Dan pouted. She waited until he noticed her and started back to his truck.

He walked on the traffic side. "Good luck. Hope you get it going."

Haddie joined Liz and they walked along the grass. "You should burn it, take the insurance money."

"Legal advice?" Liz held back a wayward section of her hair from the wind so she could smile at Haddie.

Haddie snorted. The paper could wait another day. She planned on heading back to the firm after class. There had to be some other motive to kill Mark Colman, unless the police were wrong, and the wife did it. She winced at the mental image of the burned corpse. "You need a ride after class?"

Liz shook her head and spit out hair. "Professor Arbor can give me a ride back. We talked about getting a drink anyway."

"Ooh." Haddie grinned, not looking at her friend.

"He's too old for that." Liz didn't sound sure.

"You need to check the birth date on your driver's license." Haddie swayed, bumping into Liz. Her David was what — late twenties? Handsome.

"What have you heard about this car fire murder?" Haddie asked.

"Todd's working on the car now. I can look over his report, if you want. Andrea take that case?" They arrived at the Fat Boy as Dan sped down the off-ramp.

"Yep. That girlfriend is innocent. Someone else did this." Haddie strapped on her helmet. She would need to call her dog walker, Sam, and get her to walk Rock.

"Uh-oh. I know that tone."

Haddie climbed on her bike. "What?"

"You're done with the dogfighting ring. Now you'll obsess on this. Don't you have a paper due?"

"I'm not obsessing. I've just got some research to do." Haddie fired up the engine.

Her phone vibrated and she peeked as Liz settled in.

Dad wrote, "Answer my damn texts."

CHAPTER 6

HADDIE PULLED around a black Land Rover and parked her Fat Boy on the cracked concrete of the drive that extended down the side of Mel's apartment building. Actually, it was just a large, two-story house in a residential neighborhood between downtown and West Eugene. Three kids were screaming in a neighboring yard on the other side of a small white garage.

Sarah, Mark Colman's wife, had been burned to death last night in her home in Cal Young. Haddie had heard something about a fire, but the DA had just informed them of the details this afternoon while she was researching. Andrea had not been pleased.

Haddie pulled at her suit jacket, trying to get rid of some of the wrinkles, and smoothed her hair from the ride. She had statements for Mel to sign. The woman had been unable to make it back to the office, so Andrea had done an interview over the phone.

Someone barbecued nearby; it smelled delicious, and her mouth watered. Haddie hadn't had more than a taco after class. This late in September, the night cooled as the sun dropped. A tan blanket of dying grass crunched under her boots. An ugly orange chair sat on the too small landing beside a blue-framed door. Windowpanes allowed a glimpse of a dimly lit hall inside, stretching to the back with a door on each side of the paneled walls.

A row of doorbells ran down a panel of penciled-in names behind yellowed plastic. Haddie found Mel's name and pressed the buzzer, watching down the hall through the smudged windowpanes. It took three times before the right-hand door opened and Mel walked down the hall. She wore an oversized navy sweatshirt with a white beer mug logo. It hung short over bare legs. She opened the door and greeted Haddie with a frazzled ball of blonde hair, red eyes, and a sniffle before turning back toward her open apartment.

Haddie followed, the wooden floor creaking underfoot. "Sorry to come so late."

Mel's dimly lit apartment had off-white walls and a large wood floor that needed a fresh coat of seal and maybe some sanding. A brown sofa blocked three curtained windows and held a colorful quilt, balled up against a black pillow with a sweeping insignia, perhaps a rune. A worn, wooden coffee table had a thick paperback and an empty purple mug.

Compared to the mess Haddie lived in, the apartment looked abandoned. "I've got a couple documents for you to sign; I'm sure Andrea explained."

Mel choked. "Who is doing this?"

The murders? Good question. The woman looked ready to collapse. She'd given up, her life falling apart. Earlier, she'd mentioned not showing up for work. Haddie didn't answer, though it seemed the only question that mattered at the moment. She and Andrea were looking for an alternative to offer the jury, but the police had stopped.

They had their easy target. An emotional lover, admitting to their fight the night of Mark Colman's murder, fresh fingerprints on his car door, and no verifiable alibi.

Haddie stood with papers in hand, feeling awkward. "Do you have a table?"

Tears dripping down her face, Mel pointed to the coffee table, but made no move toward it or the couch.

Obliging, Haddie placed the papers down and fished a pen from her jacket pocket. "Just read through, initial the bottom, and sign at the end. These are based on your phone call with Andrea today."

Mel just stood there, staring at the coffee table. The woman had to be chilly. "I feel like this is my fault," she finally said.

Haddie blinked and tilted her head. "Probably not a comment you want to make to anyone." She cleared her throat. "I've read through your statement. You've done nothing wrong. The police haven't contacted you today?"

Mel shook her head, strands of blonde hair sticking to her cheek.

"Have you been answering your phone?" It had taken Toby a dozen or more calls to get Mel to answer.

Turning, Mel walked through an archway into a separate area where a thin kitchen cut off the end of an empty space that should have been a dining room. As the woman turned the corner, presumably to get her phone, a buzzer rang over the door to the hall.

Haddie frowned as she stepped to the apartment door, peeking down the hall through the windowpanes of the outer door. An officer, a detective, waited on the landing, wearing a black shirt and tie with a seven-pointed star pinned over his left breast. He had light brown skin with a well-trimmed mustache and a scowl. Heavy eyebrows narrowed even further as he spotted her. Her heart started to pound. She stepped back out of sight as he motioned to her.

The buzzer rang again.

Striding into the dining room, Haddie turned at the corner of the hall, where a bedroom door lay open. "The police are here. You'll want to call Andrea." A pink nightstand had a pile of tissues reaching up to the bottom of a pleated white lampshade; the basket beside it brimmed as well. This was no murderer, certainly not a double-murderer. "Do you want me to answer the door?" She took a deep breath. How would Andrea want her to handle this?

Mel stepped into the bedroom doorway, her hands shaking but holding a purple phone. She cringed as the detective pounded on the door. Looking down, she shook her head, then nodded slowly. A large tear splattered on the wood at her bare feet.

Haddie stomped across the apartment as the pounding continued. A man's voice growled in the hall before she opened the apartment door. A wide-eyed youth, eighteen at best, stood against the wall in a pair of patterned tan boxers, letting in the police detective.

"Detective Cooper, Eugene Investigative Division. I'm here to see Mel Schaffer." He marched down the hall, fixing his eyes on Haddie's. "Who are you?"

The boy in the boxers slunk back to the apartment opposite, peering through the crack in the door as he slowly closed it.

"Hadhira Dawson. I work for Andrea Simmons, who is Ms. Schaffer's counsel." Haddie firmly blocked the doorway.

Detective Cooper stood average height and did not

close the gap between them. Brown eyes studied her. "Ms. Schaffer needs to come down and answer some questions."

They weren't here to arrest Mel for the second murder, not yet. Haddie kept her expression noncommittal and firm. "Not without her attorney present."

The scowl seemed his permanent expression. "We planned on calling Ms. Simmons when we got to the station."

"Lucky for you, I was here." Inside, she cringed. Keep humor or sarcasm out of any communication with police. Even Dad had taught her that much.

His lips tightened, sending a few hairs of the mustache down over them. He still managed to keep it a scowl as he weighed the situation. He didn't have a warrant, or he would have had that in hand, and there would be a plainclothes with him.

Haddie looked through the front door panes into the night. No police lights. He'd just planned on trotting Mel out.

"We expect Ms. Simmons and Ms. Schaffer tonight." He sighed and pulled out his card. "Have them call me."

She took the card, but said nothing.

He scowled for another moment, expecting a response before finally shaking his head and stalking away.

Haddie let out her breath, fumbling in her jacket for her phone. Andrea must have expected this to come at some point. The police would eventually arrest Mel for the second murder, perhaps even tonight, unless she had a better alibi. They had to find the actual killer.

CHAPTER 7

HADDIE LEANED on the top of the dividing wall of Grace's cubby. "Do you have Colman's financials?"

With smooth black skin and a tight head of curls, Grace had a perfect face. She looked up from her monitor with a tense expression and shook her head. "Josh is supposed to scan that in."

"Damn." That would assume he'd remember. Haddie turned toward the empty copy room at the end of the short office of cubicles. "Thanks."

Haddie's cubby had a small pile of manila folders and the list of tasks Andrea had left. She didn't mind getting stuck in the cubicle some mornings, but today she itched to be moving. She'd driven the RAV4, primarily to get Liz to work at the crime lab, but it would also make it easier to do interviews. However, she'd ended up at the office tracking phone data.

She stepped out, walked across from Josh's empty cubby, and tilted her head, trying to see into the copy room as she approached. He'd disappeared as usual. Files covered the worktable, and documents were left in the copy machine's tray. He hadn't digitized any of the victim's finances yet. So, she started leafing through the tabs of the folders on the table.

"Haddie?" Andrea barked from the office behind.

Blush warmed her cheeks as Haddie stepped quickly out of the copy room. "Yes?"

Andrea frowned, standing at the far end of the office, a plain room with three gray cubicles and set of supply shelves, no windows, and only one exit where she stood. She gestured for Haddie to follow before disappearing toward her cubicle.

Last night had turned difficult, with Andrea calling and texting to get Mel out of the house while Haddie dealt with a broken woman who took twenty minutes to get her pants on. Somehow, that had been Haddie's fault. She'd been able to go home and heat up a frozen pizza before midnight, but it had been a long day.

Longer for Andrea. Her eyes were lightly bloodshot, her face was tight, and her usually perfect bun sat slightly off-center. Two empty coffee cups from different stores sat on the credenza behind where she sat at her desk, and her purse lay between them. Even her perfume smelled weak. Had the woman even slept?

"Did you get anything on my list done yet?" Andrea asked. An accusation, as they both knew Haddie hadn't moved far down the list.

"I checked out the carrier data for the first murder, which fits Mel's account of the night." Haddie started wrapping her hair around her fist. She'd gotten sidetracked from Andrea's list that prioritized supporting Mel's weak alibis. Instead, she'd delved into Mark's history.

"You're not focused today. They'll arrest Mel on the second murder today or tomorrow, I'm sure of it. I need to be prepared for the arraignment." Andrea tapped her monitor. "I need to count on you. Focus on what I've given you, not on the murders."

Haddie resisted approaching the same argument she'd started last night. Focusing on the alibi made sense, but her gut wanted to dig deeper and find the killer. "I understand." It would take a couple hours to get everything ready; maybe by then, Josh would have done his job and she could peek at the finances.

Andrea nodded and gestured a dismissal.

Grace didn't look up as Haddie returned. She had two windows open on her monitor: one of the police interviews, and the other her notes. If she questioned Andrea pulling Haddie aside, she didn't make it her business. As a paralegal, she took her work seriously.

Haddie did too. This time she just saw the situation differently than Andrea, which wasn't why she interned here. *Focus*.

Sitting down, she noticed her phone had a message.

Terry texted, "Lunch? Cafeteria?"

Haddie's fingers slid across the phone's keyboard, replying, "I doubt it. Working on case." She added a second line, "Just got called out for not staying focused."

"So what are you obsessing on now?"

Haddie snorted. "Not obsessing. It's just that they're focused on the alibi instead of who actually killed those people."

"So what's your plan?"

"Finish the alibi work. Look into the murder." Haddie glanced up toward the office door, not wanting to be texting if Andrea came back in.

"Not obsessing then." Terry threw in a laughing emoji.

Haddie glared at the phone. He could be annoying, at least on this topic.

He added a second message. "How can I help, Buckaroo?"

Terry always did this. Busted her chops for obsessing, and then helped with whatever she'd gotten herself into.

"Can you look into the fires? I started, but it got too big. Strange fires, no accelerant." She added. "I can ask Liz for any data on the fires and get it to you."

"Sounds like my thing. The boards are already lit up on it anyway."

"Thanks." Haddie tossed her phone beside the keyboard and straightened Andrea's note with barely a tinge of guilt after being reprimanded. There were too many strange aspects to the first murder. Why did the victim stop and roll down his window at the end of the alley? How did a fire start without any evidence of an accelerant? She couldn't let it go. She wanted to dig, but instead tapped her nail on Andrea's Post-it with the hastily scribbled bullet points.

Next on the list was to follow the phone tracking for the second murder. Third on the list was to follow up on the camera at the park, the one ATM that should have a clear view of Mel's parked car. It would be the best help for the alibi. The police hadn't even checked, so the DA didn't have it.

She picked up the office phone to make the follow-up call, put it back down, and picked up her cell. First, she'd see if Liz had anything to get to Terry about the fires.

CHAPTER 8

THOMAS PULLED his white '32 Shovelhead onto the on-ramp of I-5 and headed north toward Eugene in a dull roar that drowned out the other cars. He preferred the side roads, or better yet, the small mountain highways that everyone else avoided. Sedans and SUVs scurried along the multi-lane highway, sure that they had somewhere important to go. Everyone had to be in a hurry in this era. Money flew on the wind, and they chased it. TVs blared out that they needed something new, and they danced their way to superstores and online bargains to dump whatever they earned. Then they whined and groaned about having to go back to work to fill their pockets for the next thing to buy. He'd been torn away from it long ago and learned that life could be about creating, not acquiring. So much had changed in the last century.

The people of Eugene never looked at the mountains that surrounded them. Nature in all its glory cradled the south end of the Willamette Valley, forming a paradise that they just needed to slow down and appreciate. In their hurry, they'd destroyed the river, and the air stunk. In their rush, they never looked up.

Haddie raced with them. All through her childhood, he'd taken her to some of the most beautiful sights on the west coast of America, and she'd loved them all. Now she pounded away at her school and job, sure that the purpose in her life lay there. An attorney. He never would have imagined it. She'd been born intelligent and proved to be passionate, proactive, and uninhibited. A perfect match for today's world. She'd left him behind. Usually, he was the one who left everyone else behind. Why did he stay around? It was a risk he hadn't approached in a very long time.

Driving a red coupe, a kid texting on his cell veered toward Thomas's lane, and Thomas punched forward to get past, his braid whipping the small of his back. The boy never noticed. Everyone was in a hurry to get somewhere and then spend their time with their nose glued to their phone. Each generation had their faults, and each seemed more annoying than the last.

Bikes, poker, and nature. While Thomas could escape to those, he survived.

Haddie would be pissed that he just showed up. She couldn't keep ignoring him, putting it off. They had more to talk about. More that he'd be willing to say. Why her? Somehow, it felt right. He'd reached his beginnings. The time when it all had started. *Is that why I stay?* Still, she would be annoyed when he showed up.

He took the big curve heading into Eugene, catching a glimpse of the mountains to the north, those on the east side of the Willamette Valley. This year there might be time for another ride into Montana before the weather turned bad. Haddie's questions had killed their planned trip last summer; his daughter's curiosity would just keep getting more insistent. It had happened twice before with wives he'd dearly loved and would have happily stayed with, no matter how old they'd gotten. It had never worked out. How could he explain what he didn't understand himself?

Thomas blew out a breath as he neared the exit for downtown. The highways piled together, old, and new, closing in on the Willamette River where he once swam and fished before they turned it into liquid toxins.

If he remembered Haddie's schedule correctly, he'd catch her at the apartment. Or, he just wasted his time driving into the city. He could wait, though. Patience, after all these centuries, came easy.

CHAPTER 9

HADDIE TURNED down her street and groaned. Dad, leaning against his Shovelhead, had parked beside her Fat Boy under the overhang of her two-story apartment. His riding glasses hung at his neck. His long auburn braid lay over his shoulder, and the left side of his head remained shaved. The slightly crooked nose, broken before she'd been born, added to his brooding look. Wearing the usual Harley T-shirt and jeans, he turned his head up and nodded as she pulled her blue SUV into her second assigned parking space. How long had he been sitting there?

She dragged her book satchel from the passenger seat to her lap, gritting her teeth. With a paper to write, she didn't have time for this. Besides, she'd skipped lunch and her mouth tasted foul from hunger. After dealing with Andrea, there had been nothing significant to support Mel's alibi and little time for her own investigating. The day seemed to be getting worse by the minute. She opened the car door and stepped out to face him. "Not today, Dad. I've got a paper due."

Slowly, he stood from his seat and turned to face her at

equal height. His face, tan from riding, looked young enough to be in his mid-thirties. "Expected. You're in college."

She could smell the ever-present grease on him, a familiar smell of summers spent in his garage. "Fine." Her grip on her bag tightened, and she slammed the car door closed. "You want to talk. When were you born?" His answer her entire life had been to hand her his driver's license. A lie, in and of itself.

He snorted but didn't smile. "1985. Summer."

Haddie blinked. He'd never given her an answer on this one. He didn't lie, and the age almost seemed to fit. "Really?" His birth certificate had him born in 1971, just like his license, which left him forty-five years old and looking thirtyish. But he'd looked the same age when she was a teenager. Being born in 1985 would make him thirty-five and too young to have been her father.

He shrugged. "That's the truth."

Impossible. It didn't work; he would have been seven when she was born. He'd never lied to her. "But . . ." She trailed off as the old concerns came back. She couldn't be adopted, her mother's family had been at the birth, and there were pictures with her mother. They helped raise her after Mom had died. He couldn't be right about the date.

"It's not going to make sense." He rubbed a gloved hand, cut open at the fingertips, over his head, tracing hair back to the top of the braid.

It didn't make sense. 1971 or 1985, both were wrong somehow. And he expected her to just accept it. She couldn't. "I don't have time for games and nonsense." She stuffed her satchel under her arm. "I don't have time for you right now."

He didn't look hurt; he never did, even when she acted

like a bitch. Instead, he just had that rough, brooding look. He didn't respond but seemed to be weighing whether to say something else.

Despite her statement, Haddie paused, hoping somehow that he could say something that would make everything fit. This is why she couldn't talk to him. It physically hurt to go through it. She'd pushed him away when he first started evading these questions, when she'd finally built up the courage to confront him after going through most of college realizing he wasn't getting any older. He hadn't aged since as far back as she could remember. It wasn't possible. Now — 1985. That made less sense, but she would spend the night looking up Thomas Dawson born in 1985. Every variation.

No, she said to the questions in her head and started to walk away to the stairs leading up to her apartment. When no one else usually flustered her, Haddie found her heart racing with him. Damn.

He called out behind her, "Coffee? Better yet, Fifth Street?" The tone came out casual, as if none of the rest of their conversation had happened.

Her phone vibrated, and though she should have kept going, she stopped and checked it.

Terry texted, "Your dog guy just got picked up, along with three others. Heavy records. Be careful."

She shook a little responding, "Thanks." Another thing to look up when she got upstairs. This paper was supposed to happen tonight, and it didn't look good. The case wasn't going well. Her involvement in the dogfighting ring could have just gotten dangerous. What was she supposed to make of 1985?

"Haddie?"

She didn't turn around. "I can't right now. Later, Dad. Later."

CHAPTER 10

HADDIE TURNED into the driveway of Liz's yellow-cream house and pulled out her phone. The heat in the RAV4 had kicked on during the drive and whirred quietly.

Her small, odd-shaped house sat on a corner and had a single peak high at the front that slanted from the small third floor to the second. It sat nestled amid pine trees on one side and oaks on the slope that drifted into the woods. The side street was a dead-end, unfinished at the woods.

"Here," she texted to Liz.

Scrolling down to Andrea's message from 4:40 a.m., she twisted her lips, reading it yet again. "I'm sure they will arrest Mel Schaffer today for the second murder. I'll want to be prepared. When you come in today, please focus on the tasks I've assigned and not your own agenda. I don't have time to redirect you today. Please focus."

The most recent prior message from Andrea had been from ten days ago, when she'd praised her for work put into a DUI case. The drastic difference in tone made Haddie cringe. She would do nothing but Andrea's list today, no matter what came up.

Then, she needed to get on her paper — it was due in five days. She still had the weekend, but two days would give her almost no time to research. The rest — the murders, Colman's finances, Dad — had to wait.

Dad. She'd spent the last twelve hours, waking and sleeping, in turmoil. The birth years made no sense, and she couldn't let it go. Thinking about him made her physically ache. She swallowed, trying not to hear Terry's admonishments. Maybe she did get a bit obsessive, here and there.

Liz texted back with a thumbs-up emoji, and Haddie waited, running through her schedule for the day. Andrea's text had been a slap first thing this morning and made Haddie's morning cereal taste sour in her mouth. Wednesday, she had a late class, so any time at the library would have to be done in the afternoon. She purposefully had not texted Terry to see what he'd learned about any spontaneous human combustion fires.

Liz came dashing out with a jean jacket covered in random patches from heavy metal bands. She wore sunglasses, though the clouds kept the morning light soft. It had rained overnight.

"It's freezing." Liz jumped in with a breath of cold air and the scent of orange shampoo.

"Fifty-eight," Haddie corrected.

"If you'd like to get technical, fifty-eight is well below the melting point for most of your frozen car." Liz clustered her satchel on her knees as she clipped her seatbelt. "So let me whine. I'm freezing."

Haddie chuckled and turned up the heat. "Benny says your car will be ready tomorrow."

"How much?" Liz clutched her satchel against her chest, as if it had some warmth.

"A few hours of free legal advice. I charge him 450 an

hour." She turned, as Liz had gone silent with her face wide-eyed and mouth open. Haddie laughed. "He charges me 225 an hour. We have an understanding."

Haddie pulled out onto the street and checked her phone. In order for her to get to work on time, she had to get Liz to the lab early. In this neighborhood, few cars were leaving yet. The street was empty, except for a gray SUV that pulled out behind them.

"I appreciate everything, Haddie. I hate my car."

"Because your Avenger is crap." Haddie headed for I-5; she'd jump off at Franklin, passing the spot where the Dodge had stalled.

She stifled a yawn. It had been a late night. Terry's message about the dogfighting gang had her looking up the police blotter and then tracking the man she'd outed, along with his cohorts. Petty gang activities.

Her dad's revelation had caused her more trouble. Sleep had been nearly impossible. It wasn't something she'd ever spoken to Liz about. How could she?

A minute of silence sat in the car with them before Liz spoke. "Your case at work — anything new?"

"Nope. Still working on the alibi." She turned on Brackenfern, and the gray Outback with deeply tinted windows followed.

Swallowing, she thought about Terry's warning. It was likely just another commuter heading for I-5, but she kept glancing back. She had been a little obsessed about the dogfighting ring. Terry had suggested a couple options that might have taken longer, but she'd been driven to out this gang from the moment the first dead dog had hit the news. Now she might have gotten herself and her friends into something she couldn't handle.

Haddie put on her blinker at the upcoming left. "Just going to flip through here."

Confused, Liz looked at the motel at the corner; the opposite lot was empty. "Everything okay?"

"I imagine we're fine."

The Subaru slowed behind her, but through those deep tints, Haddie couldn't make out anything. Slowly she turned left onto the street. The SUV continued straight. Just an overactive imagination.

"What's going on?" Liz looked down the street they'd just turned on.

Haddie turned through the motel parking lot and came back out to get back on track. "Nothing. I'm a little jumpy. The dogfighting ring got picked up and Terry got me spooked. Thought someone was following me. It's nothing." She gave Liz a wry smile. "So, what's up on the fire analysis?"

Liz swiveled in her seat, glancing around them. "Todd is going back to the car. Something odd in the dispersion at the house fire. I'll let you know what he comes up with." She held back her hair as they turned, and she watched a car pass. "You really think this gang might be following you? You need to be careful."

"Just my imagination. I haven't slept enough the past few days," Haddie said. She should have talked with her dad. He obviously was opening up — a little. Next time, she'd try not to overreact.

There was no sign of the SUV ahead of them. She took a deep breath and made for I-5. Andrea would not appreciate it if she were late this morning.

PART 2

I had hoped to plead with you face to face, but your recent furlough has made that impossible.

CHAPTER 11

HADDIE SLIPPED past the reception desk in the waiting room while Toby made coffee in the kitchen. From the scent of perfume, Andrea had already arrived. She'd closed her office door, but Haddie was only a minute late.

Grace looked up from her cubicle and nodded. Her lipstick matched her purple jacket perfectly. The monitor behind her flickered on. In the firm, she was the powerhouse that plowed through Andrea's work. Josh's cubicle remained empty, and the copy room still had the lights off.

I'm not late at all. The room's heat had been on for a while, and the trip in the RAV4 had been warmer than she planned. Haddie took off her gray jacket and laid it over the side wall. Andrea had pressed two Post-its to her keyboard.

Grace spoke as Haddie sat. "I've got two interviews processed that Andrea wants you to go over. They're linked in the system. Josh," she hung at his name, "will be late."

Haddie smirked, powering up her computer. "Please tell me you know the excuse."

"He called me." Grace took on a more conversational tone. The stress of the case had been getting to everyone.

"Either a wolf or a large cat, possibly a tiger, bit his tire. He has to get it replaced."

Most of the time, Josh called in to Toby, who would relay the story over coffee. No one had been able to figure out if Josh actually believed, or expected anyone else to believe, his outlandish excuses. Andrea always said she didn't care about why anyone was out, just when and for how long. Once he'd been gone three days to rescue an uncle from an abandoned mining city in Utah. When he was in, he did the mindless grunt work without complaint. Occasionally, Andrea sent him on higher-functioning tasks.

Haddie placed the Post-its on the edge of her monitor so she could log in. All five items related to Mel's alibi. Depending on when the DA wrote up a warrant for Mel's arrest, Haddie might be able to complete them before Andrea needed them. Then she could consider some of the ideas that burned in the back of her mind.

She had two items on her list ticked off before her second coffee cooled and Josh strolled in.

Blond scraggly hair squirted from under a knitted orange cap. He wore a thick red and black Mackinaw, yellow swim trunks, and flip-flops.

"Global warming, it's reversing the poles. You'll see. A hundred years from now, Eugene will be the center of the Antarctic, and we'll have to live on the coast." He went straight to Grace's cubicle and leaned over as he spoke. "Of course, once we develop time travel, we can fix all this."

"Shut up, Josh." Grace didn't stop typing.

"Love you too." He didn't leave, just unbuttoned the top button of his Mackinaw. "One hundred years. I'm looking at buying coastline now."

Haddie chuckled. "We'll be dead in a hundred years."

Josh winked and headed for his cubicle, yelling over his shoulder, "Speak for yourself. Turmeric, Baby. Turmeric."

Haddie picked up the company phone and began her third call to the bank to check on the request for ATM footage. As the phone rang, her company email alerted her that she had a new message. She missed the name of the person answering as she juggled the phone to open the email — from the bank. The requested video had been attached below a curt message.

She stumbled over her words instead of just hanging up. "Hey, this is Hadhira from Andrea Simmons Law Firm. Just wanted to thank you for sending over that footage. We'll go over it now." She imagined Grace's expression on the other side of the cubicle wall. "So, thanks."

They're going to think I'm an idiot.

The woman on the other end cleared her throat. "Yeah. Well, thanks."

Haddie groaned after she hung up the phone. "Literally came in at the exact moment I called." She waited as the file downloaded, but Grace ignored her, or at least remained silent.

Her phone vibrated on the desk, and Haddie flipped it over. Liz.

"You're going to freak," Liz texted. "The coroner says there's damage to the DNA and other biomolecules that might be from a high-emission source of ionizing radiation. Todd says he found lingering radioactivity on the car."

Haddie raised her eyebrows. "What does that even mean?"

"It doesn't make sense, unless the car and body were exposed to cosmic rays or high-energy gamma rays, like from a solar flare."

How was that possible? Then Haddie smiled. "A deadly

sunburn? Is this something someone like me or Mel could do?"

The typing took a moment before Liz replied, "Someone piss you off? JK, not without major equipment and know-how. Even then, I'm not sure how to replicate the results."

Proving that Mel couldn't be capable of causing the fire hadn't come up. It didn't fit Andrea's alibi pursuit, but she couldn't ignore it. Unable to commit a murder had been used as an alibi defense before. First, Haddie had to understand this enough to explain the defense to her boss. Then they would need to verify with experts.

"Can you call me at lunch? Explain it like I'm an idiot?"

Liz sent a laughing emoji and a thumbs-up.

Something like this couldn't be common. Terry would love it. She texted Terry the details, copying the terminology from Liz's texts.

His response came immediately. "Don't play me. This is near impossible and way too cool." Terry included a string of emojis that made no sense, except for the three fires interspersed with suns.

"Something like this would show up in an internet search, right?" she asked.

His response came in a flash. "If they even found it. Can I see the report?"

"Not until we subpoena." *If* they subpoenaed. First, she had to get Andrea to check into it. "Check around if you can."

"Yaass!"

After a frustrating night, it was gratifying to see some hope. Haddie took a deep breath as she returned to the interviews, marking up discrepancies for Andrea. If the unusual fire proved useful, then they might get Mel off the charges. Would that be enough for Haddie to let this go? Yes, but she'd follow the case.

Josh began singing in the copy room, and Haddie considered her empty coffee mug. The tension had killed some of her exhaustion. Coffee could wait a few minutes. She needed to knock the rest of the items off her list and get ready for Liz's call at noon. Then, approach Andrea with the information.

A half an hour later when Mel walked in Haddie could hear the sniffling and Toby getting their client settled into the conference room. This wasn't a good sign.

"Coffee?" Haddie asked Grace.

Smiling, Grace handed off her empty mug. "Getting close to done?"

"Yes, but is it ever done?" Haddie strode out to the hall that led past Andrea's office and behind Toby's desk.

Andrea glanced up from her monitor but said nothing. Her office had been cleaned up, but her satchel lay on the credenza, ready.

"Coffee?" Haddie asked.

Shaking her head, Andrea turned back to her screen; two olive green hair sticks seemed to look over the top her head. Her lips were tight and tense. Hopefully, it helped that she didn't have to re-focus Haddie. The woman put in unbelievable hours, but that was the job. Her half-finished mug of black coffee sat at the corner of the desk.

Haddie peeked in on Mel at the conference room door. The blonde bob of her head lay on the table, and she could have been asleep for all she moved. A large, blue-patterned purse lay on the floor beside her chair. She wore pants.

Returning from the kitchen with a cup of light coffee, Toby paused beside Haddie in the hall. "How are you doing?"

"About as good as anyone else. I —" Haddie stopped as the front door to the firm rang. Odd. The office wasn't locked at this time of the morning.

Toby swore under her breath as she moved toward the doorway of the waiting room. Andrea strode out of her office and followed behind. Haddie backtracked to Toby's desk.

They let Detective Cooper inside, along with two officers. A stiff cool breeze brought in the scents of the city and exhaust. Andrea had intentionally locked the door, and the detective looked annoyed with a scowl on his face and sharp movements. He caught sight of Haddie, gawking with the two empty mugs, and managed to furrow his eyebrows deeper into his face.

"Is she here?" he asked.

Andrea tilted her head and nodded wordlessly. She reached out for a warrant, and he gave it to her with a huff. She took long enough to read it that Haddie considered continuing to the kitchen just to avoid the awkward tension. Toby scurried off to the conference room at a nod from Andrea.

"The name of the witness?" Andrea's voice was calm, as if requesting a table at the window.

Detective Cooper looked aside. "Get with the DA on that."

"You likely took the statement." Andrea did not raise her voice. The red bun tilted as her chin rose.

He pressed his mustache down, two fingers down one side and his index finger down the other. His face still scowled, but his eyes avoided her. "You will have to get that from the DA."

They had a witness. It seemed the DA intended to draw out and delay the information, not the detective. Haddie jumped at the wail from the conference room. She placed her empty mugs on Toby's desk and went in to help with Mel.

The woman wore dark blue sweatpants and a matching top. Her yellow bob still had not been brushed out. With her hands pressed to her face, tears smeared wet across her cheeks.

Haddie felt her heart drop, and her chest felt empty. She knew that Mel would have to go with the police, but it hurt.

Toby had her arm around the back of Mel and whispered in her ear. Haddie took the opposite side. Mel didn't resist; in fact, she seemed so loose that she would fall to the floor.

"C'mon, Hon. Andrea will meet you there. You won't be alone." Toby's voice remained calm and soothing.

Together they got Mel to take a step, but she kept her face in her hands, and tears left dark drops down her sleeves and the front of her sweatshirt.

The police moved gently — gratefully — across the room as Toby and Haddie led Mel into the waiting room, where Detective Cooper waited by the door. The older officer, graying at the temples, read Mel her rights as he slowly pulled her arms down for the handcuffs.

Andrea positioned herself in front of Mel. "I'll be right behind you. Again, speak to no one until I'm there with you." She brushed by Haddie as the officers led a stumbling Mel past Detective Cooper. "Finish your work. I'll need everything sent to my drive until I know when they've scheduled the arraignment. After that, it does me no good."

Haddie raced to the back with a glance at Andrea collecting her satchel and purse. Grace glanced up and pursed her lips, turning back to her monitor without a word.

The room smelled of paper and electricity. Haddie had begun sweating.

A witness. Of what? They would know when Andrea told them, or the DA sent over files. Until then she had one job: secure Mel's alibi. She wanted to bring up the unusual aspect of the fire. Surely that would make a difference. But she had to talk with Liz first, then approach Andrea. That could be difficult, depending on when they set the arraignment and if they continued questioning Mel. For now, Haddie intended to wipe everything off her list. She had an hour and a quarter before Liz took her lunch.

She would have finished if, during her search for the last file, she hadn't spotted that Josh had scanned Mark Colman's financial records. Promising to only take a quick glance, Haddie soon had a slew of windows open. The man had another business in Portland. He lived in a house far beyond what little his mortgage company could pay for. She ached to know if Mrs. Colman's records would be coming soon. Had the wife carried the household? He surely didn't. Neither the Portland import business, nor the mortgage brokering seemed to do much more than break even. If the wife didn't have any money, then Mark Colman had something shady going on.

Liz called at noon. "How's it going? Getting everything done?"

Haddie felt her cheeks warm. "Almost. So, we can prove radiation caused the deaths?"

"Yes. When they were trying to determine the source, the lack pointed to solar radiation, which is impossible."

"Impossible?" Haddie took a deep breath. Juries and judges did not trust proof that pointed toward impossibilities. They just ignored it.

"Yes, under circumstances that it did not ignite the city as well."

Haddie closed her eyes. She'd hoped for something that would point to a technical expertise beyond Mel's capability. Maybe Terry would have a different viewpoint. She sighed. It would be tough to get Andrea to look at anything bizarre at this point.

"Then I need to focus on the first victim, go through his finances. I've already started, and some things look wonkier than I'd imagined. I need to figure out what he was into."

"Other than the girlfriend." Liz giggled.

"Yeah." Haddie couldn't shake her last moments with Mel. It was heartbreaking. She found herself dragging another document up.

Liz coughed on the other end of the phone. "How about the wife? Maybe she had a lover gone bad. Lover kills the hubby, then they fight."

It was a possibility. The wife likely knew about the affair. "Maybe. I can talk Andrea into getting her phone records. I'll get the police interview with her as well. I wish we'd had time to get a deposition on her, before —"

"Seance?"

Haddie smiled, but she found it hard to get a solid breath. "Getting goofy. Not helping."

"Just trying to keep it light. You've got schoolwork to think of as well. Balance."

That was going to be difficult. First, she needed to finish Andrea's list, then dig into Mark Colman's other business. Someone other than Mel killed the man and his wife; she had to find out who.

In the college library, Haddie sat at one of the tables near the windows. The room had the dull murmur of whispers, shuffling papers, and laptop keys. Lunch filled her stomach and the taco sauce still warmed her tongue.

The library had tall, thin windows that let in too much light during a nearly cloudless afternoon. Hints of green from trees and lawns mixed with the dull brown of the buildings outside. She'd covered the table with research books and took pictures of them with her phone as she found items that would help with her paper. The top pages of two notepads were filled with references so she could pull the paper together a few minutes before it was due. She would have to buckle down.

Mel weighed on her mind. Haddie had done what she could and finished the prep for the arraignment. Liz had alerted them that the report on the fire had gone to the DA. However, Andrea had shut her down over the radiation — as expected. Too impossible. Grace had promised to let Haddie know when they got the report from the DA.

The shady financials gave her some hope. Really, the only hope. They still didn't know what the witness saw, but it wouldn't be good. If they could prove that there were other motives, strong motives, for the attack on Mark Colman and his wife, then Andrea might be able to cast doubt on circumstantial evidence.

Haddie's phone vibrated under one of the open books.

Terry. He called instead of texted when he got excited. She really should let it go to voicemail and deal with it on her way to class in a couple of hours.

"Hey," Haddie said.

"Three dead Irishmen in a London apartment. Know what they have in common?" Terry sounded too excited.

Haddie slunk down in her chair, trying to avoid being seen talking on her phone. "No. I —"

"A sunburn." He paused, and in her mind, she could see his grin. "A really bad sunburn. Lit the whole complex on fire."

He'd found a similar case. She started to sit up and shoved herself back down. "You're kidding?"

"And — wait for it . . ." He paused so long she felt her jaw tighten. "They were part of a mob. Irish mob, of course."

Haddie raised her eyebrows. Could this be the link she was looking for? She took in a tight breath. "How do you know?" If Mark Colman had any organized crime connections, that would seriously jeopardize the prosecution's case, depending on what the witness saw.

"Interpol report. It got hacked and liberated by someone inside and then scooped up before the governments deleted it. I'll send you a copy. Does this help? Are you going to need me to testify as an expert?"

"What kind of expert?" Haddie slid lower in her chair as one of the librarians scanned the room; they seemed to hate cell phones.

"A conspiracy theory expert, of course."

Haddie sighed. "Please, yes, send me the doc."

"You owe me."

"One big, overly-sweet, citrus-smelling beverage. And my gratitude." The librarian centered her gaze on Haddie.

"I think I've talked them into getting me a fifty-five gallon drum of YellowYum. The woman at the counter says she doesn't do the ordering, but that's just a cover to avoid the salesmen."

She tried speaking without moving her lips. "Gotta go. Thanks." Haddie clicked off and opened a browser, trying to look innocent.

The librarian, a middle-aged woman with an overly tight, button-down blouse, stopped and pointed to her ear and Haddie's phone before cutting across her neck. The woman took silence seriously, at least when it came to cell phones.

Nodding, smiling, and sitting up, Haddie put her phone on the desk.

I have to get Andrea to do a deeper check on the victim. The police might not have taken his background seriously. You couldn't count on their investigation to prove your client innocent. How deep had they dug?

She considered texting Andrea, but their last conversation had been short and curt. Andrea did not want wild theories. Haddie didn't have a feel for Detective Cooper, except that he took everything seriously. Maybe he had looked into Mark Colman's background already. Grace or Josh would not have that information because the prosecution surely wouldn't want it. Andrea would not appreciate duplicating the effort if the police already had that report.

Absently, Haddie found herself opening the browser on her phone and looking up the Eugene police. With a sigh, she found the number to investigations. *This might be a bad idea.*

The librarian glanced over, prompting Haddie to get up and walk toward the door. She would be able to see her papers through the glass and no one would want her scribbled notes, as thin as they were.

The air had a solid chill, and she could smell fresh mulch from the plant beds. In the west, a dark line of clouds barely edged the horizon. It hadn't rained since last week.

"Detective Cooper, please. Hadhira Dawson." Haddie leaned against the alcove, risking the door being opened. "He's expecting my call," she lied. The phone clicked as they transferred her to his cell.

"Detective Cooper." His tone expressed annoyance.

She kept her tone professional but light. "Detective Cooper. Thank you for taking the call. This is Hadhira Dawson at Andrea Simmons Law Firm. I was hoping you could answer a question about Mark Colman's background check. Did you run an FBI inquiry? Does the DA have that file?" She knew the answer to the second question was no.

He answered after a long, uncomfortable silence. "Why are you asking, Ms. Dawson? What do you expect to find?"

Haddie blew out a sigh away from the phone. He wasn't going to answer her question directly, or he hadn't run the check. "Curious to know if he has any ties to criminal organizations. His finances are not adding up. He has an import business in Portland."

"Businessmen often have multiple businesses, Ms. Dawson." He wasn't budging. His tone had become less annoyed though. "Do you have anything that might lead to your — curiosity?"

She doubted he would tell her about any background check at this point. He'd turned this into an interrogation. Still, she might be able to persuade him enough that he would check, if he hadn't. "The circumstances of the fire that led to his death are suspicious. The specifics correlate to a similar death in Britain, where organized crime members were killed." She cringed. It wouldn't work.

He took a long time to respond and Haddie found herself fidgeting at the door, glancing toward the warm table where her paper lay abandoned. "I don't know what your boss is fishing for, but tell her it won't work. Never mind, I'll let her know myself."

"No." Haddie swallowed. This had been a terrible idea. "This is purely my inquiry. I'm trying to find something she can use. Impress her, you know." Intentionally, she'd changed tone to a desperate schoolgirl, hoping to kill it before it got to Andrea. She had to follow these leads without involving her boss until she had something solid. She shouldn't be playing this at all.

"Not very impressive, Ms. Dawson." The connection dropped.

She stared at her phone for a moment. Hopefully, he'd let this go and Andrea wouldn't find out. It had been a miserable idea. She breathed in and out before opening the door back into the library. The only lead she could reasonably investigate was Mark Colman's other business. It wouldn't stir up trouble with the police, or the prosecution, or Andrea.

Portland lay two hours north, or less. She wound her hair around her fist and stared at the open books spread across the table. First, she needed to get some traction on this paper, then class. Tonight, she could look up the address for the import business. Since all the pressing work had been finished for the arraignment, Andrea might not need Haddie at the office. If the rain held off, it would be a nice ride on the Fat Boy.

CHAPTER 13

Sitting at the light in her RAV4, Haddie checked the message on her phone. She tried to ignore the smell of spice and coconut milk from her curry takeout. Her stomach growled.

Andrea had replied with one word: "Yes."

Haddie sighed. Her three texts had been long, explaining Mark Colman's second business and the oddities that Haddie had barely skimmed in the financial reports. She'd carefully avoided the strange origins of the fire. Somehow though, they fit, just not in Andrea's defense strategy. A trip to the import business might give her a lead if it was still open after his death. The phone on record had been his cell. Going there seemed the only logical plan.

This meant skipping her morning class. She didn't worry; she would pass, but with the dogfighting ring and now Mel, she'd put herself behind. She had to catch up on the paper that was due Monday over the weekend.

The light turned green, and she followed a beige Camry, checking the traffic behind her. The odd SUV that might have been following her hadn't shown up again. It very well could have been her imagination. The dogfight gang was still locked up; they'd failed to post bail, which was a good sign that they were just a small group. Still, it didn't hurt to pay attention.

Haddie turned down her street and groaned. Under the overhang of her two-story apartment, Dad leaned against his Shovelhead, parked beside her Fat Boy. How long had he been sitting there? His long auburn braid draped over his shoulder. With the shaved side of his head caught in her headlights, he almost looked Viking, but the black Harley shirt killed that image. He turned toward her, forced a smile, and stood up.

She pulled into her parking spot next to him and stared at the design her lights made against the wood siding. Shadows grew longer at each successive layer of planking that climbed up the wall. Why did he think it was okay to just show up? She had too much going on to deal with him tonight. Sighing, she shifted into park.

Haddie stepped out and gave him a tight-lipped stare. "What do you want, Dad?"

"You said we could talk later." He wore his riding gloves with the fingertips cut out. He smoothed his hair from his forehead to the start of the braid.

She raised her eyebrows. And this was later? "I've got schoolwork." Lingering at the side of her car, she ached to find out more — to understand. Their last meeting had left her more confused than she'd ever been. Only Mel's case had helped her bury the impossible dates he'd given her.

"You've got questions. My answers will not make sense, but I'm willing to try."

"Your answers don't make sense." She pulled her hair back and closed her eyes. "You lied to me when I was a kid."

"Yes. I lie to everyone about my age. Except when I finally told you that I don't age."

She opened her eyes and shivered. *I don't age.* It had been the very statement he'd made when this all started. The answer she'd insisted he give her. The questions had started years ago when she was a teenager, and he'd managed to avoid answering for a long time. He didn't grow old. He grew beards, mustaches, shaved the sides of his head, and had changed over the years, but he didn't age. She'd managed a photo of him when she was eighteen, but otherwise he carefully avoided cameras and cell phones. He looked the same six years later. She felt weak, ready to cry; it had been a long day. She could see Mel being taken out of the office. Andrea's curt replies and arrogant Detective Cooper still weighed on her. Haddie couldn't take any more today.

"I —" She wanted to know, but she was too worn out. "I'm going to Portland tomorrow; if the rain holds out, I'll ride. Do you want to come?" *I'll be fresh — awake.* They could sit at one of the rest stops and clear this up. Her chest tightened at the thought. *This close and I'm procrastinating.*

He nodded and grabbed his helmet off the seat, a black skull cap. "Meet you here. What time?"

"Sunrise." His favorite time. She hadn't even thought the trip through.

He lifted his head as he buckled the strap. He hadn't shaved his chin, leaving reddish-brown stubble. "Can we come in through twenty-six?"

Haddie snorted. "No. I'm not taking an extra four hours to get there. This is work." She took in a deep breath, feeling like they had broken through some barrier. Weight lifted off her.

Dad grunted and threw a leg over his bike. "Sunrise. Love you."

She didn't reply as a large knot swelled in her throat. They'd become so distant. She walked around the back of the RAV4 to get to her passenger door. His Shovelhead blasted alive and the fumes filled the parking area. She had no appetite, but she'd eat. Then she had to get to work on her paper — get something done on it. Her dad pulled down the street as she retrieved her satchel and slid it over her head. She picked up the take-out bag and stared into her car. The day had taken its toll. Tomorrow promised some new resolutions, both in her case and with her dad. Revelations, hopefully.

CHAPTER 14

By 7:00 the next morning, Thomas pulled his Shovelhead onto I-5 with a comforting roar and headed toward Eugene. His bike rumbled through the light traffic. Fast moving dark shapes and bright lights spread out on both sides of the interstate. Predawn gray blotted out the stars. City lights flared to the west, and beyond, a dark, smoky ridge of clouds lay where the storm brewed. They didn't expect rain until later in the afternoon. It would be a good ride.

He couldn't be sure how the talk with Haddie would go. She was the first in a very long time; it had never gone well before. He just had to put his apprehension aside and let her absorb what she could.

The chill of the night air bit into his face and around his collar. He swore he smelled rain on the wind, but it was too far away. When the highway's curve came, he could easily make out the shadows of the mountains against gray sky. They would ride into the valley, and some of the sights would be magnificent, despite all the development along the interstate. The interstate had been there for decades, and people sprang up around any road.

He did hope Haddie was doing well in her studies. He'd have to ask. He would have preferred she'd gotten into something more creative. He saw an attorney as more destructive than creative, but she loved the idea, had since she was in her teens. He could remember the day; they'd been working on a three-wheeler that had been swiped in an accident, a red 1958 Harley-Davidson Servi-Car.

"I'm going to be an attorney, like Perry Mason." She'd had long black hair like her mother's even at sixteen. Back then, she'd worn it braided and tucked inside a blue mechanic's shirt that she insisted he buy for her, red embroidered name and all. "I could make the insurance company pay for the work on an accident like this."

"Perry Mason, who's that?" He'd heard the name somewhere. They'd been packing bearings on the new axle.

Haddie stopped, raised her eyebrows, and opened her arms up in exaggeration. "Who's that? Just one of the best attorneys. He figures out what the criminals are really doing and gets them to admit to it, tricks them. They're all so stupid."

"And you want to do that?" He paused looking up at her. "Why?"

She snorted. "Because they're smart, and they help people."

"We're smart, and we're helping people." He pointed to the bike.

Haddie tilted her head and grimaced. "Not like that, really help. Like when people have big problems."

He hadn't pushed. He'd hoped it had been a phase. The television show had been. The career hadn't.

Turning the corner, his lights lit up the back of an SUV trolling down her road, likely a driver looking to pick up someone. They rolled past Haddie's parking spot and then sped up when he came in behind them. There was no need. He could have waited. He pulled in behind her Fat Boy, which she kept in good shape, and killed his engine.

7:22. Technically before sunrise. He pulled off his helmet and rubbed his head. He didn't need to feel so nervous. Haddie would have a rough time with it. *Devil take me, I have a difficult time with it.* Still, they needed to move forward. He'd committed to this conversation when he answered her last spring, a decision he hadn't made lightly.

The air under her carport had a wonderful scent of grease and fumes from his cooling engine, crisp morning dew air, and the mulched gardens from around the buildings. Solid boots sounded on the stairs, and Thomas turned to watch the end of the carport.

Haddie wore a tan leather jacket zipped against the cold, with a red scarf wrapped around her neck and tucked under the collar. Over one shoulder, she had a light brown business satchel and a lunch cooler with a purple dragon on it. In her hand, she had a thermos and helmet. She looked like her mother with light brown skin, large almond eyes, and a long thin nose. A nervous smile lifted the edge of her lips on the right side.

"I imagined you'd be early." She crouched by her saddle bags and put down the thermos.

He shrugged. "Old habits." He'd been in plenty of armies; they all had you hurry up and wait.

She gave him an odd look and began storing her satchel and cooler bag. The dragon looked too round and cheerful, but she'd always enjoyed modern fantasy stories. Silently, he rubbed his hair flat and slid on his helmet. The sun would take a while to break over the mountains, and the first hour of the ride would be chilly. He waited until she fired up her Fat Boy into a gentle purr before he brought his baby up and it echoed across the buildings. Most of her neighbors would not appreciate their early morning start.

After pulling onto the street, Thomas motioned for her to lead. She would likely stop at the midway point, and then they'd have to talk. The remainder of the ride would give her some time to digest whatever they'd gotten through. He didn't take I-5 up to Portland, so he couldn't know how thick the traffic got, but he doubted it would be pleasant. There were so many people nowadays. Haddie led the way through apartments silhouetted against gray sky.

When they passed over the Santiam River, the sun had taken some of the chill off his face. She pulled into a rest area earlier than he expected. To the west, the clouds held a steady, dark line merging into the mountains. Dreading the conversation, his heartbeat quickened as they rolled by grass yellowing under the cooling season. Haddie led them past a small, white Ford truck with black toolboxes and pulled into a spot facing a pair of oaks and a powder blue picnic table. The next section of the lot had a camper and a red SUV with a young woman walking her dog on the grass.

He turned off the Shovelhead and took a deep breath before unstrapping his helmet. The sun felt good. Haddie had already jumped off and balanced her helmet on her seat. Aching joints didn't let him move as fast unless he needed to. The cold stiffened his fingers. The rest area smelled fresh with nearby water and grass, the city and interstate fumes left behind. A tinted Durango moved behind him toward the next section of parking, leaving them nearly alone.

He followed her to the bright picnic table and took the bench opposite her. "One question at a time."

Face grim, she jumped in. "How old are you?" She spat out the question and pinned him with a look.

He spread both hands out on the powder blue table, feeling the cold surface under exposed fingertips. "Six hundred and twenty-three years old." The last time he'd told his age, he'd been younger than three hundred. Tove had left him, taking their boys.

Haddie raised her eyebrows, and her mouth opened slightly. The dull roar of the interstate intruded into their silence. A west wind pushed at her hair, which had been flattened from being under her helmet. She snapped her mouth closed and swallowed. "That's impossible."

The last time, Tove first accused him of lying. This might be an improvement. "We'll get nowhere if you say that word. Nothing that has happened to me is possible."

"Then how about insane?" She rubbed her face and then came back to pinch her nose. "Six hundred years? You must realize how crazy that sounds."

Try living it. He rubbed his hair down and felt the tie at his braid. "Nonetheless, it is my reality. I don't expect you to immediately believe it."

"Immediately, how about ever?" Shifting on the bench and looking to each side of them, she acted caged, like an animal that needed to flee. Her eyes had widened, and the muscles around her jaw were tight.

He could let her dismiss him as crazy. In time, she'd see he wasn't lying. Tove had been with him for thirty years before she insisted on the truth. He'd loved her enough to make the mistake of not leaving her, and then made it worse by telling her the truth. She'd branded him a demon. Maybe. Haddie had been there when her mother died, but at four years old, she didn't seem to remember it.

"There's three pictures of me on the internet. From the

Great War. I served France." They'd called him a Swede, even though Norway had been independent for a number of years before that. "I'll email you the links."

Haddie stared and her face grew slack — emotionless. At least she hadn't accused him of being the devil. He'd always worried that she remembered the day her mother had died. She blinked and scurried off her bench. After two quick steps, she strolled toward the river and left him sitting at the picnic table. He waited while she wandered.

The woman walking the dog left, and the Durango sat quietly beside the camper in the next lot. Thomas didn't turn to look at the white truck behind him. He just needed to wait. Haddie might have more questions, or she might be overwhelmed and let it be for now. He couldn't imagine how the news would affect her. The more he thought he understood people, the more they surprised him.

She stood for a long time at the far edge of the fading grass, just staring south. The white truck behind him started up and left.

When she started back toward the table, he felt his pulse rise. But she looked composed, pulling her hair out to smooth it.

She tied it back up as she stopped by their table. Her mother had had the same habit. "Send me the links."

Haddie's tone sounded more like she'd agreed to review a legal document than determine his sanity. Well at least she wasn't judging the dog by its hairs. She'd given him a chance to explain, though he hadn't even gotten to how he'd been born in 1985. That, he expected, would be the harder conversation.

Ice in his stomach, he stood up. "Thank you. When we get back." He wanted to hug her, let her feel that everything would be okay, but that would have to wait.

She nodded and made for her Fat Boy.

It had gone better than he'd expected. Then again, she might just think him insane and never talk to him again. He took a deep breath and pushed slow joints to keep up with her.

They reached Portland with the sun warming the day and pulled off I-5 before they reached downtown. They cut through a residential district of old homes and older trees. The asphalt had been recently patched with dark lines that filled cracks from the previous winter. The fumes of the city held the air despite all the green. A turn down another suburban street led them under the interstate, and Haddie took them right onto a thoroughfare with businesses down the sides and a suicide turn lane in the middle.

She moved to the middle lane at a red-topped light-house and then crept forward slowly, as if searching. Hesi-tantly, she pulled down a side street to the left and then into the small parking lot on the corner, where a gray house serving as offices sat empty. A concrete-walled bar or lounge sat across the side street. He killed the Shovelhead and the city noise around him sprang up, mainly from the busy street they'd just left.

"Is this it?" he asked.

Haddie's expression said it wasn't what she'd expected. "No. Not at all. I should have pulled up the street view before driving us out here. I'm looking for 8425 Southwest Barbur Boulevard. Which would be between that building," she said, pointing toward the concrete bunker bar, "and the storage place." She didn't look him directly in the eye.

The door to the gray office had 8405 written on it. Removing a glove, she pulled out her phone and began searching.

Thomas slid off his bike and began unstrapping his

helmet. He wandered across the front of the gray building. The sparse brush on the right corner hadn't been trimmed or mulched in a while. In the drive on the side of the house, fall leaves had spilled into yellow piles from the neighbor's silver maple across the hedge.

"Damn." Haddie shoved her phone in her jacket pocket and put back on her glove. She looked first to the bar, and then stepped toward the sidewalk. "I'm going to ask the storage place next door, but I think it's a false address. I might have wasted your time."

Thomas smiled as he followed. *Hardly a waste.* They'd gotten a little further and she hadn't locked him out completely. Today had been a good day. A ride, and a little uncomfortable conversation. He'd had worse days.

She strode down the sidewalk toward the lighthouse, forcing him to follow. Her posture and speed told him she was pissed. Haddie didn't like wasting her time.

Inside the office, a middle-aged, balding man glanced up from his monitor over round glasses. "Welcome. How can I help you today?" His tone sounded anything but helpful.

Haddie stepped up to the counter, looming enough that the man visibly craned his neck to look at her. "Hopefully you can help me. I'm looking for Sirota Imports at 8425 Southwest Barbur Boulevard."

The man swallowed and tapped his keyboard with one quick stroke. "I — I've never heard of any such place. You must have the wrong information." He spoke fast and stood to check on keys and papers on the counter behind him. His back turned, he shook his head. "Sorry, I can't help you."

Haddie rested her hands on the front counter. "The business is owned by a Mark Colman."

Still checking the keys and shifting papers, the man

glanced back after a moment. With Haddie looming, he quickly returned to the rear counter. "Doesn't ring a bell."

Haddie stood a moment, then raised her hands in an expression of frustration.

Thomas waited. The man, whether he knew anything or not, had no intention of engaging her.

Haddie spun with a frown and muttered as she passed Thomas, "I've wasted your time. Sorry."

He shrugged and they made for the door. Whatever she hunted had her obsessed. He'd seen her like this through her entire childhood. Whenever she got a project, she would do whatever it took to finish it. An asset, if not taken too far.

The door opened with a chime. Haddie didn't turn around as she called out, "Thank you."

She acted as though they hadn't just had the most uncomfortable discussion of their life at the rest area. Haddie could compartmentalize, though. Probably make her a good attorney. It could have gone worse. He could let her be for a while, until she returned with more questions.

They'd reached the other building when she spun to face him. "Did he seem weird?"

He stopped. "Most people are."

"I think he's hiding something."

Nodding, he noticed a dark-tinted Durango pass them. Black, with no stickers. He turned a little late and watched it head down the thoroughfare.

"What is it?" Haddie asked.

"Nothing. It's the same kind of SUV that followed us into the rest area." He turned back to find her frowning.

"I saw a gray Outback, thought it might be following me, but that was a few nights ago," she said.

He would have to keep an eye out. There had been a

gray SUV at her apartment when he'd arrived. "What have you been up to?" What was this Mark Colman business? Sirota Imports?

"I thought it might be the dogfighting ring. I outed them, and the police picked up a small gang. But they're still in jail."

Thomas prickled, momentarily considering getting on his bike and chasing down the Durango. He'd taught Haddie to defend herself, forcing Taekwondo practice on her until she took to it on her own. Still, he had a nasty habit of trying to protect others. It had gotten him into some tight places. This was different, though. Haddie was his flesh and blood.

"Be careful," he said. "How is Mark Colman related to the dogfighting gang?"

Twisting her hair into a black knot around her fist, Haddie started back toward their bikes. "He's not. It's intern work."

He felt his jaw tighten. No matter how independent he wanted her to be, he'd be looking up both Mark Colman and the news of dogfighting rings in Eugene.

He enjoyed another bite of the sausage roll seasoned with hot mustard and looked back to his laptop. The midday numbers looked promising, but he'd have to put more pressure on the Seattle shipping. They were still behind on their payments. *I can't afford any more losses.*

On the credenza in front of a bright window, one of his phones rang among the bank of cells and chargers. One of his men, gray-haired Burke, moved across the room to answer it.

Fall had brought an early chill to the hills. However, it was warm enough that he didn't need the heat until the evening, and the pines would remain green all year long. He preferred Mexico in the thick of winter. A lively people, even if the food lacked. They used spices like garnish. All his people could cook a decent meal; it just took getting the proper provisions.

Burke pulled the phone away from his ear. "It is Milton. Manager at the storage company. Someone asking about Sirota Imports."

Who would be asking about that company? *Blast.* Mark

Colman's name wasn't off the company yet; it would take until the end of the week. Will this fiasco never end?

Taking a breath to calm himself, he waved for the phone. "Milton. Who's asking?"

"Sir. A man and a woman. Bikers." The storage manager had a timid voice.

"Describe them. Detail. What did they say? Exactly."

"Tall, both of them. The woman had light brown skin, tall — I said that — pretty, with long black hair. Dark eyes." Milton sounded more nervous than usual. Had he made some mistake?

Hadhira Dawson. She kept digging. He had people on payroll to make sure this investigation got laid quickly onto the daft girlfriend.

Milton continued, "The man had a long braid, head shaved on one side — left, I think. Light skin. Reddish hair. Messed up nose — like he broke it."

This intern might put a bug in everything. She'd dragged other people in with her now. *I need a good witness to feed the police.* Someone who would know enough to stay away from this intern and lock down the girlfriend for Mark and Sarah's deaths; then it wouldn't matter what Hadhira dug up.

"And what did they say?" He glanced outside at the hills and green treetops. This little man had always annoyed him.

"She knew the address and wanted to know if I knew anything about the company. Mentioned Mark Colman. I said no, of course." Milton said the last part too quickly. He'd likely handled it badly.

Another phone rang, and Burke retrieved it, moving toward the outer edge of the dining room before he answered it.

What had started as a good day had slowly soured. *I don't have time for this.* He pushed his lunch aside. The smell of sausage had lost its appeal.

"If she comes back, call me," he said, hanging up in the middle of Milton saying goodbye and hoping that he'd done everything right.

His men took on a cautious look when he started to lose his temper. Burke had that expression now as he held up the phone. "Dmitry."

He waved impatiently. *I expected this call.* Burke handed the phone over, muted. "Get me everything on Hadhira Dawson."

Burke nodded and pulled out his cell.

"Brother, how are you?" he asked.

"Little Brother. I would be better if you weren't causing such a scene in America." Dmitry's Russian accent came through thick. It had gotten worse since he moved there.

"I've got it handled." In truth, he'd made mistakes and had a mess to clean up. Best if the intern just disappears.

Dmitry assumed the tone of an older brother chiding his younger sibling. "I don't intend to lose everything because you can't control yourself. Ever since Guatemala, someone's been asking around about the incident there. You know that. You need to learn to clean up after yourself. You can't figure out how to hide the bodies?"

He replied through gritted teeth, "I've got it handled."

"Clean up your messes. I'll be out soon, we need to talk." Dmitry said.

I don't need your help. The last thing he needed was an older brother coming out to interfere with the situation. He threw the phone across the tiled floor. A snarl grew in his throat.

His tone rang.

Fire blossomed from his palms across his table. The sausage lit and the plate cracked. The laptop went dead and sparked.

Pain seared across his skin.

He dropped into the visions. Blessed visions.

HADDIE PULLED her Fat Boy into the parking lot of Mark Colman's office. Dad's Shovelhead rumbled in beside her.

Solidly built and tall, her dad moved slowly. He'd always complained about aching joints. He scanned the small lot with the same intensity he had always had. Everything he'd always done seemed different, shaded with what she learned about him.

She couldn't look at her dad without her stomach turning queasy. Insanity made the most logical sense, but only if she wasn't sure that Dad hadn't aged her entire life. The other option — that he actually was centuries old — What was he? What did that make her? Had her mother known?

She shivered and turned away. The lot had a white Maxima and a silver Cruze parked in it. The air smelled crisp, with a faint tinge of grease coming from the paint-peeled shop next door. The bank's drive-through had a white Ford work van stopped at it.

The camera footage had been requested and the credit union hadn't required a subpoena. It would be interesting to see the activity on the night of Mark Colman's murder. Perhaps there would be a clue.

"What are we here for?" her dad asked, smoothing back his hair.

She didn't look at him but pointed toward the office entrances. "This is the first victim's office. I want to ask the secretary here about the other business he owned. The one that doesn't exist. She might have handled something, even mail, for Sirota Imports."

Jasmine had been forthcoming and might shed some light onto the fabricated business. The company had to get mail, even if just a business license.

The stench of mold hit her as she entered. A note hung on the mortgage company door. Trying not to take a breath, Haddie walked down the hall. The mortgage company had been closed and a cell number had been left to call for service. Had Jasmine found another job, or had the son taken over? She should have gotten Jasmine's number. The résumé would have it, or at least an email.

"Damn." Haddie pulled out her phone to take a picture of the note.

"What is it?" Dad asked.

He stepped closer to read the note, and she found herself stepping away. Was she scared of him now? Her throat swelled. "They're closed. I'd hoped they might have some mail, better yet, records on this Sirota Imports."

Moving around him, she headed for the exit. Between the smell and the close confines of the narrow hall, she wanted to be back outside. She'd taken two steps when the door thumped open. Turning, she found him dropping his knife back into the sheath at his belt.

"It's open." He tilted his head and shrugged before walking into the office.

The alarm. Drawing in a stiff breath of moldy air, Haddie raced toward him. The light flicked on in the office. She reached the doorway, and the alarm pad still flashed its error message. "Dad," she hissed. What was he thinking?

He'd walked past Jasmine's desk and stood in the interior office, facing the light from the window outside.

Breaking and entering. Not something the bar association looked favorably on. "Dad, leave. Now."

He stepped into the office, disappearing from view. Haddie closed the door, making sure the jamb hadn't been damaged. She should have left her gloves on.

Dad rummaged through an inbox on a cheap office desk. Pens and a coffee mug lay on a calendar pad with circular stains and doodles. A red stapler and a pink box of tissues sat on the far side. A wood-laminate bookcase stood against the wall to the left of the window; its blinds slanted up so that she could see the sidewalk. A matching file cabinet sat on the right with a picture of Sarah and Mark Colman on a boat. A happier time of their life. Mel must have enjoyed seeing that.

"Nothing addressed to Sirota Imports," her dad said.

"We're leaving." Haddie wanted to grab him, pull him out, but she also didn't want to touch him.

"Might as well look around. You've already broken the law. Make the best of it." He waved unopened envelopes over his shoulder.

Haddie glared, but he didn't turn around. The wooden filing cabinet seemed to be the only storage in the room, though the desk likely had drawers. Raising her eyebrows, she took a deep breath. "This could be just as bad for you. What if they arrested you, checked your license? What would they find?"

He grunted and moved around to the back of the desk,

opening a drawer. "Perfect credentials. Every generation, they make them more sophisticated. But there is always someone as good as them."

"Fingerprints?" Had he been arrested? Great. Now she had something else to look up. A background check on her dad.

He nodded, as if agreeing, but then held up his right hand and wiggled fingers. He'd pulled his glove off enough to cover his fingertips.

Clumsily, she tested the filing cabinet, trying not to use her fingertips. Locked. It didn't mean Mark Colman hid something important here. Everyone locked office cabinets.

Dad had noticed her dilemma and approached, drawing his knife. She didn't stop him as he popped the latch and opened the top drawer.

He went back to the desk. "Man didn't keep much here."

She grabbed a tissue from the desk and flicked through the sparse file tabs. The one listed as business license had two documents regarding the mortgage company. In another folder, Colman kept his broker's license. There was nothing in the top drawer for Sirota Imports. She moved down to the bottom drawer, glancing at their picture. Palm trees on a distant beach — tropical. "Who killed you? Why?"

If Colman worked for organized crime, would he keep anything incriminating in this office? Maybe he'd had records at home. Is that why Sarah Colman had been burned too?

"Condoms and sweets. Doesn't even keep a bottle in here." Dad closed the drawer closest to Haddie. "Find anything?"

When she didn't respond, he moved to the shelves and

began looking through the dozen books there. Model cars took up most of the space, along with some pictures.

Haddie found nothing. The lower drawer held blank forms. The file cabinet seemed as much decoration as the rest of the room. Jasmine likely had been in charge of client records — or they kept everything digital. Did Colman have online storage?

She couldn't spend too much time in the office, certainly not enough to dig through the company computer, which was likely password protected. This had been a mistake. One that Dad had started. She'd never seen him do anything illegal before, besides speeding. Maybe a little trespassing when they'd hiked or camped. Was it just their conversation today that had him acting differently? Or was this the real him? The centuries-old him?

"Where were you born, and when?" She blurted it out before she could stop herself.

He stopped, returning a gray book to its place on the shelf. Facing her, he rubbed his hair back with a grim look, wincing as he sat on the edge of the desk. "I was born in Laconia, New Hampshire, in 1985." He stared out the window.

That was impossible. *He's insane.* All of this, some bizarre, imagined manifestation to explain why he still looked the same. A physical anomaly. Some disease that affected the brain and made him seem not to age. The room felt colder. She closed her eyes. She'd actually begun believing in some paranormal explanation.

Haddie opened her eyes and kicked the file cabinet drawer shut. Wordlessly, she spun and headed out of the office, using the tissue she held to open the door to the hall. She left it open, ignoring the stench as she marched toward the exit. She'd been a fool. The morning had been wasted. The trip to Portland: useless.

She took a deep breath of fresh air, trying to clean out her lungs and mind. Get back to the office. Thursdays were her afternoons there. Dig up some more on Sirota Imports and forget about her dad. Something in Mark Colman's business interests would link her to sketchy connections. She was sure of it.

Dad exited the building as she neared her bike. She couldn't look at him. It physically hurt. She would have to get him help.

"Hadhira?"

She turned to the voice, recognizing it. David walked toward her with bright eyes and a broad smile.

"Back again?" she asked. "What do you do? You said you had a client here."

He stepped close enough that she could see the smile lines at the edges of his eyes. "Electrical engineer. What are you doing back here?"

Haddie felt a cold chill and rescued her smile. *Oh, just breaking into an office.* "Wanted to see if Jasmine was here." Partly true.

Dad waited on his bike, helmet on.

David looked awkward for a moment, clearing his throat. "Listen, I'm just picking up some plans and have the afternoon off. Hadhira, would you like to . . . maybe grab a coffee?"

Tea, but yes. He seemed quite adorable when he was being shy. Not too shy, he had asked her out. "Call me Haddie. I can't. I've got to get back to work, but this week-end?" With a paper due Monday. *I could use a distraction.*

David beamed. "Haddie. That would be great. I'll give you my number so we can set up something."

"I'll text you tomorrow, Friday. We can pick a place and time." She opened her contacts.

Dad still sat on his bike, beside hers, as David went inside with a quick glance and smile back at her.

Haddie climbed on wordlessly, started the engine, and rolled back. They would need a little time before she could get into all this with him. She dropped into gear and angled toward the alley that led to the street.

She heard screeching tires behind her and veered back into the parking lot. A beat-up gold Taurus raced past her, almost clipping her back tire. It must have been coming down the cross alley. Had it turned toward her? As the car squealed onto the road, she caught a glimpse of the driver, a young white male with short blond hair, almost a military cut. The right rear quarter had been hit prior; the turn lights had red tape over them. It had a hand-written paper tag. Horns blared as a utility truck braked to avoid rear-ending the car.

"Haddie." Dad was off his bike, moving toward her with a concerned frown.

Turning her wheel, she checked the alley twice before driving into it.

CHAPTER 17

NOTING THE SCENT OF COFFEE, Haddie stepped into the office and took a deep breath.

"Hey, Haddie." Toby sat at her desk, scrolling through her phone, which lay beside the mouse pad.

Haddie stopped at the desk and peeked toward Andrea's office. "How's it going?" The door was closed.

"Good." Toby noticed her glance toward the office door. "She's gone." She smoothed an eyebrow. "You went to Portland?"

"Yeah. A waste." A rising anxiety pushed up her chest, and Haddie forced herself not to think of Dad. It hurt too much. Get to work. "Please tell me there's some coffee left."

"About an hour old." Toby looked back to her phone. "Grace made it. It's been quiet here, but Josh should be back soon — picking up some files from the DA."

Haddie adjusted her satchel and pulled her hair from under the strap and smoothed it out. "Any bagels left from the other morning?"

Toby shook her head. "Josh."

"Worth a shot." Haddie should have stopped and

bought lunch. She wasn't thinking straight. Tying her hair back up, she sighed and headed around Toby's desk.

"I've got Mapo tofu in the fridge, might not be too cold. You're welcome to it." Toby waved in the general direction of the kitchen.

Haddie spun. "You sure?"

Toby nodded and waved again.

"Thanks." Haddie turned down the hall toward the kitchen.

Tofu wasn't her favorite, but spices made it passable. The yogurt and apple in her cooler bag hadn't dented her hunger on the way back from Portland. Her head reeled after the trip to the mortgage office, but she needed some food. Digging into Mark Colman's finances would help get her mind straight again. Mel sat in jail, unable to raise a sufficient bond for the bail. Andrea wouldn't be in a good mood.

The kitchen — little more than a sink, microwave, and fridge — always looked clean, almost unused. She grabbed a fork from the drawer and stabbed a piece of spicy tofu before finding her mug. Her stomach rebelled at first, but she'd been queasy over her dad. Once she got settled and working, it would pass.

With a full mug, she worked her way to their back office, where Grace glanced up from her cubicle.

The delicate features of her face never seemed to wrinkle, perhaps because she never frowned and her smiles were light and gentle. "How was Portland?"

Dismal. "The building doesn't exist. That should teach me to do more research. I should have looked it up on the property appraisers to see who owned it. Would have figured it out then, I'd imagine." No notes from Andrea. Good. She could focus on Colman's finances.

"Sorry." Grace turned back to her monitor. "We're supposed to get the witness statement today from the mail carrier who saw Mel Schaffer at the Colmans' residence."

Haddie paused with her hand still on the mug handle after she'd placed it on the envelope she used as a coaster. "What?" No wonder bail had gone so high. "When do they say Mel was there?"

"Four that afternoon."

Sliding Toby's lunch onto her desk, Haddie shrugged the satchel off her shoulder and dropped it to the floor. The fire had been started at ten. Six hours later. Did they think Mel sat with the woman for six hours? Probably not. But her being seen around the woman's house would not be good, in any case. Still circumstantial.

Logging in, Haddie froze when she saw she had emails. Dad would be sending her a link — one that would prove his identity, at least back a century. And if it was proof . . . ?

Three spam and a text with a link from Terry. No email from Dad. No proof. Haddie let out a breath and reluctantly clicked the URL. It led to a sketchy website with an accident report from a Russian scientist supposedly burned during a secret particle accelerator collision of photons. *Not helpful.* She closed the conspiracy website.

Her head spun with everything she'd gone through that day. Portland had been a bust, and Dad was . . . impossible and maybe crazy. He'd actually broken into an office, though technically so had she by following him in.

Then there was David. She drew a deep breath.

It's just coffee. Still, it gave her one positive thing to hold onto in the madness. Unless, of course, he was a serial killer.

She twisted her hair into a knot before typing to Terry. "Hey. Can you look up this number? See if he's some kind of weirdo?"

"Date?" Terry replied.

"Maybe. If he's not a sociopath."

"Got it, Buckaroo."

Haddie put the phone down, lining it up even with her mouse pad. *Great, now I'm stalking him.*

The clatter of Grace's keystrokes broke through Haddie's thoughts. Taking a breath in and out, she opened Mark Colman's finances and her spreadsheet.

She'd notated his income from business accounts and had begun adding in expenses to her calculations. He ran most of his purchases through Amex and paid house bills from his checking account. Opening his bank statements, she already knew that he didn't make enough to cover a house in Cal Young — most started at half a million, and he'd had a nice one. Before it burned with his wife.

The mortgage payment was extremely low. Pulling up the property appraiser's site, she paused to double-check her addresses. Sarah Colman had purchased the property two years prior for one hundred and sixty thousand, a fifth of the appraised value. Something wasn't right. Haddie flipped through the statements just after the purchase. No major renovations, barely even furniture. Stabbing another piece of tofu, Haddie scrolled as she chewed, barely noticing the spice. She moved back to property appraiser and dug to find the corporation that had sold Sarah Colman the property.

Twenty minutes later, she'd finished her lunch, let her coffee get cold, and come no closer than a Panamanian company with no officers listed. Someone, possibly organized crime, had gifted the Colmans the house through shell corporations and left Haddie with a list of people to search through, if she ever found the time.

Her searches had led to one oddity that she put to the side to follow up on. Regular forty-eight hundred dollar checks to a vineyard in California named Jessup Farms. Perhaps the Colmans liked a fine vintage. From the company's website, Haddie dialed them.

"Jessup Farms, Ellis speaking, how can I help you?" The man sounded pleasant, and young.

"Yes, please. This is Hadhira Dawson from Andrea Simmons Law Firm. We're working on the case regarding the Colmans' deaths here in Eugene. We've found some large purchases from your company, paid via check, and hoped you could tell us what was invoiced. The last was for forty-eight hundred, cashed on September third from an account owned by Mark and Sarah Colman."

"Customers, you said. Dead? Sorry to hear. Forty-eight hundred, that's more than I've seen, except for a couple of our LA customers. September third? I'll check invoices for August."

Haddie could hear the keyboard clacking from the other end of the connection. After her latest failures, it felt good to have someone eager to help. Anything that would be a solid lead. Not that buying wine might be that, it just was an odd reoccurring cost that warranted a quick call.

Grace answered the phone on the other side of the cubicle. "Andrea Simmons — hi, Andrea. No, I asked —"

The vineyard employee cleared his throat. "Ms. Simmons? I don't show anything for that amount in August, September, or even July." The man sounded concerned. "Perhaps a different winery?"

Odd. She didn't correct her name. That hardly mattered. Who was cashing these checks, then? The owner, perhaps?

Grace stood, catching Haddie's attention. "She's on the phone. Let me see if I can get her to take your call, Andrea. Or, if she needs to call you back."

Haddie raised a finger. "Alright, well I'll follow up on this. Thank you for your help. Bye." She hung up without waiting for a response and nodded to Grace. When the line lit, she punched it. "Andrea, hi."

"Got your text about Portland. That's odd, but I don't know that it helps us without anything else." A cat meowed somewhere in the background; Andrea was at home. "What are you working on? Colman's finances?"

Haddie swallowed. Earlier, Andrea had been perturbed over the idea, but that was when she'd been tasked with working on Mel's alibi. Now, she sounded curious. "Yes. Sarah bought their home in Cal Young for one hundred and sixty thousand. Traced the seller through shell corporations to a Panamanian company."

"Okay. You might be on a good track. Anything else?"

"Yes. I was on the phone with a winery that Mark sent forty-eight hundred to nearly every month. No record of them buying anything." Haddie smiled hopefully.

"Okay." Andrea paused, leaving the sound of something scraping. "Who owns the winery, are they connected to the Colmans?"

Haddie twisted her hair into a ball and looked at it. "I hadn't got that far."

"Alright, this is good, keep looking into his finances — you might be onto something." A thump sounded over the phone. "Still waiting on the wife's phone records. Did they send over the police interview with the wife?"

"No. Want me to put a call into the DA's office?"

"Hit up Detective Cooper. If he sent them over, I want to know when. I'll bust Dillard's ass personally if they're sitting on these reports."

Haddie dropped her hair, swallowing. "Detective Cooper?" After her last call, she didn't really want to stir him up. Should she tell Andrea about the previous call? That meant bringing up the strange situation around the fire again. That hadn't gone well.

"Yes. Email me an update. I'm working from home today." The cat meowed again. "Anything else?"

My life is falling apart, and my dad is likely insane. "No, whatever I find, I'll send you in the email."

"Thanks. Good work." Andrea dropped off the connection.

Haddie took a sip of cold, black coffee. The bitter flavor made her yearn for some unsweetened tea. She could make some but didn't want to lose momentum. Pulling up the police website, she found the investigation unit's phone number. She just had to be diplomatic with Detective Cooper, and hopefully he'd forgotten about her previous call already.

She recognized his voice as he answered. "Detective Cooper? Hadhira Dawson with Andrea Simmons. Did the DA send in a request for us to get the police interview with Sarah Colman?" She could hit him for the phone records next.

"The intern?" So much for him forgetting her. He had that same annoying clipped tone as before. "I wouldn't know. Check with records. I'll transfer you."

Haddie's jaw tensed. "Wait. Have you looked at Mark Colman's finances? Didn't you see how little he, well his wife, paid for that house? And his business in Portland, it's a fake address —"

His tone became more aggressive. "Ms. Dawson. Is this an inquiry from the defense attorney, or her over-zealous intern?"

"We are looking more carefully —" *Than the police did.* Haddie stopped herself. Insinuating their incompetence would not get her the phone records, or anything else, for that matter. "At the disparity between Mark Colman's income and expenditures, as well as his business connections. I'm just hoping you might have more to offer on these topics."

"If it was relevant, it was in our reports."

Infuriating man. "Those reports are fairly thin. You still haven't said if you investigated Mark Colman's finances further." If he wasn't determined to find Mel guilty, he seemed to have no interest in following other leads.

"We've done our work, Ms. Dawson. It's up to the DA now. Put your inquiries through them. Just make sure you stay inside the lines during your investigation." She could hear tapping in the background. "Your mother died when you were a child, in '96? And your father, Ms. Dawson, he was born in Nampa, Idaho in 1971?"

The back of Haddie's neck chilled. "Yes." How did he know? All of this was on record, but why did he care?

"And he was adopted by a Ben and Laurel Dawson, deceased in '78 and '89, respectively?"

"Yes." Haddie raised her eyebrows and took in a breath. "Why are you looking up my family?"

There was a pause, then a single click on a keyboard. "I like to know who I'm dealing with, Ms. Dawson. Stay inside the lines."

The connection cut off. Was this meant to threaten her somehow? How far would Cooper dig? She'd need to mention this to Dad. No, she couldn't.

The phone still pressed against her ear, Haddie let out her breath. Shaking, she returned the phone to its cradle and pressed her fingers against the table. Her father's history terrified her. No. What she *didn't* know about it terrified her. Did that mean she didn't think he was insane?

Elbows on the counter, she pressed her face into her hands. Dad made this all worse — he distracted her. But how could she ignore it? And Detective Cooper? How had she let that devolve?

She took a deep breath and forced her concerns into a small pile. *I'm not going to let these feelings own me. Dig in.* She had work to do.

First, she had to call back and get records on the phone.

CHAPTER 18

HADDIE WALKED BACK from the kitchen, a glass of strong, hot tea melting ice cubes in a curious mix of heat and cold against her palm. A strong earthy aroma with a hint of citrus rose from her drink.

Toby looked up as she passed and nodded. The afternoon had passed with Josh's return and three new Bankers boxes for him to scan. "I can hear Josh from here. That's gotta be fun." Toby smirked.

He'd been singing since he arrived. Quietly, after Grace had talked to him.

Haddie chuckled. "It's better than him talking."

The chime for the door rang, and they both looked up to see a tall, pale man with blue eyes step in. He wore a tan three-piece suit, a red tie with thin, blue, diagonal stripes, red socks, and light brown leather dress shoes. He had curly black hair well-styled over the ears. He swaggered, as if he carried more weight than he did.

"Good evening, ladies." He had a southern, perhaps Texan, accent.

Toby sat straighter. "Good afternoon. Can I help you?"

The man stared at Haddie, somehow pinning her there with tea cooling in her hand. "I'm certain you can. First, I'd like to schedule an appointment — a consultation — with Andrea Simmons. My name is Bruce Palmer."

His eyes seemed to pierce, and his tone commanded in a way that made Haddie want to help.

Toby cleared her throat. "Ms. Simmons has a case that is tying up a lot of her time. I'll have to call you —"

Bruce kept his eyes on Haddie as he produced a card from his palm and handed it to Toby between two fingers. "Second, I would have your names."

"I'm Toby." She took the card and held it with both hands.

Bruce waited, unwavering. He had a presence like her dad, confident and ready, but he might have been forty.

She swallowed, pushing any thought of age, or Dad, aside. "Haddie Dawson." She made an exaggerated gesture to the back office, as if that might break the lock of his gaze. "And, I've got to get back to work. Pleased to meet you, Mr. Palmer."

He nodded. "A pleasure. I look forward to seeing you again, Haddie Dawson."

For no apparent reason, she shifted her drink to her other hand and squirmed uncomfortably before actually walking. Awkwardly, she moved down the hall listening as he talked with Toby. She could still imagine his eyes. A light blue that worked with the tan of his jacket.

Grace swore as she hung up her phone. "Third call today and still the DA is blowing me off."

"Damn," Haddie tested a sip of her tea as she eased back into her chair. Some client had sent Andrea a bag of Darjeeling Bergamot, which immediately got gifted to the kitchen. Lighter than Earl Grey, it made a great iced tea, or her version of the drink. She'd picked up the habit her first year in college. Cindy, her first roommate, would make sweetened tea by pouring the hot tea over sugar, then adding ice. Haddie had copied the technique for her own unsweetened version, and now she preferred it over tea chilled in the fridge. The flavor popped more, if you made it strong enough when it was steeping. Something about it being freshly brewed seemed to add to the flavor.

Mark Colman's finances had run as dry as she could get. She had a list of people and places to investigate. First, she wanted to look up the address in Portland that she'd wasted time on that morning. Worst case would be if it led to her finding the actual address; it was possible that the street or number had been recorded wrong with the Secretary of State.

Curious, she typed the address on the state website. A second business, Larrin Imports, Inc., came up under the registration of a Marino Zannetti. The business had lasted six years and ended three years ago after they failed to file. She hardly considered it a coincidence that another import company registered at the same fake address with less than a year between the two. Maybe Marino Zannetti could answer some questions.

Her email dinged and she absently checked.

Dad's email. Haddie swallowed and blinked. The past few emails she'd checked in dread; now, when she wasn't thinking of him, it came in. She opened the message.

Three URLs waited alone without any other text. She couldn't not check them out; she couldn't even wait. But apprehension soaked into her bones like ice.

The first opened a commemorative war site's photograph: a gray picture of ten soldiers in a trench lined with what looked like pallets. They had long buttoned coats, some with rifles slung over their shoulders, and one with a paper, possibly a map. Wide-brimmed helmets hung to their eyebrows, so she zoomed in until she recognized her dad's brooding face and misshapen nose. Blood drained from her neck and face.

The second photo came from a university site where they discussed the war's mental health impact. Her father, with short hair, lay sleeping on the side of the road with other soldiers.

The third caught him nearly smiling as he marched through a city street, bayoneted rifle on his shoulder.

Haddie shivered. If this was not her dad, it was a blood relative. With the same broken nose? How could that be possible? The photos had no attribution or names of the soldiers. Did she really believe her dad had lived for centuries? Then how could he have been born in 1985? She could not accept it.

The clearest image was the second photo, her dad sleeping with his head on a pack, his face clearly in focus. She took a snippet, isolating him, and cringed at the grainy quality when she zoomed in. It wasn't possible. She felt in shock, but her hand found her phone.

She texted Terry. "If I send you some pictures, can you do the recognition thing on the web, tell me what you come up with?" Maybe her dad had been caught in more recent pictures unawares.

He replied instantly, "I am a black belt in recognition-thingy stuff."

Haddie smiled, despite herself. "Great, look for my company email. Thanks."

Terry still typed. "This David looks clean. Your boyfriend's not a serial killer. Learning Japanese. Likes iguanas, which is weird." He followed it with devil emojis.

"Not my boyfriend." Haddie smiled. She could pick a time and place now; she didn't have to wait for Friday.

She shook her head. *I can't think about that right now.* So, he's not a serial killer.

Her finger poised over her phone. Her face flushed. She was wanting to flirt with some guy while Mel sat alone in jail.

Still, she scrolled back to Terry's message and stared at the picture of her dad. She pushed the phone aside, shaking. Anyone living this long couldn't fit into reality. But this *was* Dad. Haddie took a short breath, trying to force the thoughts away. 1985. How could he think that statement fit with his other insanity? The pictures could be an elaborate hoax. They did not fit Dad as she knew him. Obviously, she didn't know him. He wouldn't allow pictures. If anything, he avoided being noticed. *Stop.*

Opening a new email to Terry, she mechanically pasted snippets with the URLs. *Don't think.*

As she sent the email, her hand trembled as it touched the glass of cooled tea. She stared for a moment and blinked. What next? Her focus blurred, the white of the screen forcing her to squint.

Zannetti. Find him. She returned to the last tab, where she had Marino Zannetti pulled up. She nodded and minimized to her desktop, then clicked a red icon. Logging in mechanically, she found a place to put the man's name. As familiar as the process felt, the moment felt alien and detached, like she wasn't really there.

When the data came up, her eyes flitted down the information until she came to a date, and she sighed. Zannetti was dead. Three years ago, when the filing stopped. No interview. A dead end. She smiled, thinking that Terry would have liked that thought.

Her face tightened and she pushed away the image of Dad standing with men who were likely long dead, or over a hundred years old themselves.

She opened her browser again and pasted Zannetti's name into it.

Grace's voice caused her to jump. "Witness interview is in."

As if Grace could see her, Haddie nodded. Swallowing with a dry mouth, she answered, "Thank you." She'd felt alone. The voice of someone else brought some sense of normalcy, like she'd awakened from a dream. Still groggy, but awake.

A number of headlines came up with the Zannetti search, including "Deadly Mugging at Picc-A-Dilly Flea Market." Right in Eugene. It had to fit somehow.

"Damn," Haddie muttered.

"What? Problem with the file?" Grace asked.

"No, no. Sorry. I found another owner of an import business at the same bad address in Portland. It ended just before Mark Colman opened his import business. Strange, right?" Haddie found her hands gesturing to the gray cubicle wall and stood. "I just found out that this previous owner, Marino Zannetti, died in a mugging here in Eugene. Mark Colman wasn't mugged, but I'd like to see Zannetti's mugging report."

Grace shrugged. "Email me the date and name, and I'll get it for you."

Haddie smiled. "Thanks. That'd be great."

Two owners of import businesses at a fake address in Portland, both killed in Eugene. Too much coincidence. She needed to tell Andrea. And then? The witness.

CHAPTER 19

For the third time, Haddie picked up her empty glass of tea, sighed, and put it down.

Josh sang, mumbling out a lyric from the copy room. He'd come back with two more Bankers boxes of files and had begun scanning after a few minutes of annoying Grace. Their back office had acquired stacks of the boxes. Andrea had requested everything she could get from the prosecution, and Mel still sat in jail.

Haddie read through the short statement for the second time. Her focus kept drifting among Dad and his photos, Detective Cooper's odd statements, and checking to see if Terry had responded. She had requested the business records of the California vineyard, but those names would be difficult to get. Her coworkers had noticed; Josh had claimed she acted "itchy," whatever that meant.

The witness, a Malorie Sanchez, reported that when she delivered mail to the victims' address, she'd seen a blonde woman sitting in Mel's white Optima across the street, supposedly watching the residence. Haddie had pulled up the street satellite photos and found the curving road in Cal Young. Detective Cooper's questions had not been leading, and the interview was thorough. With no mailbox on the street, Malorie had gotten out of the mail truck, and Mel had just been sitting there. In the quiet neighborhood with tight streets, it would have been very obvious, but the mail worker hadn't noticed Mel on the way in, just when she got out across the street.

It would be interesting to see the woman on her route by the victims' house.

Terry texted, "Whoa."

Haddie's chest tightened. She picked up the phone and leaned back into the chair. "What?" she typed.

"Was that your dad's dad?" He followed with an image. "This is your dad. Right?" Dad riding on a bike toward a camera. A closer helmet in the foreground covered his shoulder and part of the bike. Color photography, something recent.

Perhaps involving Terry had been a bad idea. Still, she couldn't help herself. "When is that?" she texted.

"1981, Daytona." Terry had to think something was odd, even if he believed the war images and the bike images were separate people.

Haddie scrolled back to the picture and froze there. *Nothing that has happened to me is possible.* He'd said it when they'd started talking. She couldn't have just let the questions sit there. If this was him in 1981, then according to him, he hadn't been born yet. Each answer made it worse.

The image shifted as Terry texted again. "Was this what you expected? You found his birth father?"

That would answer Terry's questions, hopefully. "Yes," she answered. "Thanks!"

"Your dad doesn't look like, what . . . sixty?"

What was she supposed to say? "Yeah." She took in a deep breath. "Thanks. Boss here. Later."

Putting her phone down, she held her hands toward it as if to will it to stay silent. She couldn't absorb any more without breaking down. Nothing had ever made her feel this way. The world felt wrong and broken. She had to focus on something else. Anything else. The only thing she had in front of her was the testimony from the mail worker. What was she going to do, prove it wrong? The way the day had gone, she'd only make it worse.

Automatically, without thinking, she scooped up her satchel and stood.

Grace looked up and then back at her computer. "3:15. You done for the day?"

"I'm going to see if I can watch the mail lady make her rounds."

Grace shrugged lightly. "Okay. What'll that prove?"

Haddie felt like she visibly trembled. "Not much. Just curious." She ached to be on the road and focused there. No email, no text. Maybe she could clear her mind for just a moment. Malorie's statement sounded weird, though she couldn't put her finger on it. Maybe seeing the scene would help.

"You okay?" Grace tilted her head.

Her words came out too fast. "I'm fine. Great. Everything's good." Haddie tried to smile, but it didn't work. *I need to get out of here.*

CHAPTER 20

Haddie sat on the Fat Boy, twisting her hair into knots and releasing it while she stared toward the entrance to the dead-end street. The stench of the Colmans' burnt-out home permeated the air. The house behind her had someone wailing country music, but it was muffled enough that she caught only the high notes.

Across the affluent neighborhood, manicured grass had started to turn tan, and a few of the maples had turned yellow. Each house seemed to pride itself in having a variety of large trees surrounding it, except for the expansive front lawns. Around the black walls of the Colmans' house, one of the trees had lost its leaves, and another was beginning to turn yellow. Outer bushes, still green, or at least alive, hid much of the fire damage from her angle. The wind gusted, tossing leaves off trees. She parked where Mel had supposedly sat.

In the west, a line of dark clouds brewed. She'd have time to run home before any chance of rain; the RAV4 would be better to take to class.

Her phone vibrated, and she held her breath as she picked it up.

Liz texted, "Coffee? Before your class?"

Haddie nodded to herself. She couldn't exactly explain about Dad, but some company would be a good distraction. Besides, she wanted to know how this impossible radiation could be created. A fire as impossible as Dad. "Sounds good," she texted.

"Common Grounds? I need chocolate."

The university café offered baked goods, often brownies. Haddie might go for an açaí bowl. "5:15?" she texted.

"I'll be there." Liz followed with another text, "Thanks for getting my car fixed. Works great."

Biff's friend, Benny, had Liz's car ready that morning. Haddie doubted the car worked great, but at least it ran. "No problem."

Haddie stared at the burnt wall rising over the green bushes. What did Biff know about Dad? He'd only been working there about six years. Phone in hand, she felt chilled. Wind rippled through the brush, swaying them. The scent of wet, burned wood had a deeper, primordial effect, like an ancestral warning. Her mind locked when she thought of her dad. Too much impossible to process.

She was there, working, to prove Mel innocent. *Focus.* The firm's client sat in jail alone. From every indication, she had no real friends, just coworkers who she went out after work with on occasion. A sad life, truly. And, Mel had been dating a married man. Haddie tried not to judge that.

What did Andrea plan next? Since the arraignment on Sarah Colman's murder, she seemed okay with Haddie following the alternate perpetrator theories. Mark Colman's finances just pointed to shadier business practices and had given her no concrete leads. Forty-eight hundred a month or two to a California winery wasn't going to free Mel. Neither would a bad business address.

A stretch, but a lover for Sarah Colman was still an option, but how would you investigate that? Find her friends — interview where she frequented. Phone logs, emails. Perhaps Josh was scanning those, or that was what Grace fought the DA for. The DA had little information on Sarah's life because Detective Cooper hadn't looked too deeply. He had, however, bothered to dig into Haddie's life, even if for nothing more than to warn her from digging too deep. Was he that insecure?

The Irish mob who had died in a similar fire could lead to a possible organized crime connection, especially with sketchy business dealings considered. It wasn't anything they'd bring to court, but it could lead her to something else. Perhaps Andrea would spring for a deeper background check with the FBI or Interpol, if she hadn't already.

She jerked up straight. Haddie almost missed the mail truck heading toward her. Sitting in the shade of canyon live oak, she had a good view up the street before it curved, and decorative vegetation hid the entrance. If Mel had been looking to intercept Sarah, it would be a good place to park. It also would have given Haddie a good chance of spotting the mail woman, if she hadn't been preoccupied. She straddled the Fat Boy, one leg on the ground and her other on her peg so that her knee rested on the tank.

The truck must have just finished one stop. Each property took up long stretches of the road and left ample greenery around massive houses. It ambled toward the house where Haddie waited, a white-walled, modern two-story with a large circular drive in the front with low, still-green plantings and one lone yellowing maple at the street. Haddie tucked her phone in her pocket and waited. The mail truck suddenly turned into the circular drive instead of parking in the street. Stubby tires squealed as it spun around, heading to exit as quickly as it entered.

The driver, black-haired with a dark tan complexion, looked toward Haddie as she pulled back onto the street. Her face was unreadable in the distance, but there was no doubt she looked in Haddie's direction. Catching traction on the asphalt, the mail truck turned the wrong direction and headed away, leaving its route incomplete.

Because of me?

Malorie Sanchez couldn't know Haddie. They'd never met. Andrea hadn't even deposed her yet — couldn't; the testimony had just arrived that afternoon.

Maybe Malorie Sanchez had been spooked by seeing someone on the type of street where people rarely parked, let alone sat and waited. It couldn't have anything to do with Haddie directly. Still, it made little to no sense.

Haddie couldn't even be sure if it was Malorie Sanchez, though the description had been of a Hispanic female. The hair and skin tone could match. Haddie had planned to take a quick photograph to confirm later, but the truth was, she hadn't much of a plan at all. Now the witness had bailed — for no good reason. She'd acted spooked. Who was she afraid of? *Me?*

Raising her eyebrows, she sighed and pulled on her gloves. She wasn't about to chase the mail driver; that hadn't been any part of any plan. The weather had begun to look gloomy. Best to get home to change and switch to the RAV4. She strapped her helmet on and closed her jacket.

Haddie kicked the Fat Boy into life. In her jacket pocket, her phone vibrated. She sighed again, leaning back to pull it out. Andrea.

PART 3

I've admired your work since I first heard of your skills while we both served in South Asia.

CHAPTER 21

HADDIE KILLED THE BIKE, and the sudden silence high-lighted the wind rustling through the oak above her. A trio of leaves danced above her in the air as she answered the phone. "Hello?"

Andrea sounded excited — or stressed; it was difficult to tell sometimes. "We've got a potential lead on clearing Mel. A man called in to Toby and says he can prove Mel was nowhere near the crime scene on the night of the first murder. Won't come in, but he'll hand the evidence over." A cat meowed in the background, and she shushed it. "Campbell Park, bike path, in forty-five minutes. I can call Josh back in if you've got class."

Campbell Park, over by the river. Twenty or thirty minutes from this part of Cal Young at this time of the day.

"I got it." Haddie did have class, but this burned inside her. If there was some evidence to get Mel free, she didn't want Josh getting stoned and missing something.

"Thanks, Haddie. Call me back when you get whatever he has."

Haddie sucked in her breath. "Wait, who am I looking for?"

"Some man. Toby would have given me more if she had it. Weather's gonna be lousy soon, I doubt it'll be busy on the bike path at this hour."

Great, just approach any strange men you see on the bike path. "Okay. I'll call you in about an hour, I'd imagine." She let out a sigh and frowned. Her first thought was to call Dad. That wasn't happening.

"Thanks, Haddie."

The connection dropped and she stared at her phone. Rock needed to get walked. Sam took him out at noon on Thursdays, but he'd be expecting Haddie home around now. 4:15. *Damn.* Liz.

Haddie dialed. "Hey. Want to meet up at Campbell Park, in about half an hour? Something at work came up." Not much of a substitute for coffee and brownies.

"Can't. 5:15 was cutting it tight. I teach Evidence Management at 5:35, but it was a five-minute walk from the café. I'd never get through rush hour in time. What's going on?" Liz sounded disappointed.

"Anonymous evidence for Mel's alibi."

"It's going to be dark in a couple hours. You're meeting at a park? Isn't that a little . . . odd?" Liz coughed. "Listen, if you need me to come, I can be late for class — they won't start without me. How long do you think it will take?"

Haddie couldn't know if the mystery man would be waiting or show up twenty minutes late. "I'm good. Sorry we couldn't grab a minute to catch up. I could use a little break. Tomorrow?"

"I'd like that. Friday. We could grab a beer."

"That would be great." The way the week was going, Haddie might get drunk.

"Be careful."

Haddie stared out at the dark clouds. "I will. Don't worry."

She pulled up Sam's contact, stopping as a silver, dark-tinted Expedition came down the road toward her, moving at a good clip. Her pulse quickened before it passed. After the close call with the car earlier and the continued sightings of dark-tinted SUVs, she'd gotten edgy. They drove to the dead end and pulled into the farthest driveway, where a two-story sat uphill, nestled amid massive trees. The garage door began grinding open — just someone who lived there.

I'm getting paranoid.

Sam picked up on the third ring. "Hi."

"Sam, Honey, can you take Rock out for a walk? Sorry it's the last minute; I was going to swing by on the way to class, but I've got to run an errand for work."

"Not a prob." There was a rustle of movement and then a swish. "Your dad's not sitting out there. Good. I don't think he likes me." Sam lived in the same apartment complex but across the street; her bedroom window faced Haddie's parking spots.

"He needs a shirt that says, 'I Hate Everyone.' He's just like that. It's certainly not you."

Rock and Jisoo loved her, but Sam tended to get nervous and awkward around humans. Haddie thought about asking Sam to keep an eye out for odd cars, but dragging her into the paranoia would just mean a text every time a neighbor pulled in.

"You went on a ride with him this morning. Where'd you go?"

Haddie wiped off a leaf that drifted onto her tank. "Portland. Honey, I've got to go. I'm heading over to Campbell Park. I'll check in after."

"Okay." Sam sounded disappointed. She got lonely, and Haddie was one of the few people she talked with.

Stuffing the phone back into her pocket, Haddie fired up the Fat Boy and pulled onto the street. Getting around the golf courses took most of the time when navigating Cal Young; otherwise, it lay just on the north side of the Willamette River. Normally a ten-minute drive, getting to Campbell Park meant cutting across either of the two bridges at the beginning of rush hour. Her phone vibrated as she wound through the luxury houses that lined the golf course greens. The air smelled like rain. She had gear in her saddlebags and could change at the park.

She chose the Ferry Street Bridge rather than dealing with I-105. Traffic thickened on the side streets until she reached the more residential neighborhood leading toward the river. Some older, charming houses remained against the three-story apartments that dominated one side of the street.

In front of Campbell Park, maples and oaks lined the street before a thin strip of parking spaces and grass that stretched along the river. On the east end sat the community building, a squat gray and blue complex. A couple dozen cars scattered the parking lot, while others parked on the street that might have belonged to the residences across the road, red brick townhouses climbing up Skinner Butte.

She pulled into the parking lot, eyeing the bike trail that bordered the outer edge of the grass. Thick woods, oak and evergreen, lined the back between the park and the river. Picking a spot facing the bike trail and two spaces down from a blue Blazer, she killed the Fat Boy. A woman and two young children biked along the path, heading east toward the community center.

Dark boiling clouds dominated the west sky over the

roof of the Blazer. The back seat and cargo area were filled with cardboard boxes. No rain fell yet, but Haddie would have to put on rain gear for the ride back to her apartment. After stowing her helmet in a saddlebag, she checked her phone. 4:42. Plenty early. Terry had called.

Haddie sighed, looking at the dark woods that lined the bike trail. If Terry had found more photos, did she really want that on her mind right now? She could wait until afterward, but she had time to kill. Strolling across the grass toward the bike trail, she dialed Terry.

"Buckaroo," he answered.

"What's up?" Haddie stopped at the edge of the strip of asphalt that made up the bike trail and casually turned back toward the lot. Most of the cars were empty, and a couple sat eating in a blue sedan down to the left. She'd hoped that her contact would be sitting in his car, waiting to see someone approach the path.

"Nothing major — I just figured you'd be getting ready for class tonight and I'd let you know where some of my awesome skills have been spent. I found a British chat going on about your three dead Irishmen. They've got some wild theories about the origin of the fire. One is that it was the CIA and some specialized ray gun that they can fire from helicopters or planes. I like that one, personally."

Proving the CIA had killed the Colmans would be tricky. "You think the CIA is involved?"

Terry snorted. "Not really. The NSA starts tripping when someone plays in their territory. But thought I'd let you know. The next most popular is angelic intervention, or even fallen angelic intervention."

A car pulled up, two spaces from her bike, but the person inside didn't get out. A lighter flashed while their hands covered their face, and they lit something. Likely a stoner.

Haddie walked west, facing the dark ridge of clouds. "That's cool. Not helpful, but cool."

"I know — isn't it? Of course, there's the alien theories, as usual. But the Brits have a different view of them than we do. Area 51 and all." He paused a moment. "Are you home? I thought I heard a car."

"Campbell Park. Meeting someone." She smiled. "An anonymous informant."

"You are kidding me. Really?" His voice jumped up an octave. "Did you set up a camera to record it? I would have lent you some equipment."

A duck called from the woods and Haddie turned, studying the dark shadows. She liked having Terry on the phone. The sun had moved behind the clouds and the park felt gloomy, threatening.

"A camera would have been a good idea, but I didn't really have time. This was a last-minute kind of thing. They called into the office just as we closed." She scanned the parking lot again. A pinprick glow burned from the car near her bike. She didn't want Terry to hang up. "So, did you post anything about the radiation in the fire here in Eugene? Any theories about that?"

"Well, yeah. I couldn't help it." His tone sounded guilty. "But nothing really novel came up. Mostly just questions at this point. It won't gear up until after the first troll chimes in."

A man walked down the lot from the direction of the community center, pulling on a hoodie. Haddie spun in the grass and began walking back east along the bike trail. This could be it.

"Well," she said, distracted, "I'd imagine it'll be some of the same theories."

Dark hair disappeared under the hood and the man continued, striding straight down the middle of the parking lot. He didn't look in her direction, nor make any move toward the grass. Still, her pulse raced, and she shifted the phone to her left ear.

"Can't hurt to try, right?" He paused for a moment, then continued when she didn't respond. "You're not mad I posted about it, are you? I never mentioned you or Liz, of course."

The hooded man walked past Haddie's position and continued down the lot. "What? No. I expected it, Terry." She paused, facing the lot.

Terry sounded relieved. "Awesome. So, when does your mysterious Deep Throat show up?" He slurped on a straw in the background. "And when's the date?"

"Huh?" Haddie asked. *David.* "I don't know." Maybe he wanted to hang out at the park.

The man rounded a Jeep and climbed in. The headlights lit the grass as the engine fired up. She let out a long breath. The woods had turned dark; if their informant hid there, she wouldn't see him until the last moment.

"What time is it?" Haddie asked.

The lights along the path flickered on as the clouds swallowed the sun. The Jeep drove away, its red lights glowing.

"Um, 4:59."

"Then he'll be here any moment now."

CHAPTER 22

HADDIE STROLLED east toward the community center. An ice cream truck jingled through the parking lot, moving too fast for anyone to hail it. In better weather, it might have had customers.

Terry had hung up a minute before, and Haddie felt her heart pounding as she tried to look casual. The lights along the bike trail left cones of security, with stretches of darkness that extended into the shadows of the woods. It would rain any minute; she could smell it. The informant was late or had gotten cold feet and decided not to show. Had he seen her and left? Was he watching her now?

The park, slightly off-putting at first, became gloomier by the minute. Coming alone might have been a bad idea. She could protect herself, but the greater strategy was to avoid having to do so.

Haddie had resisted her dad's insistence on learning Taekwondo in the beginning. Dad had bundled her up and taken her, no matter her complaints, then he'd hand her off and sit in a dark corner behind the other parents, avoiding the cameras. Her love for the art didn't happen until she made her first belt — yellow.

She'd failed three months prior and endured heckling for each class afterward. Each jibe and insult made her angrier and more determined. Master Goh ignored her tormentors, and she never complained to him. Dad never said a word, and she never cried in front of him. Each class, she walked in with her head held high and focused on perfecting her kata, but still there were those who found something to dig at.

She sparred mainly with the other white belts, though on occasion, Master Goh let her spar the yellows. Often, she won those matches.

When the time came to try for her yellow belt, the Pumsae had become simple, and she executed each move with precision, not because of any pride of the art, but to show her hecklers that she would not be beaten. It had been a matter of ego and shame, not of learning.

When she finished, Master Goh stood up from behind his table, came to the side, and bowed to Haddie. "A black belt is a white belt that never gave up," he said. "Today, you are a yellow belt because you did not give up. It would have been easier to give up. I am proudest of you. You will become a black belt."

She'd beamed. He had seen all her abuse and watched her reactions to it. Haddie had never blown up at the other students, and it rarely showed in her sparring. She gained more from the experience than a simple yellow belt. It fit her nature not to give up; she embraced it. From that day on, she studied not just the physical aspects of Taekwondo but its tenets and history.

Terry would say that she'd become obsessed. Whatever her motivation, she'd gained confidence and a healthy respect for staying safe, which involved not placing herself in danger unnecessarily.

This day in the park, she found that necessity, even if their informant was late. *I'm not giving up. Yet.*

She'd missed class for this. It was nothing she couldn't catch up on, but the whole week had been a mess for schoolwork. She still had a paper due Monday, with little but research done. The next day she'd committed to drinking with Liz, when she should be home kicking out some of her paper. Mel still sat in jail. Nothing Haddie had done would change that. The week had been a failure, in so many ways.

And Dad was a nightmare every which way. She couldn't consider any aspect of him without getting queasy. Terry had gratefully not mentioned anything about the photographs, but he had to think they were weird.

She pulled up her phone. 5:06. How long should she wait? Sunset wasn't for an hour, but with the storm coming, daylight had vanished into the edge of blue sky to the east. Already, wisps of white crawled above her, turning the sky gray, and black dominated the west.

Two people left the community center, talking as they crossed the parking lot. Along the bike trail, the mother and her kids headed toward Haddie — she moved a step deeper into the grass. The young girl, no older than six, waved and then grabbed the handle quickly as she wobbled.

Haddie started as her phone vibrated in her pocket. Liz called.

"Hey, I'm still here. Waiting." Haddie turned back toward the cars as the mother and her kids walked their bikes across the grass toward the lot.

"I don't like this, Haddie." The sound of people gabbing filled the background behind Liz.

Neither do I. "I'm fine. There's people out here and there's lights."

"It's black outside — I can see that from in here. I wish I had my umbrella." Glass clinked somewhere near Liz. "Can't you leave?"

"Soon. I'm going to give it a few minutes." Or until it rains. Haddie stopped along the trail opposite her bike — she could get her rain gear on now.

"Will you call me when you're home, or text me at least?"

"Yeah, of course." She didn't want to hang up. "Did your friend at the lab do any analysis on the fire at the Colmans' home? Come up with anything strange?"

"Todd says he'll have a harder time because it's a house fire and firefighters doused the area with water. I've been checking with him 'cause I knew you'd want to know. Maybe in the next day or two." Someone cackled close to Liz. "You sure you're okay? I can cancel class and head over."

The lot looked thinner now. Three cars around her bike — the smoker, the Blazer, and behind them, a black sedan parked facing the street. Five vehicles were parked at the community center end, and another two spread out on the west end.

"No. I'll be leaving soon."

Had she been stood up by the informant? Maybe he got spooked and would reschedule. She didn't want to give up — Mel sat in jail. They were no closer to getting her free than the moment she went in. If only the police, Detective Cooper, would look into some of the irregularities, they might find who actually murdered these people. Haddie couldn't leave quite yet. Mel deserved someone fighting for her.

The background noise around Liz dimmed. "Keep me on the phone until you get to your bike. I've got twenty minutes before I walk into class. I'm crossing the grounds now, before the rain. Maybe Professor Arbor will have space under his umbrella."

Another call rang on Haddie's phone. Andrea. "Hey, Liz, my boss is calling. I'll call you back."

"Okay. Be careful."

The smoker opened their car door and got out. It was an old gray Plymouth Neon from the shape, though hard to tell in the growing darkness.

Haddie cleared her throat. "Andrea. He's a no-show so far."

There was a long pause. "That's a shame. Toby said he was insistent that it happen tonight."

A gust blew in, rustling the woods behind her and bringing a sure scent of rain and the distant jingle of the ice cream truck. Fall leaves rained from the trees, littering the grass. The smoker, a man in dark sweats, opened his back driver's side door and began rummaging inside.

"I'll wait a few more minutes."

"Let me know when you leave. Grace is waiting at the office in case this evidence is something we should work on tonight." A cat let out a throaty meow close to the phone and Andrea shushed it.

It made sense. Andrea might get something filed on Friday to get Mel out before the weekend. This was their last chance to get their client out before Monday. Haddie could hang on a little while longer. As creepy as the park had gotten, it would be nothing compared to jail.

A car door closed somewhere in the park, or on the street, but Haddie didn't see anyone but the smoker. He still dug in his back seat. She glanced at the gloom of the woods behind her, grateful that Andrea hadn't hung up yet.

"I didn't get to tell you about the mail carrier. You called when I was leaving Cal Young." Haddie hoped that Andrea wouldn't get upset about the trip out to the Colmans' house. "I waited where the witness said Mel had been sitting, but before they got to me, the truck left without finishing their route — like I spooked them or something."

"Are you sure they weren't done with their route?" Andrea asked.

"It's a dead end. They didn't drop off mail to any of the houses at the end. They left before they delivered to the house up the street from me. Maybe I'm misinterpreting it, but it seemed strange enough to mention. I know you still have a deposition to schedule with them." Haddie paced in a small circle now, partially to keep an eye all around her.

Andrea didn't seem upset about the fact that Haddie had gone down to the Colmans' burnt-out house. That, at least, was good. It had been impulsive and fairly useless. Most of the day had been unproductive, except for Dad, and that had poured in more than she could handle.

"Write it up for me tomorrow. It does sound odd. I'll be able to tell if she's just the skittish type." Andrea sighed. "I need a break somewhere. As it stands now, I'll have to pound in how circumstantial this all is. Some juries react to that, but not all."

The temperature had dropped. Maybe now would be a good time for rain gear and gloves. She would be more comfortable if the smoker would leave. At this point, waiting at her bike would be preferable.

A truck parked over by the community center turned on its lights and began backing out of a parking space. The smoker had both doors open on the driver's side but moved to search the front seat. What was he looking for?

Andrea spoke, bringing Haddie's focus back to the phone. "Oh, Grace said to check in with her. She got the mugging report you asked for. What's that about?"

Haddie swallowed. "The address that I went to Portland for? It's been used before, by another import company three years ago. When I looked up the owner, I found he'd died in a mugging here in Eugene. It seemed an odd coincidence, so Grace had said she'd look it up and get me the police report."

A paper shuffled before Andrea spoke. "Marino Zannetti, you mentioned him. Good. See where it goes. I know I discouraged you for getting off track before, it's just a matter of prioritizing. However, this is the time. Keep at it; you might dig up something yet. Good work."

Haddie found herself smiling at the encouragement. "Thanks. I'll call Grace now and kill a few minutes while I wait."

CHAPTER 23

Haddie raised her eyebrows, looking at the phone as she hung up with Andrea. *Good work*, she'd said. After a week of trying and failing to get some help for Mel, at least her boss appreciated the effort.

She dialed the office and punched in Grace's extension. Behind her, in the woods, the ducks sounded happy.

"Andrea Simmons Law Firm. Grace speaking." Grace often worked this late, but tonight she waited on Haddie.

"It's Haddie. No show yet on our informant. I'm going to give it a few more minutes, but Andrea said you received the police report on Zannetti's mugging and death."

"Yes. It's loaded on the network." Keys typed in the background. "You're just standing there, in the dark, in that park, aren't you?"

"Like the fool I am." Haddie shrugged.

"Let me pull it up. Stay on the phone with me and I'll walk you through the relevant parts. You are crazy." Grace didn't sound as stressed as she had been the past few days.

"Thanks." Being on the phone added some illusion of security.

Haddie stood at the edge of one of the cones of light shed by the lamps on the bike trail. The smoker had climbed back into his front seat, but both doors were still open. Lights in the apartments across the street and street-lamps had begun to glow. It seemed like night, though the eastern sky still showed blue.

"Should have sent Josh. No one wants to be near that boy," Grace mumbled as keyboard and mouse clicked.

"Thanks, Grace."

"Yeah. Here it is." Grace cleared her throat. "Victim: Marino Zannetti. American. Born 1971, Tiffin, Ohio. Last known address: 5210 Elk Ridge Drive, Eugene, Oregon, 97402." Grace hummed. "Body found in the rear of Picc-A-Dilly Flea Market, 796 West 13th Avenue, Eugene, Oregon, 97402."

That was clear across town. Haddie frowned, staring at the grass.

"Wife confirmed victim's gold wedding ring and Omega watch were missing from belongings. No wallet found at scene. Unknown contents of wallet."

Grace paused, as if picking out relevant parts of the report. "Two gunshot wounds, one to the chest, through the heart; the second to the side of the head, believed to have been fired after the victim fell."

A shot to the head after the man likely had been killed sounded more like an assassination than a mugging.

"Two 357 hollow-point rounds recovered during autopsy. Shells not found on scene." Grace hummed. "The initial call to 911 placed by Savira Maita. Security guard on duty. Shots fired. Awaited squad at gate. Four other reports of gunfire called in. Neighboring residents on West 16th Avenue were interviewed; noises attributed to fireworks or car backfire." Grace paused, leaving Haddie in silence.

"Patrolmen Clarke and Jones arrived on scene at 2:16 a.m. Detective Cooper arrived at 2:25 a.m."

Haddie interrupted. "Wait. Detective Cooper?"

"His department, right? He's probably the lead on a lot of murder cases."

Or Detective Cooper had other motives when it came to keeping Haddie inside the lines. How did he arrive so quickly? If this case did relate to organized crime, crooked cops could be part of it. The sudden appearance of tinted SUVs could be tied to her investigation. Initially, she'd feared they were related to the dogfighting ring. Haddie spun toward the lot. The Blazer, without tinted windows, was the only SUV in the lot. The more distant cars she couldn't see well enough to determine if they were tinted. The smoker sat in his front seat, both doors still open.

"You want me to continue?" Grace asked.

"Please, sorry." Haddie grimaced.

"Assumed mugging, though victim's car found in 163 East 12th Avenue parking lot. Unable to determine victim's whereabouts after wife, Cynthia Zannetti, went to bed at 11 p.m."

"That's across town, near Mark Colman's office."

"And you can't get near Picc-A-Dilly at night without getting shot. Unless he was robbing the place." Grace snorted. "It sounds unusual, but I don't know how this is going to help you."

Haddie tilted her head and absently wrapped her fingers around her hair. How did this help, other than looking like a mob hit? Detective Cooper? She couldn't start investigating him, but what were the odds that he investigated the deaths of the two people who owned import companies at a false address in Portland?

"Does it state Zannetti's occupation?"

"Accountant," Grace replied.

Haddie could look into Zannetti's finances, but even if they looked like Mark Colman's, would that get her anywhere? All she'd done was substantiate her own concerns over this shady import business with a fake address. It didn't help. Not yet.

"Nothing unexpected in the coroner's brief. It doesn't look like they had any real forensics done at the scene . . ." Grace trailed off.

A gust ripped fall leaves from the trees in a torrent. What felt like a raindrop nicked off Haddie's jacket. "All right. Thanks, Grace. I'm going to leave now. It's got to be half past by now."

"5:33."

"Then I'm out of here. I'll call Andrea when I get home." Haddie shivered and headed across the grass toward her Fat Boy. "Thanks again."

"Stay safe." Grace's connection cut out.

Haddie tucked her phone into her jacket pocket and zipped up the last bit to her neck. Leaves floated about her like snow, dotting the grass with brown and yellow. The smoker stepped out without glancing her way and leaned into his back seat again.

Far down past the end of the lot, a door opened in the community center and a yellow rectangle framed someone leaving.

She'd done what she could. Disappointing. Evidence supplying Mel with an alibi would have put the whole case on track, possibly even gotten the DA to back down before trial. Haddie had burned through most of her solid leads. They still waited for two videos that might catch Mel's car parked, where she supposedly never left. The ATM had been a bust, blocked by a truck. She still favored Mark

Colman's shady dealings, but where else could she look? The vineyard?

The smoker still had his butt sticking out of his door when she pulled her keys out and approached her bike. She'd be happy to get home, warm, and out of her work clothes.

CHAPTER 24

FLIPPING OUT HER KEY, Haddie unlocked the left saddlebag on her Fat Boy. Leaves skittered across asphalt from under the Blazer, but as the breeze waned, she could smell tobacco. She'd jumped to the assumption that the smoker was a stoner. Who came to the park for a cigarette?

He wore loose black sweatpants, and the heel of his left foot tilted up to reveal new tread on tan work boots. She'd expected a junk-filled car from all the time he'd spent digging in it, but the front tray and seats were empty. As he pulled out of the back, nothing lay on the brown seats. The car looked older, but unused. Was he digging inside the seats? Looking for change?

She laid her helmet on the bike and dug past her satchel for the rolled-up rain gear on the bottom. Uncomfortable, she considered getting wet instead of taking the time to suit up.

The smoker turned toward her. "Hey, do you have a light?"

He had pale skin, large, almost comical eyes, and a round head. He had his brown hair cut short, well above the ears. Stubble darkened his upper lip. He wore black gloves, which he shoved into the pockets of his sweatpants. He pulled out a pack of cheap cigarettes with his left hand.

Haddie shook her head, pulling out her roll of rain gear. "Sorry. Don't smoke."

He took a step toward the back of her bike and she dropped the gear back into the saddlebag. A dust devil of leaves whorled across the asphalt behind him. Slipping the cigarettes back into his left pocket, he pulled out his right hand and sprung open a black-handled switchblade with a flourish. It had tiny, polished knobs at the joint and a double-edged blade that picked up the lights of the lot.

Already tense, her heart raced as she shifted her right foot out, squaring her stance, not against the Blazer, but with her back toward the open area of the lawn behind her. She'd been edgy at his proximity in the first place. He'd been foolish though — if she had been on the bike, rolling it back out of the parking space, it would have been much harder to defend herself.

A dry leaf crunched on the asphalt behind her, near where she knew the front of the Blazer sat.

She stepped back with her left foot and spun, bringing her right knee nearly against the front tire of the Fat Boy. Her right arm swung with the momentum for an inside block. She planted her right foot near the front of the bike.

A second attacker lunged with a larger hunting knife. It had a cruel curve at the tip, like the one her dad carried in his sheath. Pulse racing, she yelled. Barked. His light brown face pulled back in a surprised expression as she adjusted her swing and connected down against his wrist with her forearm. A shiver trailed up her arm. If he hadn't alerted her, she'd have taken a knife in the back.

Dressed in dark sweats, like his partner, the man had a

long eye shape, hooded lids, and a broad nose. Black hair swung loose at his forehead. Her blow over-extended his arm downward. She clenched her jaw when he didn't let go of his knife. He would try for a back swing if he regained his footing.

She shifted weight to her left foot and pivoted, slamming her heel into his rib cage with her leg partially coiled. Too close. Extending her leg, she threw him into the Blazer.

He tried to grab onto the Blazer but skidded to the asphalt, cursing.

A risky close maneuver. Haddie jumped back to the grass to gain balance and distance.

The smoker nearly collided with his falling partner as he scrambled between bike and body, his right arm drawn back to stab or slash. Bulging eyes looked less comical and had a wide fanatical look to them. His lips parted and showed his tobacco-yellowed teeth clenched tight.

Knife takedowns had always been theoretical in class. She drew in a deep breath that rasped in rhythm to her pulse. She'd never actually been faced with someone who wanted to stab her.

As he began his lunge, she yelled and stepped back with her left foot. Shifting almost sideways to him, she slapped her left hand around the back of his wrist. Fingers wrapped tight and forceful around the stranger's flesh. Pulling against bone, she drew him toward herself, using his momentum.

He stunk of tobacco, and his eyes widened as she tightened her grip. She pushed, angling his knife hand away from them both. He grunted, seeming surprised.

Close, and committed to the move, her breathing paused. She shifted toward him, and he growled. Maniacal, bloodshot eyes didn't show fear. Attacking with her right hand, she grabbed his hand and knife, feeling the bones of his thumb under hers. The sharp, double-edged blade turned up and toward his face.

Throwing her left foot back and around, she shifted her body weight. Yelling, she used both her hands to twist bones.

He whined as he began to fall. His forward momentum carried him, but her pressure on his wrist twisted him to spin backward. Joints carried the tension from wrist to elbow to shoulder. His hips and knees dropped, trying to release the pain and pressure.

She had him. The momentum and control were hers.

Leaning forward as he spun, she yelled again. Not to shock him again, but in triumph. His eyes closed as his back slammed on the grass.

She jerked his arm back to her right knee. Forcing her thumb easily into the webbing of flesh between his fore-finger and thumb, she pried the knife out. It fell into the grass with a flash of black and silver, and she kicked it toward the Blazer.

Haddie stumbled back as she found the long-eyed man slashing at her face with his long hunting knife. In the space of a moment, she heard the switchblade clatter against asphalt and echo under the Blazer, a woman screamed farther down the parking lot, and she felt her left forearm sear with pain as it blocked the blade. A single raindrop splashed onto the back of her head.

While he held the sharp edge embedded into leather and her flesh, she pushed against him with both arms, and the man staggered backward. Once she had a leg's distance from him, she kicked in an inside crescent and connected the sole of her boot to his wrist. Finally, the knife flew out of his hand and landed in the grass past the Fat Boy's front tire.

Haddie jumped toward the front of the Blazer. A deeper male voice yelled from the far end of the parking lot, somewhere close to the community building. Blood soaked the inside of her left sleeve, and her bone hurt in a dull ache that reached her elbow.

She grabbed her forearm, ignoring the sharp slice of pain, and tried to staunch the blood.

Stepping sideways around the Blazer, she kept the bug-eyed man in sight on the ground. His partner started to move past her bike to retrieve his weapon, but stalled, looking toward the community center.

Haddie worked herself wide on the other side of the Blazer and out into the middle of the parking lot.

A woman stood near one of the parked cars, both hands on her face.

A darker male figure loped toward them from the community center. He shouted again, "Hey!"

Haddie's heart raced as she watched the long-eyed man turn and race up the opposite side of the Blazer, across the lot, and toward the street. She backed up, glanced quickly around her, and kept the Blazer between her and the other attacker. The man with the round eyes took a moment to follow his partner, scrambling and nearly stumbling. He left the car, its doors still open, where he'd parked it.

She panted, blinking with each throb of pain, and locked onto the woman who stood by her car. As Haddie began walking forward, checking the dark street beyond the parking lot, the man from the community center passed the woman.

I've never been mugged before. Somehow, she didn't think she'd be the one hurt during an attack. Master Goh always said that hubris brought down defense. He had stories of martial students who got hurt during attacks because they believed they were invulnerable. That wasn't exactly her case, but it was all she could think of. *Damn, this hurts.* She needed to get her jacket off, bind her arm, and get it stitched.

She reached the back of the Blazer, feeling woozy, as the man arrived.

"Are you okay?" he asked, slightly wheezing. Middle-aged and pudgy, he'd still been enough, along with the screaming woman, to help her get rid of the muggers.

"Thank you. I need to bandage my arm." Blood seeped through the fingers of her right hand, which she held squeezed over the cut in her leather jacket.

He pulled out his phone, then shoved it back in his pocket and started pulling off the dark green sweater he wore. "Can we use this?"

Haddie cringed. "I've got a first aid kit in my right saddlebag." *My keys.*

She'd left them in the left saddlebag. Pointing with her left hand, she moaned from the pain.

"Close the open saddlebag. There's a set of keys in the top; use the same key to open the other side. You'll see the red and white kit near the top. Thank you." She needed to sit. Her legs felt like Jell-O.

He nodded, his face paling as he watched blood drip steadily from her arm.

The woman remained at her car, but she had her phone to her ear. Calling the police, most likely. Hopefully. Haddie would need stitches. This wasn't a garage shop cut that Dad put a butterfly bandage on. And she wouldn't be riding her bike to the hospital. Haddie sighed. *Biff. Dad. Damn.* She couldn't leave her bike here.

She leaned against the Blazer, then shifted and slid her butt down against the bumper. She wasn't quite sitting, but the middle-aged man seemed to be having a difficult time getting the key out of her left saddlebag. It might be a few minutes before she got her arm bandaged or the ambulance arrived, whichever came first. The mugger had left his car. His too-empty car.

This wasn't a mugging.

Someone, possibly the same people who were driving the tinted SUVs, didn't like where Haddie investigated. *Which means I'm on the right track.* She smiled just as the middle-aged man got the key out. He smiled back and nodded.

Had they intended on killing her, or just getting her hospitalized and out of the way? If they'd burned the Colmans, then killing her wouldn't weigh on their consciences. Eyes keen, she stood and checked the park around them. She didn't need to get paranoid.

Taking a deep breath, she let go of her arm and felt the surge of pain flush over her left side, then she unzipped her jacket. Her wound wouldn't get any better until she got some stitches in it. She didn't need to spend time in the hospital because of blood loss. Wiggling her right arm out of her sleeve jostled the cut and she gritted her teeth.

Someone is trying to kill me.

She couldn't feel the cold; her heart still raced too fast. The black clouds were directly above. Only a drop or two had loosened from their grasp, but she could feel them, oppressive, waiting overhead.

Headlights shone on the middle-aged man as he worked the lock on her right saddlebag. The car moved slowly toward them and she made out the woman's face from before. She crawled toward them, glancing out of her windows as if the thugs would race back onto the lot and attack her. Haddie couldn't blame her. In fact, she owed her a debt of gratitude. If the woman hadn't been getting into her car, who knows how the attack would have turned out?

She grimaced in pain. Her jacket sleeve stuck on her arm. Blood already glued her blouse to her skin and the leather. With her fingers firm on the cuff and her left arm straight, Haddie yanked.

CHAPTER 25

Twenty minutes later, Haddie grimaced with the bounce as the stretcher dropped to its wheels outside the hospital. Raindrops beat on the metal roof over the ambulance.

A low overhang made a dark entrance to the hospital. A pale-skinned paramedic, climbing from the back of the ambulance, grasped the stretcher with both of her hands and gave Haddie a wink. Dark beams supported the ceiling. Outside it looked like night had fallen, but they'd only been five minutes from the park. Haddie knew where the medical center was, and although she'd driven by often and seen the signs, she never noticed the alcove or emergency entrance.

The wheels of her stretcher rattled across the pavement, and she felt her chest tighten. Bright light flared ahead, and automatic doors whispered open, unleashing a clamor and light from inside. Haddie blinked as she tried to look to each side. She imagined them running a needle and thread through the gaping cut on her forearm, and her stomach turned. Blinding lights alternated with blank white panels in the ceiling.

Relax. *I'll be fine.* Cart wheels, voices, and machines added to a chaotic, but consistent noise.

She'd have to call Andrea and explain. What was she supposed to say? That Mark Colman's actual murderer had put a hit out on her? What if it was organized crime? In the movies, they just leaned on you and told you to back off. Was that what Detective Cooper meant by coloring in the lines? He could have been clearer, but would she have dropped it? Let Mel take the fall?

The pale woman startled Haddie when she spoke. "You're going to be fine. They'll have you stitched up in just a bit."

They had turned down a corridor.

Haddie offered a weak smile. "Just thinking about having to tell my boss."

They entered a room and passed a curtain hanging from the ceiling along a track. Antiseptic, and worse, permeated the air. She found herself thirsty.

The paramedic offered a cross between a shrug and a grimace. "Not your fault. Wrong place at the wrong time. Normally we don't get calls from that park."

Andrea might actually be mortified that she sent Haddie. However, this had been a setup. It had to be. The anonymous call — with just the information they couldn't ignore. How did they know she'd go? Maybe the warning was for the whole agency. No. Haddie was the one digging where no one else was. Would they have ignored Josh and tried to get at her some other way? Were they done now? Message sent. Was she? *Can I let it go?*

The radios on the paramedics crackled, and the man at

the foot of her stretcher answered. "Victim at Sacred Heart, Hilyard Street."

She leaned up to see as he began speaking to a nurse. Tall and square-shouldered, the woman looked over and smiled, but nodded at his description of Haddie's wound. She pointed to one of the curtained stalls by the wall.

As Haddie rolled past, the woman turned and headed across the room toward a pale boy who lay in a T-shirt. He locked eyes with Haddie, and she could feel his panic — terror. The woman at his side, possibly his mother, scrolled through her phone.

Only once had Haddie been in an emergency room, a much smaller version in Montana. At thirteen, she'd traveled on the back of her dad's bike. Dad liked Montana and always took her biking and camping in the summer. He'd close the garage, and they'd pack up gear until his saddlebags bulged.

They would end up near Canada, or even take 93 up over the border. They'd been on 93, south of Missoula, when she'd slipped getting off the bike. Wearing shorts, a point of contention with Dad, her left calf got stuck on his pipes. She'd cried for a while, even after he'd gotten her to the doctor, and she'd been embarrassed of the scars through most of her teenage years. Jeans replaced shorts and skirts.

The emergency room had been small compared to this room, but they'd been personal and caring. Here, she felt as though she'd been assigned a number and they'd get to her when they had time.

The paramedics got her settled, and a different nurse, with brown skin and thick eyebrows, dropped in behind them. She placed a clipboard on Haddie's legs and showed her a hospital wristband. "Ms. Dawson, can you confirm your name?"

Haddie raised her eyebrows and focused on the writing. "Yes."

"I'm Aisha. I'll be taking your vitals and getting you set up to see the doctor. We'll get you taken care of right away." She strapped the bracelet around Haddie's right wrist. "Nasty cut, I hear. Mugging?"

Haddie felt embarrassed for her assumption of a cold, uncaring staff.

The paramedics had arrived just after the middle-aged man, Jeff, had finished wrapping her wound, and they'd cut it off as soon as they had her in the ambulance to dress it again. Haddie had gotten to see the top edge twice. It split open wider than seemed right or possible.

"Yes, a mugging," she lied. They had tried to kill her. She was sure.

Aisha slipped a cuff on Haddie's right arm, clipped a monitor on her finger, and began rolling up her right sleeve. "I'm going to get an IV started. You've lost some blood."

Haddie's left sleeve had changed from a watercolor blue to a black knot where it rolled up at her elbow. Blood had dried on her arm and down to her wrist. Her jacket lay in a clear bag at her feet, blood smeared across the plastic.

She'd gotten Jeff to tuck her helmet into her saddlebag and lock it before he gave her the keys. The bike couldn't stay there.

"BP 111 over 73. Good pressure. Heart rate and oxygen are good." Aisha tied off Haddie's upper arm at the elbow and got out a needle. "This'll prick, not the worst part of your day."

One arm throbbing and the other pinned, Haddie focused impotently on the bag between her feet. Her phone would still be in her jacket pocket. Splatters of dark blood stains dotted her black slacks.

Aisha grabbed the bag and tucked it under the bed before pulling out a white blanket and draping it up to Haddie's middle. "I'll be back in a couple minutes." She closed the curtain as she left.

Haddie frowned and sighed. She should have just said something, but she'd been in for tests where they had signs for no cell phones. There weren't any here.

Reaching over the side with her right hand, she watched the intravenous line as she fished around with her fingertips. Shifting down until her boot heels hit the bottom rail, she inched sideways and waved below the bed. She felt a flap of plastic and returned, pinching in the area. Her index finger touched something, and she strained to get her thumb onto the bag. Grunting, she snagged the edge and dragged it closer to get a better grip.

Blood smeared where her left sleeve rubbed against the Ziploc. Using her left hand sparingly to steady the seal, she opened the bag.

Haddie texted Biff. "I had to leave my bike at Campbell Park. Can you pick it up and bring it to my apartment?" She didn't imagine she'd be in any shape to ride for a few days. He could do it without questions. She'd just have to be firm.

Each text came through separately. "Why?" "Where are you?" "Wait. Did you drop it?"

He baited her with the last line. She hadn't dropped a bike since she was seventeen.

Be firm. "Can you do it?"

"East 11th Avenue now. Be there in four."

He was close.

Damn. Haddie groaned. The police would still be there. Biff would tell Dad. There was no getting around it now. Nothing would stop Dad.

Haddie closed her eyes and sighed before typing out the

text. "Tell Dad I'm at Sacred Heart downtown. Emergency room. Tell him I'm okay. Just a couple stitches."

She really didn't want to see Dad. The images of the WWI pictures were too fresh and left too many questions with answers she did and didn't want, but he'd be here. Soon.

Dropping the phone to her stomach, she planned a text to Andrea. Haddie didn't want to make it out to be accusatory, even though she'd been at the park for business. Truth was, she'd have gone on her own in a heartbeat. Should she go into the whole "they're trying to kill me" theory or just stick with the mugging? The minute she'd had with the police, before the paramedics had whisked her away, she'd left it at a mugging. They were following her to the hospital to get a full report.

She typed slowly, rereading before sending. "Our informant never showed. I stayed too late and got mugged in the parking lot. I am getting a couple of stitches. Nothing to be worried about."

It took only seconds before Haddie's phone rang. Grimacing, she answered at the start. The curtain stopped about a foot above the floor and she watched the tiles to see if anyone approached. "Andrea."

"What happened?" Andrea sounded furious.

Haddie held the phone in front of her face so it covered her mouth as she spoke. "I was leaving. Two guys tried to mug me. I got a little cut." Her mouth was dry as she whispered. She wanted tea. And to be done here, and home, nestled with Rock on the couch. Or asleep.

"This was a setup, then. I should have guessed. You shouldn't have let me send you alone. No, it's not your fault. Have you told me everything you've dug up?"

Haddie paused, trying to remember all their conversations over the day. "I think so." She felt tired — groggy.

Andrea was mad, but not necessarily at her. It just felt like it. "I'm getting the police to trace that anonymous number."

Detective Cooper. Haddie didn't want him involved. "No."

"What? Why? What aren't you telling me?" Andrea sounded angry at Haddie.

Haddie went through her concerns, without bringing up the detective's curiosity over her dad, but mentioning his "in the lines" comment. It all sounded so weak, childish, and paranoid when she finished.

"He's not involved, Haddie. But I've got another resource that can get the information for us. Probably a burner anyway." Andrea yelled at her cat, who for once hadn't been meowing. "I'm going to go now and get some of this started. Text me when they release you. Do you need me to get you a ride?"

"No. My dad is coming." She felt like she was fifteen again — stuck at the dojo after practice.

Haddie breathed in and out as the line dropped. Tucking the phone face down, she held her hand on top of it. She wasn't about to tell the police that she thought someone might be trying to kill her. It could get to Detective Cooper. Trusting him was not an option; he might very well be one of them, no matter what Andrea thought.

The curtain pulled aside. Detective Cooper stood there, tilting his head.

HADDIE SWALLOWED. "DETECTIVE COOPER." She gripped her phone. The two officers who had taken her statement had been clear that they would be following up with her at the hospital. No mention had been made of a detective, let alone Detective Cooper. She imagined it had been little over half an hour since then, and somehow, he was here.

She felt queasy and thirsty. The antiseptic smell didn't help either. Her little draped off area suddenly seemed small and confining.

His light brown skin looked paler in the intense lighting. The scowl seemed diffused by the lack of shadows. "Ms. Dawson. You seem to have gotten yourself into some trouble. Campbell Park usually does not have these difficulties, yet you managed to find trouble there, end up in the hospital, and leave us with a stolen car." He remained at the edge, not stepping inside her space. "Witnesses described events that could be construed as you attacking at least one of the men, though they later changed their stories to insist that you had been the victim and had merely been defending yourself — with admirable form, according to the woman."

He didn't ask a question, but some of his comments stirred her to respond, overriding her original shock and even trepidation at his sudden arrival. "I —"

"What I am most interested in is why you were at this park during this time of night."

He'd turned everything around to insinuate she was somehow to blame. But how much was she willing to tell him? She took a deep breath. He hadn't said anything that might be considered a threat, so if he worked for someone trying to scare her off, he wasn't doing so now. If he was part of it, then he would know about the ruse and the call.

"Following up on a lead. We had a call and I went out to meet with them." Her grip relaxed on her phone.

"And . . ." He placed his thumb on his mustache, waiting. "Did you meet with them?"

Would he ask that question if he were involved? Maybe — it would be a good lie to keep her guessing. She sighed. *Or I've gone full over into paranoia.* "No."

"Descriptions."

Of the person she didn't meet? She hadn't even taken the call.

His heavy eyebrows dropped deeper over his eyes, furthering the scowl.

Haddie blinked. "Oh, the muggers?"

His expression changed quickly, lips turned thin, his head ticked, and one eyebrow inched up. Not quite rolling his eyes, he seemed to become annoyed with her lack of understanding. "It would be helpful. If you'd like us to find them."

Her pulse rose, not in the fear and apprehension she had

on his arrival, but indignance that he implied she was dim-witted. He purposefully zigzagged his comments to disorient, and she was in no shape, or mood, for games. Between the meds and the stress from the night — the whole damned day — she had a hard time focusing. She took a deep, calming breath.

"Man in car: white, smoker, five foot ten, one hundred and eighty pounds, round face, large eyes, no visible tattoos or piercings, short brown hair, right-handed, new work boots — possibly Wolverines." Angry, her voice rose. "Second assailant: light brown skin, five foot nine, one hundred and sixty pounds, thin face, long eyes with an outside slant and hooded eyelids, full nose, no visible tattoos or piercings, short black hair — bangs, right-handed, black Reeboks." Haddie glared at Detective Cooper and empha-sized her last sentence needlessly loud. "Both men wore black gloves, unlabeled black sweatpants, and sweatshirts without hoodies."

Detective Cooper sighed, pulled out his phone, and began taking notes.

Haddie didn't let up. "The smoker — the driver of the car — did you find a cigarette butt?"

He didn't look up. "Should we have?"

"He was smoking in his car. I never saw a butt on the asphalt. Did you check for an ashtray?" She paused. Did the '96 Plymouth Neon even have an ashtray?

He kept typing. "So, you watched the mugger case you?"

Infuriating man. "At the time, I didn't know."

"Obviously." His scowl had lightened. "How long did he keep you under surveillance?"

Aisha whipped the curtain open. Even though Haddie jumped, she was pleased to see Detective Cooper start as well. "Out. I've got to prep." The nurse shouldered into the detective.

"I'm not finished —"

Aisha turned inside the circumference of the curtain and, still holding the edge, whipped it in front of his face. She turned with a wink and spoke over her shoulder. "Wait outside in the hall, Detective. We'll let you know when the victim is ready for you to resume interrogation." She mouthed, "Dick."

Detective Cooper didn't press the issue.

Haddie laughed silently and lay back to stare at the ceiling. Apprehension about her arm flushed through, and she wanted to ask for water, but she tensed as Aisha began undoing the bandage. Her thirst could wait. She spent the next half hour getting poked and questioned for information on her chart. Pain medication in her IV started to ease some of the duller aches.

The doctor turned out to be a young man with orange hair and freckles. He barely spoke, except to ask Aisha about medications and required equipment. Despite shots around her wound, Haddie found her teeth clenched at points.

She found Master Goh's admonishment about hubris clear. A sweep behind her assailant's knee would have left her room to run for the community center; instead, she'd taken the time to disarm one of two opponents. Not her brightest moment. It had been a long day. She would be happy to curl up on her bed with Rock at her feet — or across three-quarters of the bed if the mood took him.

Her phone, which Aisha had moved to a stand, vibrated in two sessions while the doctor worked. His expression never changed, though Aisha's eyes went wide in mock concern. At each opportunity, the nurse smiled or touched

Haddie's shoulder or hand for comfort. Any misgivings she'd had about the care had been presumptuous and unfounded. Haddie would have felt ashamed if she didn't have to keep gritting her teeth.

Water finally came after the doctor left. Haddie's forearm felt like hamburger, and it ached to the armpit. Aisha promised a few minutes before she unleashed Detective Cooper that she'd make sure to accompany him, in case he got too annoying.

Haddie only got a few sips before a commotion started outside.

A young orderly squeaked out an objection before Dad bellowed from somewhere in the middle of the room. "Haddie?"

She rolled her eyes. "Here, Dad." The meds had her calmer than she expected. What did it matter if her dad had lived centuries? He likely had some cool stories.

The curtain rippled as it was prodded for an opening. His misshapen nose and piercing brown eyes peeked through. "How bad?"

He barely took a step in when Haddie recognized a familiar voice. "Mr. Dawson," Detective Cooper said, "I'm glad we've got a chance to meet."

Dad stopped and turned with a squint. He wore a graying 1999 Sturgis shirt that had once been black. "Do I know you?"

Haddie couldn't see the detective. He stood on the other side of the curtain, farther out in the room. His tone sounded anything but pleased. Snarky, maybe.

"Detective Cooper. I'm looking into your daughter's mugging — among other things." Detective Cooper stated the last part with a particularly chilling emphasis.

"What other things?"

"She was mugged tonight, during her investigation into a case that I have already closed. One that the DA is prosecuting, and your daughter's employer is attempting to defend. Two particularly brutal murders." Detective Cooper sniffed. "She should be careful where her questions put her."

Was that a threat? She still couldn't trust him, no matter Andrea's opinion.

"I'm aware of her case." Dad looked over to Haddie and stepped inside to inspect the bandaging on her arm. "It sounds like you're implying this is more than a simple case of mugging. I doubt her client is a threat; she's in jail. If the danger is still free, roaming the streets, then perhaps questions are necessary." He gently touched her shoulder. "You okay?"

"Drowsy. They gave me some meds." Haddie nodded toward the IV bag on her right side.

Detective Cooper moved to the opening in the curtain with pursed lips and his persistent scowl. In his left hand, he held a tablet with a black cover over the screen. "Perhaps she'll take a break and let the courts handle this. It seems everyone has gotten a little heated over the situation. Mark Colman's son believes that someone broke into the office."

Panic fluttered in Haddie's chest. Did he suspect her — them?

He looked her square in the eye. "Burglary didn't find any evidence that anything had been taken or tampered with. Leave the questions to the professionals."

It sounded like a threat. Her head too foggy, she didn't trust herself to comment.

Dad snorted. "That's her job, Detective Copper. Questions."

"*Cooper*," Detective Cooper corrected, overemphasizing

his name. His eyebrows dropped down and he pulled up the tablet into both hands.

"Whatever." Dad smirked. He rarely engaged anyone to this level, unless they were playing poker.

"She needs to be careful, obviously."

Detective Cooper's subtle comments on her safety added up. His warnings had become clear. He wanted her to stop investigating. Was it usual police behavior, or some tie to the murderer? Haddie stiffened, and her dad noticed.

Stepping toward the detective, Dad looked threatening. "Maybe if you spent your time investigating, she wouldn't have to."

Detective Cooper shrugged, stepped around the end of the bed to the opposite side of Haddie, and flipped the cover off the tablet.

Aisha arrived, striding to the open curtain and surveying the two intruders with as fierce a look as she could muster. "No visitors yet. I need consistent vitals. The both of you — out."

"I have mugshots for the victim to look at." Detective Cooper waved the tablet, already queued with a set of six pictures.

Haddie peeked curiously and then waved her right hand toward her dad. "This is my dad, Aisha. Thomas. He'll escort Detective Copper out once he's done showing me the pictures. Is that okay?"

Aisha winked lightly, gave the scowling detective a grunt, and smiled at Dad. "Don't let him get her upset." She left the curtain open when she headed away.

Detective Cooper cradled the bottom of the tablet from behind, giving her a clear view of the two rows of three pictures. The second picture was the wide-eyed man, the fifth the long-eyed man. They sat in the middle, one above the other. Detective Cooper knew them from her description. This pack was just to confirm.

"The top middle for sure. He's the smoker. The one who drove the Neon." Pointing, Haddie inadvertently touched the image, and it opened to a page where the mugshot sat on the right and details populated the left. The man's name was Louis Mattes.

Detective shifted the tablet and swiped, returning with the six pictures. "Anyone else?"

Haddie barely pointed this time. "The man below, in the middle."

Detective Cooper grunted, flipped the cover over the tablet, and studied her.

What was he thinking? She started to squirm inside, feeling his proximity too close in these confined spaces.

"Time to leave, Detective Cooper." Dad used the man's proper name, and his voice sounded thoughtful.

Cooper nodded slowly, as if thinking about something. "Thank you, Ms. Dawson. Be careful."

Another comment on her security. It would be hard not to think he had some part in this. If so, why had he led them to the muggers so easily? She almost asked him why he came instead of the two beat cops who had answered the call. She feared she knew.

Dad leaned down and kissed her forehead, like when she had a fever as a child. It felt good, and in all the stress, she'd almost forgotten that he was . . . impossible.

After they closed the curtain and left, she leaned with a grimace to retrieve her phone. Every movement seemed a dull pain. They'd put up the little gates, so it was more difficult, but safer. Her mind didn't seem to register gravity until she'd overextended against the rail and had the phone between her fingers. Texts from Liz.

"Are you home yet?" The second text came shortly after the first. "Text me back. I'm worried."

"Hey. I'm okay." Haddie texted. How could she explain without getting Liz hysterical?

Liz responded immediately. "You're home?"

Best just to be blunt, but play it off. "I wish. Hospital with Dad. I blocked a knife the wrong way. Couple of stitches."

"What?" Liz typed for a few moments and only managed to text, "What happened?"

"Mugging at the park."

"I'm sorry. I should have come down." Liz continued writing. "I want to come now. Can you drive? How bad? I can give you a ride. I owe you. What hospital?"

Haddie tilted her head in a nod. She wouldn't enjoy a bike ride with Dad, for numerous reasons. The hospital wasn't far from the university. Besides, Liz would be a comfort right now.

"That would be great. Sacred Heart downtown." It gave her an easy out with Dad.

Aisha walked in, glancing at the phone in Haddie's hand. "Your dad's gone home to get his car. Says he rode here. It'll be a while before you're discharged anyway. How are you feeling?" She poured water from a cheap blue pitcher into Haddie's cup. "Drink." She didn't seem to care about the texting.

Liz texted, "omw."

Aisha checked the monitors and IV bag. "How's the pain?"

Haddie put the phone on her stomach and leaned for the water. "Bearable. I can't handle the pain meds. Making me groggy."

"You can get through it with ibuprofen. The doctor will

set up discharge instructions. Your father will likely be back by then."

Haddie's phone rang. Andrea. Aisha nodded to it and headed back out the curtain.

Did Dad go to get the Jeep or Cooper Mini? She glanced at the time and then answered. "Hi."

"Haddie, how are you doing? Have they gotten to you yet?" An unusual tone from Andrea — worry.

"Done. Pumping me with antibiotics. Codeine too, I'd imagine." She leaned over to see under the curtains. How long had Detective Cooper been standing outside the last time they talked? She hadn't noticed when he arrived, but she'd had her voice low anyway.

"We'll cover the hospital costs; this happened on the job."

Is that what this call was about? Workman's comp?

"I just want to make sure you're okay."

"Yeah. Shook up, but that should be expected, I'd imagine. Detective Cooper came and showed me mugshots. I picked out two of them."

"Well, that's good."

It might be. If Detective Cooper didn't work for the murderer, then he could actually investigate and find out who hired them. This mugging might have given them a lead. "We can pressure the police to find out who hired these thugs. It might lead us to the actual murderer." Haddie shifted up in the bed. "We're onto something. Mark Colman had business dealings that someone doesn't want us to know about. We need to dig deeper into his financial records and his wife's. Mel is just convenient for the DA; they aren't even looking. There's something odd about the fire —"

"Hadhira." Andrea's cool tone splashed like ice water.

Haddie blinked, sucking in a quick breath. She'd been ranting.

"Haddie," Andrea continued, "sometimes we get a little close. We're digging, we've got some time. I want you to take a few days, heal and rest. Let this go for a bit."

The outlet across the room had four data ports and jack ports for oxygen or other equipment. Haddie stared at them. The antiseptic scents suddenly felt — tasted — acerbic. Andrea was pulling her off the case. Just for a few days? Not permanently? Had she gone too far?

"Okay."

"I'll check in with you in a couple of days."

"Mm-hm." Haddie felt cold.

The line hung quiet for a moment. A voice beyond the curtain laughed.

"Let me know if you need anything," Andrea said.

Haddie didn't reply, and the connection dropped.

CHAPTER 27

AT SEVEN THAT EVENING, the rain drenched him and lightning lit black clouds. Thomas pulled his Shovelhead onto East 11th and headed west toward Jefferson Westside. He ignored the weather as his bike rumbled, competing with the storm. Red lights from the cars ahead flickered in the downpour. Even the lamps and traffic lights were dimmed. The city's illusion washed away with the rain; dark square shapes of cement surrounded the asphalt, the people huddling inside or in the cars around him. The neon signs and happy posters couldn't shine through this weather. Mother Nature rolled down from the western mountains, but it could never fully cleanse man's ambition. A car squealed ahead of him and horns blew. It would be a miserable ride.

He'd lost too much family over the past six months. *I'm not losing Haddie.* His last family had thought him dead, long ago. They'd moved on to grandchildren and great-grandchildren, second cousins and weddings. Then, six months ago, the funerals had started. All of those who died were related to his last identity. He didn't — couldn't — be part of that family. Haddie was different; their bond, no matter how strained it had become, had remained intact longer than most. She had become the only real familial connection in his life and the only one he'd attempted to retain after the centuries. Usually, he would've already moved on to a new life.

As a light turned green, he wove through a line of cars, letting the water bite into his face and pour in through his collar. Even the rain could not wash the fumes from the air. It tried, smelling alive and fresh one moment before the miasma rolled in around him. Eugene tried. The city had planted trees, and only a few of the buildings reached the multi-story height of most American cities. He rode past old wooden homes, preserved among two- and three-story growths that took up full city blocks with their parking. The greenery came as an afterthought, accentuating the buildings like tassels on a cloak.

Haddie had gotten herself into something more than mugging. She and the detective both knew it. Thomas had seen his share of corruption and street violence.

However, Haddie's headstrong single-mindedness couldn't be controlled. He'd tried. At seventeen she'd taken on the administration at her high school. The cafeteria had changed their procedure by separating the children who paid for their lunch, such as her, from those who received assistance.

It seemed a small thing to him at the time, but she'd explained it differently. "They make Angela stand with everyone else who gets free meals. They have to merge in with us after we pay. Everyone knows. Before, most of us didn't pay attention. People say mean things, won't let them in until the cafeteria lady says something, or we push them ahead. It's cruel, Dad."

"Do they say why they made the change?" He'd been breaking down a carburetor for an '84 Buell Warrior on his bench when she'd come bursting in from school. He'd had a full beard back then. A lot easier to take care of.

Haddie had raised her eyebrows as if incredulous. "They said it was to streamline the lunch line."

He'd started to speak, but she'd cut him off. "It can't, Dad. Everyone has to merge to get their trays and food anyway; we just stand there waiting. It's like they're on display. It's just cruel."

He hadn't been surprised when two days later he'd gone into the garage office to find a message from a vice principal, complaining that his daughter had started a poster campaign and that a food strike had been organized for Friday. Evidently, fish filet day. Probably a good day to schedule it.

In the end, they'd capitulated. They'd caught Haddie red-handed taping up one of the proscribed posters and sent her home. Instead, she'd taken her sign making to the street in front of the school that afternoon.

She'd never been one to let things go. Haddie wouldn't stop just because she'd been jumped in a park. Maybe for a day or two. Then she'd be back out.

And she wouldn't be happy knowing that he'd gotten involved, especially right now when she didn't know what to make of him. Like her though, he had a hard time letting go — when it came to family. A trait that did not serve his life well, considering the circumstances.

He'd traveled into the west end of Eugene where many of the old houses remained. Traffic had gotten worse, and the weather relentlessly pounded around him. A block of old concrete strip malls opened up on each side and the light for Chamber Street hung dimly in the deluge. The turn brought him north into houses that fared worse than most of the city.

He'd had little cause to go to this part of Eugene over the past two decades. Now, he pulled down a gloomy side street and crawled past, searching for numbers on mailboxes or doors. Avoiding a black minivan, he turned around and came back to a yellow-beige house with dead grass and a gray Ford sedan parked deep in the back by a white garage. A pitched-roof porch had straggly plants along its walk, as if lovingly cared for at one time, but left to their own devices.

The driveway had remnants of asphalt giving way to mowed weeds, so he positioned his Shovelhead's stand before testing it. Water dripped down his forehead as he took off his skullcap helmet. Blinds shifted in the window beside the porch; they'd noticed he'd arrived. He would have had to park down the street to surprise them, and it would be easier if they opened the door for him. He pulled his other gloves from the pocket of his jacket and slipped them on as he climbed off his bike. Metal studs capped the knuckles.

Wincing from pain in the joints of his knees, he climbed the steps. The door opened and a small man with pale skin and a Scandinavian or Russian look to his nose and cheekbones stepped onto the porch. Neither of the men who had attacked Haddie. His right hand hung back at the hip of his jeans, likely resting on a gun in his back belt. He couldn't have weighed more than one hundred and fifty pounds.

Cool light, like the blue-gray of a TV, bathed the room behind, lighting a couch facing the door and a littered coffee table. Shadows behind included a dark, open doorway in the back to the left. The other occupants would be to one side or the other of the door, or in the back.

"You're in the wrong place." The accent was American. Second or third generation, then.

Thomas came to the top of the steps, just free of the rain pounding overhead, and wiped the top of his head slowly, as if to squeegee it dry. "Are you sure?" As his hand reached the tie of his braid, he whipped his fist around and clocked the man under the chin.

Barely one hundred and fifty.

The body tumbled off the porch and landed into some bushes they were trying to kill anyway. The punch had been spot-on; he'd be out for a while.

Behind the door is the best bet. Thomas stepped forward and slammed his boot heel into the partially open wooden door. A satisfying grunt preceded a gunshot. A small nine, by the sound of it.

The door swung back to its midpoint, leaving some visibility. A bottle of Black Label nestled among empty cups and a wrinkled takeout bag.

Leaning inside and darting back out, Thomas checked for an attack from the other side. All he heard was a scramble from behind the door. He kicked a second time. No shot rang out, but a muffled cry came when the door stopped suddenly. Thomas kicked a third time and entered a moment later as the door swung wide.

The TV, wedged in the corner behind the door, had been muted, or they just watched it in silence. The gun lay under the short table that held a too large screen with a set of men pounding at each other unrealistically. A man, holding a bleeding nose, lay struggling to right himself from where he rested against the wall. Still not one of Haddie's attackers.

No one else seemed to be in the room, but they could have been hiding behind the couch. Heel first, he stepped down onto the man's crotch, helping him sit up. Keeping an eye to his right where the back door and couch lay, he knelt down on the groaning man's chest, shoving him back down, and stretched to reach the gun.

A dull glint of silver moved in the black rectangle of the back doorway.

Thomas reacted. Instincts had developed over the centuries. He grunted. A short, deep, guttural vocalization like any man might do. Embedded into it, surrounding and accompanying, was a higher note. It came from inside. Not a specific location, but as if his body rang like a bell.

Windows nearby cracked. His right hand flinched, as if directing the sound. It wasn't necessary. Intent drove whatever force he wielded. Right now, he envisioned the gun held there and wanted it gone. He could survive a gunshot wound. An experience he'd survived many times, but, it would delay him from finding those who threatened Haddie. The pain of his abilities could be as debilitating, so he relied on them sparingly.

He knew, without seeing it, that the gun disappeared — spread out into some other place or time. His joints and skin seared with pain. His vision blurred for just a second, until the next heartbeat would bring fresh blood. Nerves screamed across his flesh and his mouth opened in a silent gasp.

A flash came from the black doorway, lighting a bearded man standing there. The bullet, fired at the moment Thomas called out, burned the man's hands.

The nightmare images flashed in his mind, as they always did when he used his ability. An older white-haired man, disintegrating as he protected a teenage girl in a sack-cloth tunic. Thomas shivered and pushed that and the other horrifying images to the back of his mind.

Grabbing the gun from under the table with his left hand, Thomas swung it precisely across the temple of the man under his knee. The body turned limp and relaxed, with its head braced against the wall.

Thomas didn't pause as he pushed aching joints to launch himself toward the man in the back. He swapped the gun into his right hand with effort. His fingertips felt as though they'd been seared across flames. The pain would lessen. It always did. The hellish memories never went away. It had been decades since he'd last used his power. His joints never lost their pain, but the skin would clear up in a couple of days. His tongue tasted metallic.

The bearded man had been dazed from his burns and only started to run as Thomas barreled toward him.

The doorway led into a dining room and a kitchen farther in the back. The smell of spent gunpowder filled the air beside a small round table and two wooden chairs. Thomas had momentum when he slammed into the man running between a cluttered sink under a window and a white stove with a pot and pan stored on top.

The bearded man rebounded off a matching white refrigerator, and Thomas maneuvered him to the floor onto his back. Straddling his chest, he placed the muzzle under the man's chin.

"Louis Mattes." Thomas paused, listening to the noises around the house. There could still be others in the bedrooms or the bath off the dining room. No noise. The neighbors might have called the police after the first shot. He had little time, and his intended quarry didn't seem to be there.

His silence unnerved the bearded man. "He's not here."

That had become obvious. "Where is he?"

"He moved south. Works for someone there. Never

said." The man's hands had red streaming marks from the bullet blast.

"Who?"

"Never said." The man's tone pitched higher. Nothing in his voice indicated a lie.

Devil take me. Thomas growled. "Give me something, or I will heat up that stove and finish off your hands."

Those burns would be hurting enough that any thought of heat would make the man cringe. Thomas had wasted his time and would pay for using his power. Relying on any police force was next to useless unless they were motivated. He wasn't about to lose Haddie.

"Anything." He spoke through gritted teeth.

"Tommy Cho. He left with Tommy Cho. I haven't seen them since. Used to hit up the Silver Dollar. Haven't seen them there in three months."

"Hell." Thomas jumped up.

The kitchen ended at a pantry beside the back door. He moved across the dining room to the bedroom door. Nobody hid in there, and it looked as though they barely slept there. One of the new nightmares flashed in his mind: a woman, screaming as her arm slowly evaporated. Thomas shook the thought out of his head and took a breath in and out, trying to calm himself. The images brought on by using his power were worse than the pain.

He returned to the man on the kitchen floor who had started to roll over, using his wrists instead of his hands. "Just stay still. I don't want the neighbors to hear any more gunshots."

The man flattened slowly, his face on the linoleum.

The back bedroom and bath were empty. Thomas pocketed the magazine and left the gun in the sink, heading for the side door. "The police are on their way. You might want to clean up."

The trip had been a bust, and if Detective Cooper came out to investigate, he might just hear the story. Hopefully, the boys here would take the hint and be gone before that happened. His skin burned and his joints ached, but he'd made his choice. Biff had never seen him with the bruises, and Haddie wouldn't remember. None of that mattered until Haddie was safe.

He had some bikers to visit in southeast Eugene. There was always a chance they knew of these fellows.

CHAPTER 28

HADDIE CLIMBED in the passenger side of Liz's Avenger. On the floor between her legs, she put the plastic bag containing her jacket. The car smelled of overly-sweet, artificial lavender from the air freshener. Liz slammed the door closed and ran with her black umbrella bouncing over her already wet brown hair. The storm pounded a gray wall around them. Haddie blinked as lightning lit the corner of one of the buildings.

Liz scrambled in, trying to shake off and close the umbrella in the rain. She and Haddie both were sufficiently soaked from trying to get into the car. The umbrella got tossed into the back seat before the door closed.

"Monsoon," Liz said. She shoved her purse beside her against the door.

"Thanks, again." Haddie reached for the seatbelt over her shoulder with a wince.

Liz buckled in and noticed Haddie trying to snap the buckle under her bandaged arm. The nurses had taped a plastic bag over the bandages for her to wear until she got home.

"Here, I got it." Liz clicked the buckle in and looked up. "Damn, Haddie. What's going on? A mugging? Seems messed up."

"It is." Haddie tried not to let everything crash down on her: job, Dad, Detective Cooper. Rain pounded the roof and windows of the car.

"Is it a coincidence that you were out there, supposedly to meet with some mysterious informant, then bam, these muggers show up?" Liz still hadn't started the car.

Haddie wanted to go home, snuggle Rock, and listen to Jisoo complain that she wasn't getting enough food. "Detective Cooper is looking into it. I was able to identify their mugshots."

"You'd said. It doesn't sound like you think he'll follow up on it." She pulled out a pair of sunglasses from her tray, looked at them, and put them back. "What's going on?"

"I don't know if I can trust Detective Cooper. Is it possible he's dirty?" Haddie turned her eyes from the storm and searched Liz's face.

"Detective Cooper? I've never heard anything — well, about any of the detectives — that would lead me to believe that. Two patrolmen were brought up by internal last year, but that had to do with some missing property. I never know, but nothing that comes to us would make me think that. We're sort of kept to the side in the department." She frowned. "What makes you question him? Are you sure it isn't just your attorney kind of thing when you have a client at risk? Attorneys often accuse the investigators, saying they're not looking hard enough for evidence that suits their case. Once the DA gets involved, it's sort of out of their hands. Unless we come up with something forensic."

Haddie nodded, too tired to really dig in. Besides, Andrea had told her to drop it. "Probably just that."

Liz smiled. "Do we need to pick up anything on the way to your apartment?" She dug into her purse, and keys jingled. "Medication? Do you have a prescription? Food?"

"Nope. Home. Bed."

"I can't believe this." Liz fired up the Avenger, and the headlights emphasized the deluge outside. "I'll see what Detective Cooper files tomorrow."

Traffic moved slowly along the roads. In some places, only the red lights of the cars ahead gave any indication of where the street ended or began.

Haddie wouldn't have to worry about work tomorrow. Andrea had seen to that. Would Haddie get dropped off the case permanently? She'd failed. Part of her wanted to believe that the mugging might get them a lead, but it didn't seem likely at the moment. *I'm just pouting.* She never would have imagined getting pulled from the case. Admonished for not focusing on her work, yes, but not excluded. It left a hollow, empty feeling in the pit of her stomach.

Dad hadn't returned to the hospital. He never answered her text when she told him she had a ride with Liz. Still, she expected he would have shown up anyway, being Dad and all. Or at least text. She should be happy she could avoid the uncomfortable questions looming between them, but it hadn't been bad at the hospital. In fact, she'd appreciated him being there with Detective Cooper.

"Should you be going home?" asked Liz.

"What do you mean?" Haddie tried to check the streets, to make sure they were still headed toward her apartment. She hadn't been paying attention but recognized an auto shop.

Liz pursed her lips before speaking. "I mean. If — if this was an attempt to make you stop investigating, then how do you know they'll stop? What if they're waiting for you to go home?"

"I've got Rock. Besides, if you think Detective Cooper is straight, won't he be looking for my assailants? Won't they be hiding?"

"I suppose." Liz rocked her head from side to side as if arguing with herself. "Still, I could give you my bed. I could sleep on the couch, at least for a night."

Haddie sighed. She just needed her bed. The meds had her head fuzzy, and she wanted her pillows. "I'm going to be fine. I'll call you first thing when I get up tomorrow."

She had a growing list of people to contact in the morning. Detective Cooper had disappeared, along with Dad, but he left her a message that he expected to follow up in the morning. Did that mean he would actually check into those thugs?

I shouldn't complain. She'd be in her bed in a few minutes sleeping, while Mel went through who knew what. The sad little blonde likely would have been processed into the population. That couldn't be good. *I need to stop whining.*

Liz pulled up to the apartment building, stealing someone's spot under the overhang. Some parking places were empty, but others might be left open by neighbors coming home late.

Sam had been livid after she'd seen Biff drop off the bike, and she texted Haddie at the emergency room. Rock had been taken care of, and evidently Jisoo had been hungry. The cat should be the size of Rock with all she ate. Once Haddie agreed to allow her to come over in the morning to walk Rock, Sam had calmed down. Likely, she was watching their arrival from her apartment.

They were soaked after climbing the stairs to her door.

Liz's attempt with the umbrella became almost comical. Haddie followed shakily, using the railing like she never had before. Her key seemed too thick in the lock.

As she turned off the alarm, Rock kept trying to sniff the plastic bag over her bandage. "Hey, Boy. Mama's home."

Liz stood unsure with the dripping umbrella. "What can I do? Do you need help getting out of that shirt?"

Haddie's sleeve ended in a soggy black knot from the dried, then rain-soaked blood. "Yeah, sure."

Jisoo strolled from the living room into the kitchen and complained.

Rubbing Rock's ears, Haddie yelled into the kitchen. "You've been fed. Don't lie." It should have felt good to be home, but she fought tears.

Jisoo lied with a long mournful cry. Haddie motioned for Liz to drop the umbrella by the door and led the way to the bedroom. Sam had left the living room light on, but the rest of the house remained dark. For the first time in a long time, Haddie felt uncomfortable in her apartment. Rock would not have let anyone come in except Dad; he had a way with dogs, any dog.

She flicked the light on and kicked a path to her bathroom. A bath would be good, but the bed called dibs. Dropping the bag with the jacket on the floor, she began unbuttoning her blouse. The shirt wasn't worth saving. Besides, this was not a memory she needed.

Liz stood awkwardly waiting to help. "I'm serious. You shouldn't be alone. Do you want me to spend the night?"

Haddie doubted Liz would be more intimidating to any intruder than Rock would be. A nice offer, though if she seriously thought there was danger, she wouldn't bring Liz into it. "I'm going to be fine, but if you want, I'll give you Sam's number; she's right across the street."

"Okay." Liz meant it.

Haddie shrugged off the right sleeve and straightened her left arm so that Liz could begin unrolling the bloody knot and slide the shirt off. The moistened blood stained the plastic bag covering the bandage with dark streaks. A nauseating mess. She let Liz rinse off the paste of blood inside her elbow and then peel off the tape and bag.

"What else can I do?" Liz found the garbage can and laid the plastic bag on the pile mounding on top.

"Nothing. I swear, the moment you leave, I'm dropping the rest of these clothes on the floor and heading into bed." Haddie pushed Liz out the bathroom door.

Rock hovered, concerned.

Liz let herself be escorted to the front door. "I'm going to worry."

"That will make me feel much safer."

"You should —"

"Liz, I just need to sleep. Go. I'll call in the morning."

Rock had joined them at the door and nuzzled Haddie's hand. Liz took the umbrella and, with two last protests, left. Haddie leaned against the door after she locked it, staring across the living room to her bedroom. Her computer sat on the wall beside the door. She still had a paper due Monday, and time to work on it, thanks to fouling up her job. How many classes had she missed this week?

Nothing she'd done had helped Mel. The most useful thing she might have done was get mugged, if Detective Cooper followed through and investigated. She still couldn't make up her mind about him. However, him showing up at the hospital had been beyond weird.

Haddie stumbled toward the bedroom. There was nothing she could do for Mel. Even if Andrea did let her work on the case in a couple days, it would be tightly monitored. No more trips to Portland, stalking mail trucks, or breaking into Mark Colman's office. *They're right. I get obsessed.* She didn't think things out. Tears stung her eyes, and she shook her head and wiped them away.

The storm pounded against her bedroom window, dulled only slightly by the curtains. When she turned the bedroom light out, the living room spread a dull glow through the doorway as she slipped out of her bra and tossed it to the floor. She unbuttoned her slacks and sat on the edge of the bed — she had one good arm and calf-high boots. They were her habit when she rode the Fat Boy, the scar on her calf a childhood reminder. Damn, she should have let Liz help with the boots. She probably should have taken Liz up on the offer of company, but she couldn't leave Rock home alone if there was any danger.

Tears welled again as she loosened laces. *Now you're just feeling sorry for yourself.*

PART 4

Our work there acted as a catalyst and an inspiration to bring me to the conclusions that drive my passion and mission today.

CHAPTER 29

HADDIE WOKE to sharp thunder echoing in her bedroom. She sat up, crying out as she stretched her bandaged arm. In with the wind came the scent of rain and gunpowder. Rock growled and whined from the living room.

She stumbled from the bed, trapped in blankets and groggy from sleep. Dressed in only her panties, she froze at the sight of the front door open. Haddie grabbed a yellow sweatshirt, slipping it on before snatching her phone and creeping to the doorway.

Rock growled, crouched on the floor of the living room in an awkward position. The open door was pinned by the wind. Papers rustled and folders flapped. Rock crawled toward the open door.

Haddie peeked into the kitchen. Jisoo sat, wide-eyed, on the counter and gave her a quick glance. No one was in her apartment. Rock had scared them off. Liz had been right.

As the wind shifted, the door slammed shut, nearly causing Haddie to drop the phone. She opened her cell and hit the first number — Dad. Bringing it to her ear, she gasped and dropped her phone to the carpet.

Rock was bleeding.

They shot him. Haddie stumbled and fell to him. He whimpered, seeming almost embarrassed. His left front leg splayed out to the side, and a hole bled in his chest at the edge of the shoulder. She instinctively reached to press her hand there to stop the bleeding.

I caused this. Liz had been right, and she hadn't listened. She should have taken Rock and Jisoo and gone somewhere. Dad's.

Rock growled and flinched, then whined and licked her hand, pushing it away. The white giraffe on his chest was smeared with blood.

She had to get him to the vet. *I need help.* She couldn't carry him to the RAV4 alone. Scrambling on her knees and one arm, she reached her phone. She'd been calling Dad. "Dad?" Silence replied. Voicemail. Haddie swore and hung up.

Sam. She dialed her number and stood up to return to Rock. He lay on his side, looking up with dark eyes. She knelt, laying her hand gently against his muzzle and cupping his chin. Sucking in a ragged breath, she brought her face close to his. Haddie fought tears, breathing through her nose in stiff bursts. He couldn't die. She wouldn't be able to live with it. He whined, blinking slowly.

Haddie drew in a scent of gunpowder and felt her jaw tighten. She wanted to hurt whoever did this to him. They'd been after her; Rock didn't deserve this.

"C'mon, Sam. Wake up." She set it on speaker and left it beside Rock to grab a pair of yoga pants off the floor beside her desk.

"Hello?" Sam's voice drawled over the phone.

Haddie slid the leg of her yoga pants under Rock's head,

pinning the bulk behind his neck with her knee. She shifted it down with her good hand. "Sam, I need you. Right now. Can you come help me?" She couldn't say anything about Rock's condition; Sam might lose it.

Rock whined when Haddie got the legging under his good shoulder. He had to hurt terribly. Had the bullet hit his lung?

"Is that Rock? Is he okay?" Sam's voice cleared and shuffling sounded over the phone.

"Sam, please." Haddie pulled out enough of the leg to wrap Rock's back.

"Okay. Okay. I'm coming." The connection ended.

Haddie pulled the pant leg between his legs so that it angled against the wound. Dark and angry, it welled blood. How much could he lose?

She tried to hold the end with her left hand, pain searing to her shoulder, but she couldn't get enough strength between her fingers. With her index finger through the fabric, she clenched her fist and felt woozy. Looping the ankle of the legging around with her good hand, she pulled and formed a single knot. Adjusting, she felt some pressure against the wound area. It would have to do until Sam arrived.

Stroking down his muzzle, she whispered, "You're going to be okay. You have to be." His eyes closed and she sobbed. "I need you, Honey. Stay with me." Tears rolled down her face.

There was a pounding on the door. Sam must have run the entire way.

"It's open," Haddie yelled.

Rock stirred, and she put her hand on his neck to keep him from rising.

The door opened and she could see an officer's uniform and a gun drawn, pointed toward the floor. "Police, are you okay?"

Haddie raised her eyebrows. Of course, someone would have called the police. What she'd thought had been thunder had been the gunshot. "I'm fine. I'm alone."

An older man with dark brown skin and black hair leaned in, looking around. "You're alone?" He squinted toward the back bedroom. "Can we enter?"

Rock struggled, too weakly.

Haddie swallowed. "My dog's been shot. If you come in, he'll try and get up to defend. I'm waiting for a friend, to get him to the vet. Can you wait there — a moment?"

He turned away.

Sam's voice called from outside. "Haddie?"

"Let her in." Haddie called out. Rock was getting agitated, fighting against her to get back up. "Please."

Sam took one step in, wearing a pair of pink jeans with a trans pride patch on her left knee and a loose, crumpled T-shirt. Her typically straight black hair was rumpled from sleep, and she stood wet, pale, and shaken, until she saw Rock lying on the floor beside Haddie. Turning with a snap, she faced the officers outside. "Did you do this?"

Haddie pushed Rock down. "Sam, no. Help me. We've got to get him to the vet."

Rock weighed about forty-five pounds. With two good arms, she could lift him. Getting down the stairs with Sam would be difficult, but she didn't imagine he'd let one of the officers near him, or her.

Sam skidded to her knees in front of Rock. "Who did this?" She cupped his chin.

"I don't know. Can you help me carry him down to the RAV4?"

"Of course," Sam said. She brushed bangs from her eyes and looked at Haddie's legs. "You're going to need keys —"

Haddie looked down. She wore only the sweatshirt. *I'll need pants.* Remembering Mel, she stood, tugging at the hem before heading into the bedroom. She'd worn less in front of more people. Grabbing the closest pants, a pair of red jeans, off the floor, she stuffed her keys and wallet into the pockets. She shoved her feet into her slip-ons and made for the front room.

Sam had tied the second leg of the yoga pants into a tighter bandage.

One officer had stepped inside and stood peering into the kitchen as she came out of her bedroom. "Miss, I'm going to have to know what happened here." His partner blocked the doorway.

Haddie reached into her pocket and handed him her purse, then strode to Rock. "My ID's in there. Someone broke in and shot my dog. You're welcome to search the apartment. I saw nothing when I came out, except that my door was open and my dog was shot." Her voice cracked. "You can get a full statement at the animal clinic if you want to follow me there. Don't let the cat out. Lock up when you're done." She stuffed her phone in her pocket.

Rock stirred as she knelt and slipped her good arm under his back legs. Sam, a little over five feet, raised Rock's neck and head to her chest, trying to support his left leg as well. He'd lost too much blood to fight them. He managed a whimper that broke her heart, but she couldn't allow herself to cry again. He needed her to be strong.

They passed the officers, who stepped back, though Rock didn't show any indication that he recognized they were there.

It took longer than Haddie wanted to get down the

stairs and through the downpour to her RAV4. The police car, lights still on, waited in the alley. Red and blue splashed in the falling rain. Her Fat Boy faced forward, a reminder that Biff had dropped it off and of the events of the evening. Someone had broken into her house with a gun. Did they intend to shoot her? Liz would be livid. The day blurred with all the failures. It wasn't midnight yet.

Haddie would have to call the clinic during the ride. They had overnight emergency service, but she'd need one of the veterinarians. Hopefully Dr. Stevens.

Sam managed Rock's full weight while Haddie opened the back. Together they got him in, his breathing too shallow. His wet, dark eyes were barely visible between lids, and he whined and licked weakly. *I can't lose you.* Her heart broke as she closed the back hatch on him. She choked back a sob. Tears welled in her eyes.

"I want to go." Sam paused, despite the statement, at the back of the RAV4. She rarely left the couple of city blocks surrounding their two apartments. "Wanting" to go could have different meanings.

"Can you stay here until the officers leave and check on Jisoo?" Haddie moved toward the driver's door as she spoke.

Sam nodded, looking ashamed. "Call me."

Haddie yelled out the door as she climbed in. "I will." Starting the car, she called back to Rock. "Hang in there, Boy. We're getting help."

Sam stood under the overhang, watching as Haddie backed out. The pain in her face made Haddie cry worse. Arm aching, she put the RAV4 into reverse and turned in three one-handed pulls to get out into the alley and heading toward the street. She could see the officers stopping at Sam in her rear view.

What monster shoots a dog? Rock had likely attacked.

He rarely barked, and not in warning. Dad had worked with her to train him and said that Rock had been born to protect.

She paused at the end of the alley to dial the vet — something she could have done at the apartment if she'd been clear-headed.

A drowsy voice started to answer over the car speaker and Haddie interrupted. "This is Haddie Dawson. My pit bull, Rock, is a patient of Dr. Stevens. He's been shot. I'm on my way now."

The man on the other end stuttered. "Um, I, well . . . I'll call now, but Dr. Stevens is not on call."

"Please call someone in." She dropped the connection before getting on the street. Hopefully, that would spur the man to wake up and focus.

The rain had settled into a solid downpour, gutters streamed with runoff, and the streets had emptied. The RAV4 cut through abandoned streets, sheeting water to the sides. She came to the first red light and peered both ways before running it. They could hand her a stack of tickets if they wanted.

Did Mark Colman's killer really mean to see her dead? Botched muggers and hit men? This sounded more like a local gang than organized crime. *What do I know?* She'd never come across either, really. There were stories about some of the bikers Dad did work for. Biff made jokes about them. Was there a chance that the dogfighting ring did have a larger gang?

Haddie could see the animal clinic. "We're almost there, Boy. Hang on." A round male figure stood in the doorway, looking into her approaching lights. The overnight tech, she imagined.

Whoever wanted her harmed, they had shot her dog.

That did nothing but make her angry. Right now, she needed to get Rock taken care of. After that, she had no intention of letting them get away with it.

CHAPTER 30

HADDIE SAT in the veterinarian's waiting room; tears rained down her cheeks in hot rivulets. She hated the smell — odd antiseptic and remnants of animal urine.

A duplicate row of blue plastic seats lined the wall across from her by the door. Scratched and polished yellowish tiles made up the floor. Only the lights over the counter were on, leaving darkness and the light under the exam door to shine in a thin line in the shadows. Rock lay somewhere behind that line.

Very little noise from the back could be heard over the rain pouring off the roof. The grass and plant beds outside had flooded so that waterfalls splashed off the top of the building. She'd seen the lights of a car arriving, a door closing, and voices in the back. *The veterinarian, hopefully.* Haddie wanted to go in the back and make sure they were taking care of Rock. He shouldn't have to be here, not like this.

A second set of lights cut through the gloom outside. Another veterinarian, an assistant, or had the first car not been the doctor? The thought of Rock lying in the back dying, without them trying to help, wrenched her heart apart. She stood and walked to the glass door.

A dark sedan parked beside her RAV4. The interior lights of the new arrival turned on and she pressed against cold glass to make out a face. The veterinarian would likely park in the back, where the other car had gone.

The light flickered out as the car door opened and a shadow stood up. Face down and hands thrust into the pockets of a long black raincoat, the figure strode toward her.

Haddie backed up and swallowed, finding her pulse quickening. Was she going to be scared of everyone now?

Detective Cooper looked up as he reached for the door handle. Brown hair matted wet over his scowl; his eyes picked her out before he stepped inside. "Ms. Dawson."

He didn't belong here. The officers had already talked with her; they'd taken her report. "What are you doing here?" Anger tinged her voice.

He didn't answer immediately. After wiping rain from his hair and face, he smoothed his eyebrows and mustache. "I've found this an interesting night. Your ability to be in the middle of so much commotion has me curious."

The merest hint that he might be involved with Rock's shooters made her want to kick him, to smash him right through the glass door he'd just come in. Her arm ached under the bandage. She had not filled the prescription they'd given her, just so she wouldn't be tempted. "What are you trying to say?"

"I'm beginning to think you've annoyed some people," he said. "Didn't give up after they warned you, perhaps."

Haddie tensed, shifting a foot absently so that her body squared. Had that been a threat?

Detective Cooper continued, "Your little foray into the

dogfighting world certainly would have caused some enemies, if they knew you were involved. I've considered that, somehow, they might be responsible." He took a deep breath and shifted his eyes to the door leading into the clinic. "There is also the possibility that your investigation of Mark Colman has disturbed someone. What have you learned that might cause someone concern?"

He didn't mention apprehending her attackers. What if he warned the muggers that she'd identified them? Then why make these statements? Why ask his question? It didn't line up, unless he was purposefully misleading her. Haddie froze. For a moment, she'd considered her misgivings unfounded. Did someone send him to find out how close she was? Or had she finally gotten him to consider that there could be more to the case than Mel?

"I haven't —" She started to dismiss the little she'd learned. Perhaps though, it would be better if she kept them guessing, whether the detective was directly involved or not. She couldn't decide at this point. "You'd best bring that inquiry up to my employer."

If he was clean, she wanted to persuade him about all the minor inconsistencies, but they were just that — minor. The detective did not seem to do well with the possible or improbable. He seemed, at some moments, as driven as she to find the truth. Or he played that part, all the while covering his own agenda. With no sleep, groggy from the drugs, and stressed over Rock, she couldn't think clearly.

"Ms. Dawson, I don't have time —"

A familiar rumble cut through the splashing water from outside, and the headlight of her dad's Shovelhead shone through the door. It lit the back of the detective. Her body relaxed in relief as Dad cut the engine just outside the clinic. Still, how had he found her? Sam?

Even the detective recognized Dad's bike without turning; his eyebrows dropped, darkening his eyes. Rain-soaked hair clung as he turned to look out the door. "I had expected that he would already be here when I arrived." He took a step backward, standing just in front of Haddie, but didn't turn to face her. "If you believed these conspiracies, why did you go home last night?"

Because I'm stupid? Why had she not listened to Liz? Rock would be somewhere else, safe and sleeping. "I assumed you would have taken the assailants in by now." Not exactly the truth, but he angered her.

She glanced from the back of the detective's head to Dad unstrapping his helmet, leather jacket slick and black from the rain.

"Hmph." Detective Cooper seemed amused.

Dad kept his riding goggles on and wore a black neck gaiter over his mouth. He opened the door, sucking air out of the room. Ignoring the detective, he strode two steps to face her and inspect her. She wore the bright yellow sweatshirt and red jeans, a combo that surely made a statement.

"Sam said you weren't hurt," he said.

Tears welled up. "They shot Rock, Dad."

He pulled her into him and she sobbed. She dreaded the door opening from the back of the veterinarian clinic — imagined a sad tech bringing her dreadful news. Losing Rock would crush her. Too much loss in one night. How would she ever go home without him? The apartment would never be the same.

Detective Cooper turned and coughed. "Where were you tonight, Mr. Dawson?"

Dad tensed and pulled back, putting his hands on her shoulders, and spoke through the wet gaiter. "Southeast

Eugene, playing cards with some friends." He had a tiny dark bruise on the side of his misshapen nose.

Haddie blinked and raised her eyebrows. That didn't make sense. Dad remained facing her, eyes dark behind the tinted glass. On the smooth surface, water droplets joined together and raced down to the rims.

"An alibi. Very convenient. I imagine these 'friends' will vouch for you, right after you left your daughter at the hospital." The detective obviously alluded to something.

Dad turned, facing away from Haddie, and confronted the detective. "It took a few minutes to get there. Haddie had a ride home with her friend Liz."

He wouldn't have known about the ride until much later, when she texted him. She felt a chill and folded her right arm across her chest. What had he done?

"So, you would not know anything about the gunshot at Louis Mattes' last known address? The disturbance there?" The detective glanced over to her, as if trying to read her reaction.

"No. Did someone shoot this Louis? Why would you think I'm involved?" Dad asked.

Haddie turned from them, looking at the slit of light coming from under the door to the back and wiped her eyes. Had Dad gone after Louis Mattes? Had he seen the information from the mugshot? She wouldn't have been surprised. It would explain the card playing story. He wouldn't have just abandoned her. Lie to the detective — likely — but he wouldn't leave her.

"They reported a motorcycle arriving at the house just prior to the gunshot and leaving soon after." Detective Cooper sighed, his lips turned at the corners in what seemed frustration.

Dad smoothed the top of his head. "A Shovelhead? Those are rare up here."

Detective Cooper wiped his mustache and chin. "The witnesses did not see the motorcycle or rider."

Haddie took a step to the side and sat back down, her body weak, her thighs trembling. Dad had gone looking for her muggers. Had he found them? If so, then who shot Rock? Maybe he hadn't found them. She spoke to the discolored tiles. "Did you find my assailants, Detective Cooper?"

"Not at this time, Ms. Dawson. I did have a patrol meet me at their residence. However, there was no one there. It seems someone had just left — after a brief disturbance." He took in a deep breath. "I must warn you both to stay out of the investigation into Ms. Dawson's attack at the park, and now, the incident at your residence."

Anger boiled in Haddie. At her dad, for risking himself and possibly harming the attackers. At Detective Cooper, for being pompous and righteous while doing nothing but warning her off. At herself, for not listening to Liz and keeping Rock safe.

"If you just did your job —" she said, biting off her tirade.

His voice remained calm. "If you'd let me."

"Look how well that has worked for Mel Schaffer." Haddie snapped. She would have stomped out, if there wasn't a downpour outside and if her legs didn't wobble.

"Despite your presumptions, stay out of my way. I won't hesitate to bring obstruction charges — on either of you. Stay inside the lines." His calm voice turned to a growl.

"The attorney of record has rights to investigate where they believe the police failed." It wasn't exactly the stated code, but close enough. The anger sharpened her mind, but it still felt thick.

"In regard to the Colman case, to a certain extent." Detective Cooper's black shoes shuffled slightly. "In your own case, please do not attempt to apprehend or approach any suspects."

Haddie closed her eyes, head hung down, resisting the urge to lie on the row of chairs. She didn't have the strength to argue. *Just be okay, Rock.* "Whatever. Why are you even here, Detective Cooper?"

"First to see if you have anything to add to the report on the shooting at your house. Thus, my previous question about your investigation. Have you uncovered anything that might concern someone?"

Haddie took a deep breath and looked up. "And your second reason for being here?" She still could not decide whether to trust him or not. She certainly didn't like him, but dislike and trust were not the same.

Detective Cooper looked to her dad. "I think we've already established that." He pursed his lips and shrugged. "Please leave the detective work to the police department." Turning, he headed out the door.

The storm blew in wet, brown leaves and wrestled with the door as it tried to close. Dad stood there, still in his riding glasses and gaiter. Odd.

"Did you really?" she asked.

Dad shrugged. "Best you remember that I was playing cards."

The door to the clinic opened and light streamed from the back. She could make out a silhouetted figure. "Ms. Dawson?"

CHAPTER 31

HADDIE JUMPED UP. The room seemed silent, the storm outside just a murmur. "Rock?" she asked of the figure.

She didn't recognize the doctor, an older man with white, close-trimmed sideburns and gray hair. He had a mask hanging at his neck and a white apron over a white coat. A long smear of red blood stretched along his waist.

"He's safe. He'll be fine."

Haddie sucked in a breath and sobbed it out. Her father laid a glove on her shoulder, and she curled into him. Rock had survived her mistake. Tears streamed hot down her cheeks. At what point would she start taking suggestions?

"I want to see him," she croaked. Her eyes felt glued shut from tears and sleeplessness.

"Give him a few hours to get out of the anesthesia. You're welcome to stay here — with your friend." The doctor turned around and opened the door, flooding the waiting room with bright light from a short hall.

Dad still had on the gaiter and glasses, as if ready to go. However, he maneuvered her to the chairs. "Lie down; use my lap for your head."

Exhausted, she sat down in the middle of the row. "I want to see Rock."

"You will. He's okay. Sleep. I'll be here." He sat on her right side at the end and tugged her shoulder. "Sleep is the best thing for you."

"Just going to rest my head." She lifted her legs up, wincing as she protected her bandaged arm, and rested her head against his leather pants. He smelled like rain, grease, and gunpowder. What had he been up to? She would need to ask . . . later.

Rock being safe was all that mattered. She'd let Sam know soon. So much had happened tonight. Her breath snorted out as she remembered the attack at the park: the knife and the bulging-eyed man's intensity as he attacked; the woman screaming; Jeff, the pudgy, middle-aged man who couldn't manage her saddlebag key; Detective Cooper, always there, sneaky and arrogant, and always digging; Liz, trying to put on her sunglasses in the storm at night. It all melded into a swirl. Black clouds and rain.

She awoke and found Dad answering his phone.

"Yeah?" His chin looked wrong — splotchy. He needed a shave. "No, just find out where they're holed up. Thanks, Trig."

The ringing of his phone must have awakened her. The storm poured outside. The thunder had stopped. Nothing but grayness.

"What time is it?" She lifted her head up, grimacing as her bad arm shifted. Her head felt like it weighed a hundred pounds.

Dad frowned and tucked his phone into his jacket. "Sleep. It's not even one."

His glasses and gaiter were around his neck, and she could see his face, marked up with dark splotches randomly dotting chin, jaw, and even lips. He looked like he had a rash of tiny bruises.

"What happened to your face?" she asked. Her hip complained about her makeshift bed.

"Nothing. Go back to sleep." He turned away but toward the light over the counter so that his markings became more evident.

Foggy, she raised her eyebrows, trying to remember something familiar. Had he looked like this before, when she was a child? Was Dad sick? "Dad, tell me. What's wrong?"

He stood, pulling up his gaiter to hide his face, and pulled on his riding glasses. "Maybe we should just head over to the garage. Get you settled in your old room for the night. You're not going back to your apartment."

"No. I'm waiting to see Rock." She didn't intend to go back to her apartment, not yet. It depended a lot on what Detective Cooper did. She didn't intend to leave at all right now. Rock wouldn't be ready to leave right away.

"That's hours from now. You need a good sleep."

"No. I need to know what's going on with you and to be here when Rock wakes up." Haddie resisted reaching up and pulling down his gaiter. Why did he always have to hide things from her?

"Where are you going to stay now? You can't stay at your apartment, not until this is resolved." He wore his full gloves, with the metal caps on his knuckles. He'd come back from a fight once with those on.

"What happened? What was Detective Cooper asking you about?" *Louis Mattes' residence.* "Did you find the muggers?"

Dad shook his head. "Nope. Just some scumbags. They didn't get me any closer to them."

"What were you going to do?"

He frowned and tightened his lips, pacing to the front door to stare into the gray night. Dad had a rough reputation with some of the tougher bikers, and they respected him. She'd never seen him do anything too bad. Clocked a man at the garage once, and came back a couple nights with torn clothes and bruises — mostly on his knuckles. But she'd never seen the splotches. Had she?

She'd learned impossible things about him. How could she not know her own dad?

"Dad?"

He spoke quietly to the glass. "I don't know what I was going to do." He shrugged, flexing his fingers at his side. "Stop them."

"Show me your face."

Dad didn't move for a moment, then he turned and stared into her eyes. "Let it go, Haddie."

"Show me your face," she repeated. When he didn't react, she reached up and tugged at the side of his gaiter. The light from the counter clearly lit his face. His jaw had a purplish spot, and another splotch hid along his cheekbone near his ear. *Familiar*. "What is this? Have you had this before?"

"You wouldn't remember." He sighed and pulled the gaiter down to his neck, and with two hands stretched out the band on his glasses and dropped them down. "They're called purpura. It happens when your capillaries shatter under the skin."

Blood. The purplish bruises dotted across his face. The one by his nose had not been considerable. However, now that she could see them all, they disturbed her. She'd seen this lately. On the British man, Harold Holmes, at Mark

Colman's office. He'd been cute, except for these marks. She flushed, feeling petty.

"What causes this?" She pointed to his gloves. "Hands too?"

Odd that she had never seen this condition before, and now twice in the past couple of days. Her dad never got sick. A fact she found curious now, especially considering what she'd learned about him lately.

"It's not something we're going to want to talk about. You still have other aspects of my . . . life that you need to accept." He didn't remove his gloves.

She tensed and her jaw tightened. He did not get to keep all these secrets. "Tell me, Dad."

There was more. A panic inside, an old fear, and old painful memory in her childhood. These marks were familiar. More than Harold Holmes. What couldn't she remember?

"What causes it, Dad?"

He sighed. "If we're going to continue this conversation, I'd like a drink. It's been a long night. I didn't sleep much the night before."

"Just tell me." Haddie took in a deep breath, holding her ground.

"A drink. Bars are open until 2 or 2:30 here. We've got time." He put his hand on the door and swung out, inviting the storm in. "You can't say you handle what I tell you very well. A drink is a small price to ask."

She wanted to argue. He couldn't expect what he'd told her to go over well. But she had been childish, scared. Would she handle this better? *I can't know that until he tells me.* She needed to know — before she mentioned Harold Holmes.

Haddie huffed, tucked her bandaged arm under her sweatshirt against her stomach, and stepped into the storm.

CHAPTER 32

By this time of the morning, the storm had cleared all but the most adventurous off the streets of Eugene. Thomas drove Haddie's SUV east toward a dive bar he knew just a few blocks from her veterinarian's office. On the dash to her car, she'd argued to drive; he'd escorted her to the passenger side.

Without speaking, the thrum of windshield wipers added a beat to the puddles that scrubbed the underside of the car. Water sprayed onto the empty sidewalks from under the tires. Almost no red lights from the cars ahead flickered in the downpour. A dull haze surrounded streetlamps and traffic lights. The city had been beaten into submission under the dark fury of the storm. The consistent downpour gave him strength to face the darkness that Haddie wanted exposed. He'd always liked storms.

I don't want to lose Haddie. He would survive the loss, if it happened. He always had. The unexpected deaths of his previous family had taken him by surprise. He always outlived them, but these had died so young. His ex-wife had been seventy-three, but their daughter had been only fifty-four, and her son — his grandson — in his early thirties. The great-grandson survived. A twelve-year-old boy who lived now with his mother's family, an aunt that had no bloodline to Thomas. He'd been distracted by the deaths and had been giving Haddie her space to deal with his . . . revelations. Now, she wanted it all. Her life had turned dangerous. He didn't want to lose her, too.

At the stop sign, he turned left. A wave from his tires flooded over a gray sedan parked by a white picket fence. The rain had scrubbed the residential neighborhood. Debris piled at drains or drifted onto lawns. Even in the gray, it looked greener. A storm was good for the city. Perhaps he needed to look at Haddie as a storm — pushing the debris of his life to the corners and edges where it could be seen. He didn't have to like it. This transition into understanding his life would never have been easy for her. The danger that crashed into her life made the timing wrong. He didn't need a storm right now. She didn't.

At the light, he turned right and pulled against the curb. Turning the engine off left them with the rain pounding on the roof and their silence. The bar's neon light flickered in the window.

"Ready?" he asked.

Haddie grunted and opened her passenger door. A gust brought in the scents of rain and wet earth. She'd refused his jacket, but she had to be cold. Keeping a jacket in her car would be a good plan. He'd avoided mentioning the suggestion when they'd left the vet.

Various sports lit the screens that dotted the walls, and one of the TVs blared a commentary while a seventies song played on speakers somewhere. Stale beer and fried potatoes scented the air. Three young people sat at the bar, while two older couples played pool. The tavern had been livelier the last time he'd visited. Years ago.

Gaiter down and glasses around his neck, Thomas led them to a table tucked in the corner. He could watch the door from there. Over the music, no one would hear their conversation.

A man with a tightly trimmed orange beard followed them and dropped two coasters on the table as they settled in. "What can I get you tonight?" He noticed the purpura but didn't flinch.

Thomas pointed to Haddie. She shouldn't be drinking on antibiotics, but she didn't tend to drink heavily. Maybe she'd sleep in the car.

"Two Hearts." She pulled out her hair and twisted it around her fist.

Thomas nodded. "Aquavit."

The waiter shook his head. "We don't have that."

Thomas gestured toward the bartender, an older woman with dirty blonde hair tied into a ponytail. "They've had it before. Check."

"Vodka?"

Thomas sighed. "If they don't have aquavit, a good vodka."

"Grey Goose? Absolut?"

"Yes." Thomas likely would not get aquavit, even if the bartender did have a bottle hidden. He waited as the waiter scurried off. "Rock's gonna be okay."

"I know." Haddie closed her eyes. They were rimmed from crying.

Rock had been a gift when she was seventeen. His dog Tabitha had died, and Haddie had taken it hard. Thomas had found a friend with a litter and surprised her. She'd loved the pit bull pup and did well learning to train it.

They'd been inseparable since. A gunshot wound couldn't be taken lightly. The pup would need care and attention. Haddie would need help with that.

They sat silently; he waited on their drinks before starting a conversation he wanted to remain private.

She resembled her mother, Nyra. Even his Anglo-Saxon genes hadn't diminished her tawny skin, large eyes, and pitch-black, straight hair. Outgoing and vivacious, like Nyra. He'd left Haddie with his obstinacy, and hopefully nothing worse. Each child he fathered, he worried about. None had ever developed his particular afflictions.

Their waiter returned, carrying a shot and a bottle of Haddie's beer. "Sorry. You were right. Said she hadn't opened the bottle in a couple years."

"Thanks." Thomas tapped the rim with a gloved finger.

The waiter paused a moment. "Okay. If you need something, let me know."

Haddie ran her fingers down the label of her bottle, wiping glassy beads of condensation into a drop.

Thomas took a sip. A good bottle, notes of caraway. Sometimes he lost his sense of taste after using his power. He stopped procrastinating. "Go ahead."

"How did you get those bruises, the purpura?" She spoke quickly, jumping into it.

"I used my power. I try not to." He knew it didn't fully answer her question. She needed to absorb it slowly. He wouldn't believe it if someone told him.

Haddie closed her eyes, her fingers tightened on the bottle, and she took a sip. "Power?"

"I don't understand it. Somehow, at first, it only came when I was frightened or angry. I do something." He spoke slowly, pausing between each sentence, though not long enough that she would think him finished. "It came with a shout the first time. There is another sound that comes with it. A higher note, like a bell. I can control it better now. It causes my skin to get these and my joints to ache." He wouldn't tell her of the images yet. They were nightmares from someone else's life; they weren't his memories.

Haddie stared at him. She likely thought him insane. How could he explain this? He'd struggled with the reality for centuries — with his own experience as proof. Now, she had minutes to absorb. She pulled the beer to her lips and left it hanging there, not drinking.

Without taking a sip, she returned the bottle to the table. "Okay." She swallowed and gestured in the air. "What exactly does this *sound* do?"

Thomas finished his aquavit and moved the empty shot glass to the edge of the table. He'd welcome an interruption. "Things — and people — disappear."

Haddie laughed. An outburst that caused a man at the bar to look over and smile. She continued in short bursts, ranging from chuckles to cackles. She didn't believe him. *She thinks I'm insane.*

"Okay," she said. "So, one day — I'm assuming centuries ago —" she paused, taking in a breath, "you shouted and made someone disappear."

Actually, three people. "Yes." Thomas considered asking for the bottle.

"You realize, I'd imagine, this sounds improbable — impossible — insane." She took a swig and looked up to the ceiling.

"Very much so. Precisely why I've never told anyone." He glanced as the waiter started toward them. "But not just for that reason." He tapped the edge of the shot glass when the man reached them.

"Another?" The waiter pointed to the beer Haddie clutched.

"No. No, I need to stay sober for this." She chuckled but took another sip.

They sat in silence while the waiter retrieved another aquavit. Haddie wouldn't look at him. Holding her beer, she stared at the table.

The shot glass arrived, and Thomas took a sip. "You've asked for these answers. Asked me to be honest. I understand you can't accept what I say. I love you, Haddie. Where do we go from here?" He took a deep breath to quell the anxious tightness in his chest. *I can't lose Haddie.*

"You're right. My bad." Her tone resigned, she shook her head slowly.

This wasn't like Haddie. She didn't give up. Something brewed under the surface. The clipped, excited commentary from the TV sank in around them between songs. The aquavit warmed him, but didn't soothe the aches in his joints.

"No," she said, "you can't just be insane." She tapped the table. "Go ahead. Do it. Use your power, make something disappear." Her tone said that she didn't believe him; not that he wouldn't do it, but that he *couldn't* do it.

"No, not here, certainly. I will, though. We just need to be somewhere private." He didn't relish the pain. It wouldn't make it any easier for her. How could he expect her to come to grips with this?

She closed her eyes. "Okay. Let's go with how you ended up centuries old but were only born a few decades ago. That actually seems easier to believe. How, I don't know."

"I was biking in Iceland. I have — had — friends there." Technically they still lived there. "I got in an accident, and when I awoke, I was in a different time. The roads were gone, my friends were gone. All I had was the bike and my supplies."

He'd never understood any of it, so how could she? Decades had passed before he'd resigned himself to acceptance, not understanding.

"Surely there was something more than an accident?" She had an angry tone.

There had been the woman standing on the roadside, dressed in a parka or some hooded cloak, glowing. How crazy did he want her to believe he was? "A woman on the road." He finished his second aquavit.

"Of course." Haddie finished her beer, placed it on the coaster, and stood up. "Ready?" She had an odd strain to her words and a flinch of her shoulders.

His shot glass hung in his fingers, forgotten. "That's it?"

"Dad," her face threatened to crumble into tears. "I . . . just can't." She stumbled around her chair, more frantic than anything else.

His heart dropped. She thought he was crazy. He needed to let her think on it a bit and come back with more questions. He would end up giving her a demonstration. Too close to the last, his skin would not fare well. It didn't matter. His clients hardly cared what he looked like.

"Okay." With protesting knees, he winced and stood. "Let me clear our tab."

Haddie walked away as if he hadn't spoken, heading for the door. He pulled his wallet out and headed for the register at the bar, flagging the young waiter across the room. Patting the keys to her SUV in his pocket, he watched her head into the storm.

Haddie pulled up to the clinic, and the lights of the RAV4 shone through the rain against the wet chrome of Dad's Shovelhead. She turned off the engine and sat staring at the glass door of the building. "I want to be alone. I'll be fine."

Dad's face had been so serious during their discussion. Marred with bruises and his misshapen nose, he acted as he always did, deliberate and concise. He hadn't raised his gaiter or glasses again. If she turned, he would be looking at her with dark eyes and strong features, unaware that he lived in a delusion. Somehow, he seemed older. *Why was I so sure he hadn't aged?*

They sat in silence for a moment. Aquavit made for a familiar scent in the confined space. She could still taste her beer, and her stomach felt queasy. She waited. If she got out and went into the vet's, he might follow. Haddie couldn't deal with him — with the swirling, staggering feelings about him. How long had he believed all those things he said?

"Okay. I'll check in a few hours from now." He pulled

up his gaiter and settled the glasses over his eyes. Wiping a gloved hand over his hair, he paused as if she might reply.

She hadn't expected him to agree so readily. He wouldn't let her go back to her apartment, and she didn't want to. *I can stay with Liz.* Haddie sat silently.

Howling wind gusted in as he opened the door. He strode past her headlights, oblivious to the downpour. His skull cap helmet had been sitting on his seat the entire time.

When the rumble of his Shovelhead faded as he rode away, she tucked her bandaged arm under her wet sweatshirt and stepped out. She felt numb, as if her emotions had been washed away. Rock slept in the back somewhere. Safe. Blue chairs waited for her. It would be hours before they would let her see him. She stood dripping on worn, yellowed tiles when the tech opened the door to look into the waiting room. His plump face nodded in recognition and disappeared, leaving her alone.

Had she imagined that he didn't age? With all the bruises, he looked older. What about Harold Holmes? Did his bruises, this purpura, mean anything? Maybe in her dad's mind. She tried to put it in the little box with her feelings, but it nagged at her. She should have interviewed the British businessman. He had an office in the same building as the deceased. If she didn't believe her dad, then why did the matching bruises matter?

I'm tired. I shouldn't be thinking. Haddie dropped down to one of the chairs, exhausted. Rock was safe — for the moment. Liz would be waiting for a call in the morning and likely be gracious about being right. Later, she'd berate Haddie for not listening.

The constant waterfalls outside sung in a soothing rhythm like waves on a beach. It hadn't been a day since she'd ridden to Portland at sunrise. The calls and internet searches swirled with the mugging and Rock being shot. Dad's face, grim and serious as he drank aquavit and spouted nonsense.

Her phone vibrated in her jeans pocket, and Haddie blinked her eyes open. Crusty and dry, they fought her. She lay on the row of chairs, the lip of one biting into her hip where it peaked to the gap between the next. Her bandaged arm ached and pinched sharply as she rose. She had dreamed of Dad and Mel — of purple faces and fire. Her clothes smelled wet and her tongue tasted like paste. How long had she slept? It still looked dark and gray outside. Water poured off the roof.

Sam's name showed on the display.

Damn. Haddie had never called her. "I'm sorry, Hon. Rock's okay. I — I fell asleep."

"Good." Sam sniffled. "I was sure he was."

Haddie blinked, trying to focus. The images from nightmares still danced in her head. She'd been unfair to Sam. "I'm really sorry, Sam. Have you slept?" What time was it? She couldn't see the screen. She stood with effort, stumbling; the bathroom was at the opposite end of the waiting room.

"I couldn't sleep, not really. I'm really scared for you — and Rock. You're not coming back, are you?" The question sounded painful to Sam.

Haddie planned on calling Liz. Beyond that, she had no idea how to deal with all of this. "I'll probably sleep at Liz's for a couple nights. Could you bring Jisoo over to your place? You said she gets along with everyone over there." Sam had a menagerie going on in her apartment.

Sam's tone brightened. "Of course. I'll go get her now." Sounds of shuffling echoed through the phone. "Will you call me later?"

"Yes." Haddie rubbed her eye with the back of her thumb, bringing the phone back to her ear quickly. "I'm really sorry for not calling."

"No worries. I'm heading over to your apartment now." Sam sounded excited. "Oh, you're not mad about your dad, are you?"

"What about my dad?" Haddie stared at the bathroom door. What had he done?

"He pulled into your apartment when I was heading back to mine after checking on Jisoo. She was hungry, but she seemed okay. He seemed upset about the shooting."

That's how he knew I was at the vet. "Oh. No, it's okay. I thought you meant you saw him this morning." Haddie imagined him camped outside her house.

"No. I've been watching. Let me go get Jisoo, she'll love playing with everyone. Bye."

Eating their food is more like it. Haddie yawned. "Bye." She could finally focus on the screen: 6:12.

She hadn't had enough sleep. Frowning at herself for letting her friend down, she pocketed the phone and opened the bathroom door. It was a small, white-tiled room with a sink and toilet, and it smelled of flowery disinfectant. Her body ached from the stiff chairs. She'd have done better in the RAV4, but she hadn't planned on sleeping. Dad had been on her mind. What was she going to do about him? Taking a deep breath, she turned on the faucet and pushed him to the back of her mind.

She was still a mess when she came back out to the waiting room, but she'd at least washed her face. The storm outside still poured off the roof, and a coffee would mean a drive through it. Did she dare poke her head in the back and ask about Rock? Surely, he'd awakened by now.

Tentatively, she tapped on the door to the back. No one

answered. She couldn't just pound on it; Rock rested back there. *I could call.* She pulled out her phone and saw Liz in the call list. They needed to talk anyway. Liz would be up. Haddie dialed the number.

"Hey," Liz answered immediately. "I didn't think you'd be up yet." Music in the background stopped. "How'd you sleep?"

Haddie grimaced. "Well, you were right. I should have stayed with you last night."

"Haddie, what happened?"

"Someone broke into my apartment when I was sleeping. All I know is that they shot Rock." Haddie spoke quickly, ignoring the sense of shame and getting it all out before Liz could interrupt. "He's okay. I'm at the vet's now."

"What? Where? I'll call in to work and get the day off. I'm almost dressed, give me fifteen." No recrimination in her voice, Liz was prepared to drop everything.

Haddie shook her head. She couldn't drag her friend into her mess or have her skip work to deal with her. She didn't know when Rock would be released. "No, no. I've got things I need to do this morning. I'll be over when you get off work. I'll have to get Rock over there at some point." How, with one good arm, was she going to move him? "I might need your help with that."

"They're releasing him? That's good."

"I haven't talked with them about that. I'm here, waiting." She didn't want Liz to miss work. "I've got errands."

"I can help. What do you need to do?"

Haddie took in a breath. Usually, she'd be at the law firm Friday mornings. "I've got an interview with a potential witness."

"Who?" Liz sounded skeptical. "I thought you said

Andrea wanted you to rest for a few days. Gave you time off."

Haddie paced across the waiting room. She didn't want to lie to Liz, but she didn't want her taking the day off work either. "I'm thinking about tracking down Harold Holmes; he has an office by the victim. I'd imagine he might have some insight on Mark's business dealings, maybe people who visited the office regularly."

It actually made sense. Mark's secretary, Jasmine, might not have realized that a frequent visitor could be important. Haddie had never thought to ask. She still had the woman's number.

"Haddie, shouldn't you be resting?"

"I slept here, at the clinic." Haddie twisted her back, wincing as the movement tugged on her bad arm. "I've got to find out what the plan is with Rock and grab a bag of stuff from the apartment, if we're doing a sleepover."

Liz laughed. "Okay. But drop by my work when you need a key to get in."

There was no reason Haddie couldn't take a nap at her apartment in broad daylight. She'd be out before dark. "What time do you get off?"

"5:30."

"I'll probably just see you then."

"Okay," Liz said. "Stay safe."

Haddie strode to the door at the back of the clinic and tapped on it again. Still no answer. The employee probably had an office deeper within. She scrolled back to find the call she made to the vet on the drive over. She'd called Dad just before that. Why hadn't he called back? What had he planned to do when he dropped by her apartment in the middle of the night? Sam just said she intercepted him. He likely would have slept outside and guarded the apartment.

A little late. Her cheeks flushed warm. He cared about her, always had, even if he was delusional. If she'd listened to Liz, she'd still be sleeping, and Rock would be fine. This was her fault, no one else's.

Voices sounded in the hall beyond the door, and Haddie stepped away. The doctor, or the next shift? The door opened.

A middle-aged woman with a sly smile and light brown skin opened the door. "Are you Rock's mom? He's up if you want to come say good morning."

PART 5

I can only hope to persuade you to join me in this endeavor, a revolution against the afflictions of this present society.

CHAPTER 34

HADDIE FOLLOWED the woman down the hall. A thick miasma of antiseptic and medicinal scents filled the air.

"I'm Rona," the woman said. She had a round figure under her white coat. "I'll be watching over Rock today. He's in good hands."

Haddie smiled. "Thank you."

Rona led them into a room with two cages lined in metal; they'd put Rock in the one to the left with blankets. He had a cone over his head, and his chest had blue wraps over white bandages. Seeing her, he lifted his head but didn't try to rise. He seemed so weak.

"Oh, Baby." Haddie's chest hurt just seeing him.

Rona opened the latch, letting Haddie kneel at the edge. "He's a tough boy. I checked his vitals before I let you in. He's doing well, all things considered."

Haddie slipped her hand inside the cone and caressed Rock's jaw. He didn't exactly whimper, but he cooed as she rubbed his face. His tongue licked out as she scratched through short black fur. Big, wet eyes studied her, almost regretful, though she owed the apology. He would have been safe at Liz's. Silent tears trickled down her cheeks.

"When will he be able to go home?"

Rona chuckled. "Not for a while. Dr. Stevens will check on him today and give us a better time frame. I'd bet he'll have an answer to that midday. We're just going to let Rock rest."

Haddie got a few more minutes with Rock before Rona kicked her back to the waiting room. "He needs to rest. He can't when his mom is here. We'll call you, I promise."

Haddie stepped back into the waiting room, smelling coffee.

Another employee, a young woman with tight black braids, had arrived and sat behind the counter printing documents. She sipped from an oversized mug and then smiled. "Good morning. You must be Ms. Dawson. Can I get you to sign some papers?"

Haddie's hand shook slightly as she signed documents and eyed the coffee, searching the area behind for the coffee maker. She had time to find a coffee shop, or even head home. Yesterday jumbled in the back of her head and she needed to focus. Rock and Liz wouldn't happen for hours. Without work, she felt lost. Her paper still needed to be finished, or at least started.

The rain followed her in a steady pour to her car and pounded on the windshield as she started her RAV4. There was a coffee shop down Hilyard. She put her car in reverse, then turned toward the coffee shop. If they weren't open yet, they would be soon. It was nearly 7:00, and the commuters would need their coffee.

Mostly residential houses south of downtown didn't give her much traffic to contend with. Grace would be at the office soon. Would she know about the mugging? Andrea had likely sent an email.

Haddie didn't want to go home. Sam would come check on her, and there would be Rock's blood to clean up. The apartment felt unsafe. The memory of Rock being shot bothered her most of all from the past twenty-four hours. She could deal with being attacked and Dad's delusions . . . somewhat.

Andrea's uncomfortable, forced time off made it seem like Haddie had made some mistake. Had she? The attack hadn't been her fault. What would Andrea think about Rock getting shot at her apartment? She might not take Haddie back at all. A chill ran up Haddie's spine. *I've made a mess of this.*

Haddie pulled up to the front of the coffee shop, jumped over the stream in the gutter, and dashed in. Windows lined the front of the building, and wood paneled walls stretched around the inside; an older couple already sat at one of the tables to the left of the counter. A wondrous aroma of roasted coffee scented the air.

A young man in a green apron smiled from behind the counter. "Can I help you?"

"Large black coffee, please." She eyed one of the pastries, but her stomach still felt off.

She picked a table by the window and sipped the too hot coffee. Blowing on it, she watched the rain and the traffic as commuters headed to work. She couldn't spend the day at the coffee shop; she'd have to make a plan, but there wasn't much *to* plan. There was no work, and home didn't feel safe, so she might just end up back at the vet's waiting on Rock.

A man in a black raincoat dashed in and shook droplets onto the wood floor. She could go home and get changed. It wouldn't take long, and she could grab her satchel, dust off the laptop, and bring it to the vet to get started on her paper.

Her phone vibrated and she put down the coffee to squeeze her good hand into her damp jeans.

"Hey, Sam. What's up?"

"Um. I think they saw me." In the background, fabric shuffled. "There was a car like yours, but silver with tinted windows, and they pulled into your parking space. I thought they might mess with your motorcycle, but when they got out, one guy, the passenger, looked up here, and they left."

"Did you get their plate number?" Stunned, Haddie stared at the steam rising off the black pool of coffee. *They were not done yet.*

"No. Sorry. Should I call the police?"

"Yes. Yes." Haddie wouldn't be able to live with it if Sam were hurt. How had she not insisted that Sam hang up and call the police? "Call me back." She hung up, hopefully forcing Sam to act.

What were they doing at her apartment? Who was after her? They hadn't gone after anyone at the law firm, so it had to be her investigations that someone wanted to stop. Most of that had been done on the internet or through records the DA sent, except for the trip to Mark Colman's office and the ride to Portland. No, she'd seen the tinted SUV before the ride north with Dad. It had all started when she interviewed Jasmine at the mortgage company office. Jasmine's resume and phone number sat in her satchel at home. They had to be concerned that the secretary knew something — or someone — who associated with Mark Colman.

She took the last swig of coffee, then stood and nodded to the young man before hurrying out the door to her RAV4. Part of her wanted to go home and get Jasmine's number and change, but she planned on going to the mortgage company office first. She was close to the truth; otherwise, they wouldn't be after her. Her friends were in danger. They'd already shot Rock.

By the time she got to the mortgage company parking lot, it was after 8:00. For all the rain they had in Eugene, people still couldn't drive in it.

The red Porsche Cayman Harold Holmes drove sat alone, while a white Durango and a blue Taurus parked together at the back by the alley. Haddie pulled in beside the Porsche. If nothing else, she could see what Harold Holmes knew. She had hoped someone would be in the offices; even the tellers at the bank might know something. Digging had gotten her into trouble, so more digging seemed the only way out. Andrea might not appreciate it, but if Haddie came up with something tangible, it might clear everything up concerning Mel's case and the people hunting Haddie.

The stench of mold hit her as she scrambled through the door to get out of the rain. As she tested the door to the mortgage company, she thought of Detective Cooper and Dad. Locked. Taking a picture of the note with the son's number on it, she headed back to the door that Harold Holmes had exited.

Liz texted as Haddie reached up to knock.

"Detective Cooper filed a report on the mugging, including two suspects."

Haddie nodded to herself. "Thanks."

"Rock okay?"

"Yes." Haddie leaned on the wall, then grimaced at the smell and stood straight.

"Still at the vet? You should come get the key," Liz texted.

"At Mark Colman's office." Haddie felt ashamed lying to Liz, but she was trying to interview someone. It wouldn't be a total lie, and Liz had gone to work. "I'm trying to interview his neighbor, Harold Holmes."

"Maybe come by after and pick up the key? You should be resting."

Haddie wasn't about to bring up Sam. Liz was already overprotective. "I'll see you tonight."

"Okay. Be careful."

Haddie sighed. Detective Cooper did seem to be investigating; at least he'd put the suspects on the report. She would like to see the report. Did he actually try and find them? He'd gone to their residence evidently. After Dad.

She stopped at the door marked "Kupatal Imports." She knocked before opening it.

Dressed in a sharp, black business suit, Harold Holmes sat at his desk with his cell phone to his ear. He smiled and motioned to the padded chairs. Considering the condition of Mark Colman's office, the decor was luxurious. The room stretched the full depth of that side of the building, leaving a walk from the door to where he sat. The desk looked like an antique, perhaps mahogany. A matching dark bookshelf stretched across the back wall; scrollwork marked the edges and top. Amid bronze statues and books, an old clock painted with hummingbirds sat in the center with the correct time. A dark blue curtain hung over the window, leaving the long fluorescent light in the ceiling to brighten the room.

His blue eyes watched her. "At 12:12 this afternoon. Delta. Got it." His handsome face was freshly shaved, but he still looked sickly with dark splotches. The rash had diminished, but she could still see them as she sat, suddenly conscious of the garish yellow and red clothes she wore.

"Family." He gestured with his phone. "They can be quite troublesome." Texting, he focused on his phone. "Ms. Dawson, if I remember correctly."

"Yes. I'm sorry to just drop in." *Looking like a clown who hasn't slept.* "I was wondering if I could follow up with you about Mark Colman."

He glanced up from his text, finishing, and put the phone face down on his desk. "I'm pleased you're here. What questions do you have?"

Haddie sighed. She'd barged in here, looking like a mess, and still he was polite. "I've been looking into Mark Colman's business dealings. Have you ever noticed if there was anyone he dealt with regularly? Maybe a business partner?"

His phone dinged and he pulled it up, smiling at a text. "Now that you mention it, yes. I believe he did have a business partner."

Finally, a lead that might get her somewhere. "Do you know who it was?"

The door from outside opened, and someone shook their coat as they entered the hall. Perhaps Mark Colman's son?

Harold Holmes smiled. "Of course. Me."

The door behind Haddie opened, and the man from the coffee shop, in his long black coat, stepped in. He pulled his hand from his pocket and pointed a small gun, possibly a 9mm, at her. She focused on the round muzzle.

Harold Holmes laughed. "I do want to thank you for stopping in, Ms. Dawson. We've gone through a lot of effort trying to pin you down. Your phone, please?"

CHAPTER 35

Thomas rode his Shovelhead south on Bailey Hill Road. He'd followed Haddie to the coffee shop but left her there when he got the call from Trig. The rain had settled in, leaving a gray blanket of clouds for a sky. He could smell the earth soaking up the water. Tires hissed through puddles from the traffic around him. He wouldn't have chosen rush hour to make the trip, but the chance to find Louis or Tommy made the ride unavoidable. Rain on a mountain highway he had no problem with, but city people tended to take too many chances, trying to hurry in conditions they weren't skilled to handle.

Haddie's situation had gotten worse, and her stubbornness would lead to her death. He'd dealt with people like her stalkers before. They'd hunt her down and kill her, just for their own convenience. Often he'd been surprised how little was at risk before they'd resort to violence. A smarter organization avoided such demonstrations. He'd dealt with a small-minded petty gang or leader who reacted, rather than acted. Sloppy. *I'm not taking any chances.*

Cars slowed at the larger puddles building up. He

watched the addresses on the west side of the road. The houses there fit the type he might suspect: worn and forgotten, while new developments ate up natural lands. Trig had warned that his information came from a random player without any verification. Not the best lead. However, Thomas would have to take what he could get.

In the rain, he nearly missed the address despite black letters on a faded white house. The lawn had grown tall with yellow and white flowering weeds. The beat-up car in the driveway could have been the one that nearly sideswiped Haddie as she was leaving the mortgage company office. He should have been suspicious then.

He pulled onto the sidewalk to the left of the driveway. As he killed the Shovelhead and removed his helmet, he could see the top of a white trailer behind a weather-worn fence on his side of the house. The roof looked ragged. Half the front of the building was a two-car garage, which had the only paint that wasn't peeling. The architecture said it wasn't that old, something out of the seventies or eighties, but no one had ever taken care of it. At this early hour, any inhabitants could be asleep. No one in the neighborhood seemed to be out in the weather.

The porch had no lights on, and the windows remained dark. He walked north along the sidewalk and headed to the opposite side, where there was no fence except the neighbor's. Pale blue boards covered a window beside an air conditioner hanging out of the wall. He could try entering through the back. Wet weeds clung against his jeans, reaching his hips in some parts of the backyard. A peeling, dark blue back door tilted slightly in its frame, and a screen door lay on the ground nearby, filtering smaller grasses. The trailer had been rusted through years ago. Another board covered the window on this side; someone didn't like nosy neighbors.

The house looked abandoned. Thomas strode to the back door and tested the knob. Locked. Hinges on the outside meant that the door swung outward. He pulled out his knife and worked it quietly against the doorjamb.

Car doors opened somewhere out front. He paused, listening above the rain. Had he just missed the occupants? Were they leaving?

The distinctive sound of two AR-15s being loaded came from the front. Thomas sprinted toward the trailer. Bullets tore into the house, shattering the glass in the front and splintering the wall where he'd just been standing. It only took a couple seconds before they finished and he rolled behind the trailer, using the rusted rims for cover. He only heard one magazine replaced, but again the house spit splinters of wood, and a back window collapsed. Had they set him up? In this rain, it would be easy to follow him. However, Trig wasn't beyond a bribe. Maybe the player had worked Trig.

They fired a third set of magazines into the house before he heard two car doors slam shut. Mud slipped under his boots as he ran for the far side of the house. The car squealed its brakes on the road in the rain and a horn sounded, long and angry. By the time he rounded the front corner of the building, traffic again moved evenly through the dull gray haze.

He reached his bike and a neighbor tugged at the edge of a curtain, obviously spotting him. The detective would likely hear about this. *Not my worry at the moment.* He'd left Haddie alone and needed to find her. Even the neighborhood around the veterinarian clinic wouldn't be safe. He'd have to get back.

CHAPTER 36

HADDIE HAD BEEN OBSESSED with the case. Terry was right. She hadn't been able to ignore the oddities like Mark Colman's fake business in Portland, the strange nature of the fires, or those marks on Harold Holmes. Her heart pounded in her chest.

Harold Holmes was British. The Irish mob had died, burnt in England. Now people in Eugene were dying in the same way.

Worst of all, her dad might not be delusional, and that scared her almost as much as her current predicament. Her stitches had opened when Harold Holmes forced her to lie on the floor of his office at gunpoint while he zip-tied her wrists. She could feel a warmth to the already-wet bandages. At least she knew who Mark Colman's secret partner had been. A faint victory, considering the circumstances.

The thug in the raincoat, a man in his thirties with well-styled dark brown hair and a neatly trimmed beard, had evidently been tailing her from the veterinarian clinic.

Escorted out of the building at gunpoint with wrists

bound, Haddie met his partner waiting at the Explorer parked by the exit. A man with graying hair, he didn't look older than forty, with a strong, clean-shaven jaw, a long face, and tight, intense eyes. He wore a similar black coat over a dark gray suit with a blue striped tie. He looked unhappy with the rain as he opened the back door. They used zip tie restraints on her ankles, which cut against the cuff of her short boots. Then they'd hog-tied her and left her face down on the seat so that her thighs cramped. The car seat smelled almost new.

The gray-haired man spoke on the phone, arranging to have Haddie's RAV4 moved. "He says to move it north. A rest stop will be fine."

No one had seen them kidnap her, not in the deluge. She'd disappear. Her car would be found miles away, and no one would think to look at Harold Holmes. She swallowed. *They're going to kill me.* In her whole life, she had never truly been in fear of dying, until she lay with her face pressed against the cool, smooth seat.

She swayed as they accelerated. An onramp, possibly I-5. How far away were they taking her? What did Harold Holmes plan for her? Kill her and drop her body in the mountains?

Her muscles ached from tensing on the seat. She barely avoided being tossed onto the floor each time the bearded thug braked. She could see the side of the gray-haired man's face. He texted on his phone and glanced back at her with little concern. If she hadn't been bound wrist to ankle, she could have kicked the driver, but she could only glare, trying to keep from oozing spittle onto the leather seat.

She couldn't see much through the front window except flashes of highway signs, dim in the rain through heavily tinted windows. That and the trucks they passed gave her a hint that they were on the interstate. The weather made it impossible to determine which direction they traveled, but she imagined they headed south. Otherwise, why hide her car in the north?

There were plenty of isolated ridges and ravines to hide a body in the south. She should have fought at the office. They would have shot her, but they might have run off at the noise and left her in the city.

The gray-haired man answered a call and shifted to glance into the rearview mirror outside his window. "No trouble. She's just lying here. Nice and quiet."

He'd looked behind them. Likely Harold Holmes followed. She hadn't been able to see what he did once they'd told her to climb in the back seat and lie face down. They'd finished tying her and closed the door, leaving nothing but muted voices outside.

Did Harold Holmes plan on doing the job himself? Or just want to watch? Maybe he lived out here. She should have had Terry look up his address. What would it matter? No one knew where she was headed. She flushed, thinking of Dad. She wanted him to come to the rescue. She'd grown to hate it as a teen, and even in college she'd trained him to not stalk her or her lovers. Considering the marks on Harold Holmes and the way those people had died, Dad might just be a match for two armed thugs. Maybe she'd become delusional as well. Perhaps it ran in the family.

They slowed about fifteen minutes after getting on the highway, which could put them near Cottage Grove. *Maybe they're dumping me in one of the lakes.* Her heart started racing again. The bearded man slowed along the ramp and turned left, where they kept going without a sharp turn. She couldn't remember the name of the main road, but it went out to Dorena Lake. Anywhere out east would be good to dump a body.

She nearly rolled onto the floor, her muscles cramping, as they came to a stoplight. With the fingers of her right hand, she felt at the zip tie connecting the restraints. It stretched taut. What would it take to get it to break? Then she could roll over and kick the driver, make him crash while she ditched onto the floor and they took all the impact.

They turned and her face pressed against leather, spittle pushing out the corner of her lips. She wasn't going anywhere at the moment. Maybe when they cut the ties so she could walk. Or maybe she was supposed to drown this way?

No, they were going up, into the hills. Tall pines lined a small, paved road as they drove up a noticeable incline. The forest opened, and she could make out the curved roof of a building with large glass windows instead of walls, like a modernized cupola. The Explorer lurched to a stop, toppling her onto the floor.

CHAPTER 37

THOMAS PULLED up outside the vet's clinic, idling his Shovelhead. Still no sign of the RAV4. He turned off his bike and stepped off, ignoring his burning joints. As he unbuckled his helmet, he noticed his gloves smelled of fresh gas that even the insistent rain hadn't washed off. Leaving his helmet atop the bike seat, he kept his gaiter up and glasses on as he stepped inside.

A young woman with tight black braids sat behind the counter, looking up and smiling as he walked in. An older woman sat with a paperback in the middle of the row of blue chairs.

"How can I help?" the receptionist asked.

"I was here earlier with my daughter, Haddie Dawson. We're waiting on the status of her dog, Rock. Has Haddie been in?"

"Your daughter." The woman frowned. "No. I haven't seen Ms. Dawson since early this morning. She probably won't be back for a couple of hours. Why don't you call her?"

Trying to avoid that. Thomas nodded. "I will."

He strolled to the opposite end of the waiting room, near the bathroom, and texted Haddie. "How's Rock?" She had to expect he'd have some concern.

He'd done a loop by the vet earlier, then the coffee shop, and finally checked to be sure she wasn't back at her apartment. Haddie wouldn't stray far from Rock, so he'd come back here. Eventually, she would show up.

He ached from using his power last night, and standing didn't make it much better. The blue chairs were designed to be uncomfortable. *I don't like not knowing where she is.*

Pulling up her contact, he punched the icon to dial her. It went to voicemail. Likely, she just wanted some space.

"Just want to make sure you're okay. Text me." He grimaced. She hated messages like that.

Telling her so much about him in such a short time, she might never speak to him again. She rightfully thought him insane. Given the same scenario, he would. It still hurt. He'd have to move on from the garage and his present identity at some point, no matter what. Even Biff would begin to question his age. He just hoped that he could stay connected to her. It wasn't the first time he'd raised his children alone, but she'd been different somehow.

The past few decades had been different. His prior self had been born and lived on the east coast of the United States. He mused about the idea of warning himself not to go to Iceland. What would that cause — not going back in time? He'd ridden with himself three times already. Once in Daytona, and twice at Sturgis. A surreal experience. His former self had never seen his face. But they'd been doppelgangers, a hand's width apart. He could unravel all his centuries just by having one conversation — one warning. A theory, at most. But he wouldn't do it, not risking Haddie. She would never have been born.

He glanced down at the phone still in his hand. 9:40 a.m. She hadn't answered. He scrolled his contacts and dialed again.

"Hey, Boss. What's up?" Biff answered in what sounded like a restaurant with gabbing and clinking plates in the background.

"You got a number for Haddie's friend Liz? She works at the police department and teaches at the college? Drives that beater that Benny keeps fixing?" Thomas had kept Biff out of Haddie's business as much as he could. He was a good man, but didn't know when to keep his mouth shut sometimes. She'd gotten him involved last night, though, to tow her bike.

"Blue-eyes? Nah, she's got better sense than to give her number to me." Someone at Biff's table laughed. "Let me ask Benny. He might have it." The phone muffled. Then Biff's voice became audible, though distant. "Hold on, hold on." Someone, likely Benny, called out a string of numbers. Biff repeated them absently, as if to himself and not to Thomas. Still, he caught most of them.

"Biff?" Thomas frowned and started to complain, before he received a text from Biff, a phone number.

"Ya get it?" Biff's voice returned to the phone, clear.

"Yeah. Thanks, Biff."

"What's up, Boss?" The outside sounds shifted, as if Biff turned and cupped the phone. "How's Haddie?"

He hadn't told Biff about Rock yet. "Okay. Listen, I got an errand this morning. I'll be late."

"Sure." From his tone, Biff had questions, but he let them drop. "See ya when I do."

"Thanks." Thomas hung up and opened the text. Taking a deep breath, he dialed the number.

The woman's voice sounded polite with a lightly curious tone. "Hello?"

"Hi, Liz? This is Thomas Dawson, Haddie's father –"

"Is Haddie okay?" the woman interrupted, sounding terrified. He'd met the woman before, though he couldn't remember where. Her voice sounded familiar.

His pulse rose and he ran his hand over his hair. "I'm sure. I'm just trying to get her on the phone —"

"She's not answering. Detective Cooper just called me. No one can get a hold of her."

Why was Detective Cooper looking for Haddie? A follow up to last night? "When was the last time you talked with her?" Thomas kept his tone flat, not wanting to excite the woman any more than she already was.

"Let me check . . . 8:16 this morning. We texted." Liz replied, with barely a pause between her words. "She was at the mortgage company doing an interview with Harold Holmes. I didn't know, but Sam had called the police, and Detective Cooper is looking to talk to Haddie. Have you seen her?"

Thomas stood, glancing at the older woman reading her book, but she never noticed him. Sam — Haddie's dogwalker. Why had she called the police? Who was Harold Holmes? "Not since before 8:00. Why did Sam call the police?"

"Suspicious activity outside Haddie's apartment. Her door is secure. A patrol went out there. I'm worried, though. Usually she'll text me back. This interview couldn't have taken — what — two hours?" Haddie's friend had built herself into a near frenzy by the end.

His cell read 9:43. He'd wasted over an hour following a

lead that had been a trap. Or at least, useless. Then, while Haddie had gone missing, he'd driven around looking for her. All this time, where had she gone? He took in a deep breath, trying to calm a rising dread.

"Do you have any contact information for this Harold Holmes?"

CHAPTER 38

HADDIE SAT ON A MODERN, bright red chair with thin metal legs; beside her sat a zebra-striped couch, luxurious and empty. Restraints still bound her ankles and wrists. Her bandaged arm felt wet behind her back. Her jaw ached, and her lip bled from the pistol-whip that the gray-haired man had delivered. When they released the zip tie binding her wrists to her legs, she had to make a try for it. She didn't plan on dying without a struggle.

Harold Holmes stood at the top of the stairs leading from the glassed-in foyer. He spoke to someone on his cell, his expression perturbed. "I understand you are paying me a visit, Brother?"

From the foyer, they'd carried her down a set of stairs to a lower floor; she considered herself a healthy weight, but the gray-haired man had no issues flopping her over his shoulder. He'd smelled like alcohol and curry.

A luxurious mansion in her standards, the ceiling rose above two stories to a rounded peak above the foyer. Its white walls and beams were sparse compared to the number of windows. The tips of some trees rose around the mountain top, but few enough that she knew the building sat at the crest. The view would have been amazing if rain didn't cloud the horizon in gray and she weren't about to die. She could taste salty blood.

Harold Holmes took a single step down. "It is not your business, and it is handled." He glanced over, noticed Haddie was listening, and winked at her.

The bearded man stood attentively by a black wood stove at the bottom of the stairs. He'd taken off his coat and wore a light gray suit. Arms crossed, he watched Haddie without emotion.

She had no doubt he would kill her at a moment's notice, though not likely in this nice sitting area where she would make a mess. The gray-haired man stood behind and to her left, between white columns that reached the ceiling. Holmes had given her phone to the gray-haired man when they were at the cars. She could only see him if she turned. He scrolled through it; she'd given up the passcode, kneeling in the rain with a gun to her forehead.

Holmes took another step, bringing himself midway down the stairs. "Very well, Dmitry. I'll make sure someone meets you at the airport." He smirked at whatever response came over his phone. "It's no bother, Brother."

He hung up, paused on the stairs with his cell phone raised, and said, "Families, right?" Taking another step, he stopped and smiled. "Not something you need to worry about anymore." Holmes finished walking down the stairs and turned to the bearded man. "Did Casey and Todd get confirmation on the body?"

"Not yet. They had to evacuate – too many witnesses." The bearded man swallowed. "They're monitoring."

"Twits. I don't have time for them to monitor." Holmes flipped his hand in the air. "Make sure they don't miss my brother's flight. I don't want that knob to make it here. We're done."

When she'd been carried in, there had been a third guard with dirty blond hair acting as a doorman. She hadn't seen him since they'd hauled her downstairs and dropped her into the red chair. Whatever Harold Holmes had planned for her, it wasn't a quick death. They would have done that in the driveway. What had he meant by not worrying about family? That she would be dead soon? Or was this some threat against Dad? Which of these men shot Rock? She flushed warm at the thought, not that she was in any position to do anything about it.

Holmes walked toward her. The bearded man accompanied him, drawing his gun — a bodyguard.

Stopping three steps from her, Holmes gestured. "Hadhira Dawson. This whole situation has gone to the dogs because of you. Now I've got to clean up all the bits and pieces. I lost two somewhat useful men because of you. Not good for business."

He paused, as if waiting for a response, and shrugged. "Sorry about the bracelets. Tommy had said you can be a little rough." Harold Holmes turned toward the gray-haired man. "What do we have?"

"There's a lot here. The attorney and the detective. Her father —" The gray-haired man scrolled quickly.

Holmes turned and winked. "Not a problem anymore."

Haddie's chest dropped. Her pulse, racing just a second earlier, now seemed to skip beats. They couldn't have killed Dad. However, on his bike, streets flooded, he'd be an easy target. She'd been horrible to him last night. *I should have handled it better.* How could she believe he was anything but insane? Rain pounded on the windows behind her.

"No." The gray-haired man drawled, delaying as he

scrolled. He shook his head. "Nope. I've got calls and texts from him after Casey and Todd hit that house."

Harold Holmes spun on the bearded man. "You said they saw him enter."

Haddie couldn't help but smile. *Now just disappear, Dad. You said if it weren't for me, you would.* She wasn't going to make it out of this, but it might save her dad. Maybe Holmes would let it go, once she was dead.

When the bearded man responded with a slight tilt of his head, Holmes turned back to her. "Don't be too happy. We'll get around to him. Who else have you told your concerns regarding Mark Colman's mystery partner? You visited Portland with your Dad. Who else knows?"

It might not end with her death. Dad, and maybe her friends, were still at risk. She should have taken a bullet to the head in the driveway, before they got into her phone. *I'm not that brave.* Haddie looked down. Harold Holmes wore loafers with what seemed an inordinate number of tassels. How had she not noticed these before?

The gray-haired man cleared his throat. "I've got four other contacts here with plenty of activity. A Liz, Sam, Jerk, and Terry. I'll dig through their text threads."

Haddie chilled. Rock had been shot, they'd tried to kill Dad, and now her friends — and Biff. Harold Holmes might consider them all a threat.

"What about them, Hadhira?" He paced to the side, keeping a distance from her and leaving room for the bearded man to shoot her if necessary.

She couldn't let them hurt her friends. Her mind scrambled, trying to remember what texts she'd sent to Liz and Terry. Haddie raised her head. "I can't discuss my case with anyone outside of work. That includes my dog walker, teachers, and classmates. Detective Cooper has everything I know."

If the detective worked for Holmes, then that might satisfy him. If the detective didn't, then perhaps she had just put Detective Cooper in danger, but he was at least equipped to handle it. Had she just put Andrea on their list? Dread rose in her throat.

"And your boss," Harold Holmes added.

Haddie deflated. Andrea would never expect these killers. "She didn't want me pursuing this angle. Her focus is on the alibi." She hoped the truth would sound genuine. "She put me on leave because of all the trouble."

Harold Holmes frowned, almost pouting. "Sorry, don't believe you."

She could charge at him now, make the bodyguard shoot her. Would that end this — despite what he said? She'd dragged family and friends into this, and it still wouldn't free Mel. It wouldn't end with Haddie's life. She shifted her bound legs under the chair and flexed on her toes.

"This is going to get painful, but I need to know who you talked to and what you told them. I've already had to cut some loose ends, and that's hurting my business. I can't just indiscriminately destroy everything I've built." Holmes smiled. "I'll know when you're finally telling me the truth. People eventually get there with enough pain. It'll save me time, and resources, in the end."

"Boss." A voice came from the foyer above. "We've got company." The dirty blond guard had a nervous tone.

Holmes rolled his eyes, gritting his teeth. "What now?"

Pushing on her toes, Haddie launched from her seat, sending it toppling across the wood floor. She gained height but not much distance. Landing a good pace away from

Harold Holmes, she skidded to her knees, off-balance. Metal slammed into her temple, likely from the bearded man's gun, and she spun from the impact, falling to her side.

Holmes looked down at her. "Drop her in the hole."

Stars blazed in her vision. She blinked, trying to clear them. He was walking toward the stairs. She felt a rough yank on her arm and cried in pain as they pulled her up, nearly dislocating her shoulder.

"It looks like the detective," the voice of the dirty blond guard called from above, as the other two hauled Haddie to her feet.

CHAPTER 39

AGAIN, the gray-haired man threw Haddie over his shoulder. Surprisingly, they carried her up the stairs, behind Harold Holmes, and into the foyer. *Toward Detective Cooper?* Blood rushed to her head, and the stars brightened her vision. As they turned at the top, she could see only the gray rain outside. Over the pounding in her ears, she barely heard it beating on the windows.

The bearded man led the way down another set of stairs. She wanted to struggle, to cause a commotion in case Detective Cooper had actually come looking for her, but she could barely orient herself over a pounding skull. She'd tried. Now, unless by some miracle the detective freed her, she'd have to endure whatever torture Holmes had planned and then lie enough that her friends might survive.

Her head spun when the back of it tapped a beam or corner as the gray-haired man navigated the house. She caught bright blues either from a couch or wall, then they turned again into a hall or another room. Lightning flashed through wide windows, and she blinked before they dropped her to a black mat beside an exercise bike. They wouldn't bother hiding her if Detective Cooper worked for Harold Holmes. She might have been wrong about him. Was he here looking for her, or, had he found the connecting evidence from Mark Colman to Harold Holmes? Was there some bit that she'd missed?

The room turned at a slant. No. The exercise bike lifted at an angle, tilting back until the seat touched the floor. Rough hands lifted her head, and as she gasped from the pain, a strip of white flashed in front of her eyes before a gag cut into the sides of her mouth. Detective Cooper certainly didn't work for them.

Under the floor where the bike had been, a dark hole cut a rectangle. With her head still spinning, she had barely noticed it. The hatch had hinges at the back by her feet; the equipment attached to it. This, evidently, was the "hole" Harold Holmes referred to, and where she would be stowed.

Gag tied, Haddie felt a foot on her hip. With a shove they rolled her in.

She screamed despite the cloth between her teeth. Her heart stopped as the freefall began. Haddie saw the set of wooden stairs descending by her face. Her chin only dropped a foot before it jolted down onto solid wood. Her chest hit a lower step as her body angled, but by the time she landed on her left forearm she rolled toward the edge of the stairs. Her hips hit steps and rail with a crash. When her knees and boots hit, she began sliding on her side.

As she jolted against steps, she could make out an expansive basement and a dim wall of carved stone. The only light came from the opening above, but the room seemed empty, reaching out to dark curves where the floor met chiseled walls. Musty, it had a tinge of ash to the scent, as if there were a fireplace nearby.

The hatch above slammed shut, and the room turned pitch-black. She slowed to a stop on the stairs, sure that her feet were only a couple steps from the floor. It was a hole. She placed her hand into thick pungent dust that covered the floor.

Her side burned from scraping, and her head pounded so hard she dared not move it. The stars of light still danced across the blackness. Her arm felt as though every stitch had been pulled free. What if she just bled to death? Harold Holmes would still go after her friends. Her only chance was to endure the torture and lie to Holmes. Liz, Terry, and Sam's lives depended on it.

Over the pounding in her ears, she heard an odd, rhythmic whining. Someone was exercising on the bike above.

CHAPTER 40

Haddie lay on the stone floor beside the stairs at least an hour before the hatch above opened. She sucked in a breath and her heart raced. Dust covered the floor in drifts. The room stunk of dust and decay.

"Ah," Harold Holmes said. "It seems we can finally get to business."

He let one of the other shadowed figures lead the way, a handful of zip ties dangling from their fingers. A silhouetted arm raised, and lights flared on. Haddie blinked, seeing the bearded man above her and long fluorescents in the ceiling. The room stretched in a large circle into which the stairs descended. Black metal columns supported beams of the floor above. She lay in what seemed the center. A heavy black chair sat against the curve; bolts skirted the legs. Dust or dirt piled below it. It smelled of ash.

The bearded man yanked her up and began shuffling her across the floor toward the blackened chair. Bolts held the legs bracketed to the stone floor. He pushed her into the seat. Using her hair, he pulled her head back and moved behind her. He wrapped a zip tie around her neck and tightened it so that Haddie sat straight-backed. She could breathe, but there was no moving without choking.

Harold Holmes walked to her left side where a metal stand waited, and he took off his coat carefully. "Detective Cooper seemed quite interested in me. Even after I assured him that you left the office soon after our short interview. He seems to share some of your habits. Persistence being one. I may end up having to set up a crime scene for him to attend."

Haddie felt metal at her wrists and flinched, but the bearded man only cut one cuff of her restraint and pulled up a scraped, cramped, and nearly limp right arm. Efficiently, he wrapped a zip tie over her elbow and secured it to the chair.

Holmes rolled up the sleeves of a pale blue shirt. "You seem healthy overall. I'm sure you'll do as well as can be expected. Sarah Colman did not prove up to lasting long enough for me to be confident in her answers." He turned toward her and shrugged. "Unfortunately, I lost my patience with Mark Colman before we even got started."

The bearded man had her neck, elbows, and arms strapped to the chair. Holmes motioned toward her legs. She wouldn't be able to move except to swing her legs out straight. Kicking shins would not get her out of this. Swung to one side, her ankles were bound to the right leg of the chair. She imagined she would not survive this chair. Her only hope would be to die without giving up her friends. For a moment, she wanted to beg, promise something that would make Holmes change his mind, but his eyes lit with determination and eagerness.

Some of Haddie's texts surely incriminated Terry or Liz. What would Holmes deem worthy of death? She hadn't been close to knowing it was him, and he'd tried to kill her – was *going* to kill her. What chance did her friends have? Dad might survive. If he had lived as long as he said he had, and truly had some strange ability, then he might live. If he gave up on her. But he couldn't give up any easier than she could.

Harold Holmes nodded to the bearded man. "Her gag, too. Then, we are both going to need some water. I think she'll make a few rounds."

A knife pressed against her cheek, and the cloth tugged, then loosened. Dropping his remaining ties beside her chair, the bearded man walked for the stairs. Gray ash coated his black dress shoes.

"Let's get this started, shall we?" Holmes rubbed his hands together. "I've got family coming in today, not that I expect him to make it."

Haddie imagined the blackened corpses and sucked in a breath. *I don't want to die.*

He made a soft hum, almost melodic, with high notes that seemed to spring from the air around her. An aura of light surrounded him, leaking from his skin and dulled by his clothes. He held his palms up for her to see, and they lit with bright fire that curled out into short flames which flickered and licked into the air as if hungry to burn. She choked and instinctively withdrew, but the most she could manage was to turn her head. He grimaced as if it pained him, but his flesh didn't burn. She could feel the heat. How was he doing this?

He placed his palms on the back of her wrists and hummed.

White light seeped from under his hands, illuminating Harold Holmes and the room. Skin crackling and scorching, Haddie screamed. The pain burned up her arms, though the burning fire had doused into the flesh around her wrists.

The smell of her own burnt skin had her retch into her lap. She gagged and sobbed. A blackened circle extended a couple inches from the beginning of her forearms toward her knuckles, barely the width of her own hand. The pain felt so much larger. The edges of her wet bandage smoldered, and embers died out.

He breathed deeply in and out and smiled. "Realize," Harold Holmes said, "the different parts of your body that I'm going to burn. Each one will have a unique sensitivity. I'm going to have to work my way through at least a couple of them before we even start with the questions. Just so that I know you're taking us seriously."

The pain dulled her mind. She couldn't survive another. How had he done that? *Is this what Dad does?*

Without fire, Holmes reached down and touched her pants at her thighs, as if to gauge his next target. Reeling, she barely realized what he was doing, jumping only as he made contact. He winced at his own movements; somehow this hurt him as well. Dad had said something similar, but she couldn't remember his exact words through the pain.

He positioned his hands just above her knees, and smiled. "There is so much flesh on the thighs, I find they work well."

Haddie sobbed in quick inhales. She could see the burns on her wrists. The pain extended up her entire arms. She couldn't imagine what her thighs would feel like. Anything to stop it. Even if she lived, she couldn't imagine it would ever heal. Her legs shook at his touch. Sam had to survive; she'd take care of Rock. Tears rolled down Haddie's cheeks. She couldn't betray Terry or Liz, but he'd barely started, and she was desperate.

Holmes began to hum.

Harold steeled himself for the pain. The intern sobbed; she'd tell him everything after this.

The tone had just begun to ring when Burke called down from above, "Hey Boss, we got company. Big guy on a bike."

Harold pulled his hands back with a grimace. He took a deep breath and frowned at her.

She'd caused so much trouble. *Look at her now*. Hadhira trembled in the chair, tears running down her face. Helpless. Afraid. She should be. He would clear up this cock-up now. Anyone she'd been talking to would need to be handled. Rather convenient that her father, the git who'd been at the storage facility, showed up here to rescue his daughter.

"Aw, Father, how sweet." He yelled over his shoulder, "Kill him!"

She reacted to that, blinking away tears to stare after Burke. Nothing she could do. Maybe yell out a bit. Even with the hatch open above, sound didn't travel well across the rest of the house. Might be fun, having her father know his daughter was being tortured, just before he died.

Harold smiled. *No theatrics.* He'd need to wait, make sure the father had been taken care of. Each use of his skill wore on him. Two or three usages and he could barely move. The ancients hadn't had that drawback. He'd had four visions from one battle, and never once had there been a hint of fatigue or difficulty. He would learn how someday.

Dmitry would be dead by now, or soon. The two men Harold had sent had been warned. *They know my power.* They'd been told to make it quick, right outside the airport. A shot through the spine while they drove. He wouldn't be expecting an ambush at that point. His brother didn't deserve this skill.

They'd both used it to get established, but only Harold had realized the power it truly had. The visions. They'd both experienced the same ones. Those first few had been too shocking, and he'd missed details, he was sure. He had recognized immediately that they spoke of a mastery of the skill, not the shoddy mess of his first use.

Dmitry had called them nightmares, but still he used his skill. It had built their enterprises. Harold had just seen a greater purpose to it. Knowledge.

"Why?" Hadhira asked.

He glanced over and smiled. The next session would be enjoyable. Experience told him that few could survive, at least enough to speak, more than two bouts. Their bodies shut down quickly from the burns. She'd have a couple hours of lucidity left after he burnt her thighs.

He glanced up at the gunfire. Perhaps that was the end of it. Pacing, he kicked through dust, more than he remembered being down here. A wet stain spread out in the middle, a few steps from the stairs. Did he have a leak?

Turning, he strolled toward her, leaned down, and placed his hands on her thighs. He hummed, just to watch her eyes widen.

No, not yet.

CHAPTER 42

THOMAS PULLED up in front of the modern estate atop the mountain. The rain thrummed in a dull, indistinct beat around him.

Rising two stories, wood and glass walls were topped with a white roof and rounded peak. A clean deck stretched to the right, with a neat dining table and counter-height chairs. He parked to the right of a Porsche, where the brick driveway sloped down a path to the back. There was no sign of Haddie's RAV4 — only a tinted SUV.

This had turned into his last lead on Harold Holmes and it seemed hopeful. Liz had mentioned the red sports car as one of those owned by his company. The pricey mountaintop estate was titled in the name of a related company.

Thomas left his helmet on his seat and headed for the front door. Only his bike smelled warm. The cars had been sitting for a while.

Something had happened to Haddie. His gut instincts and her friend Liz seemed sure of it. A heavy breath of dread had settled in his chest for the past hour. Her absence this morning had gone on too long. *Am I too late?* He'd lost those he'd loved before. He'd lost Haddie's mom. The world could be horrible and cruel.

A sandy-haired guard opened the front door and fired a gun.

The tug on his left leg caused Thomas to stumble, even as he stopped to react. The gunshot echoed against the walls of the house. He sang out, barely raising a hand toward the figure before it blinked away.

Light poured from the empty doorway. Pain roared through his joints, and fire washed his hands and face. A horrific image, someone else's memory flashed across his mind.

An elderly woman knelt, screaming as her tunic and the skin of her stomach faded into non-existence. Thomas knew it had been caused by someone wielding this very power. He saw through their eyes. She clutched her stomach as exposed intestines rolled outward. His teeth clenched, focusing on the house, and he put his right hand against wet pavers to steady himself. The nightmares were sometimes more incapacitating than the pain.

He'd dropped to his right knee. The bullet had gone through his upper thigh, leaving a hole in his leather pants. Water washed away the blood.

Harold Holmes, the British immigrant-turned-business-man, held Haddie, had killed her, or was involved. Thomas would have to be more careful and leave witnesses, someone to ask questions. His burning rage would have to wait.

Lurching up, he clenched his teeth against aching joints and the nagging burn from the gunshot. Sprinting for the door with barely a limp, he ran past the opening and slammed into the angled wall on the opposite side. Gunfire echoed from inside the house as three shots splintered the doorframe and shattered the thin glass window on his side of the doorway.

The shooter stood to the back of the entranceway, midway in the building, partially hidden by standing on steps so that only the top half of his body was exposed. A black piano and a couple light chairs seemed the only furniture; bright artwork colored the white walls. A railing to a second set of stairs heading down blocked a clear path from the door to the back where the guard stood. Behind Thomas, where his back rested against a wood wall, adjoining rooms had doors leading back to the entry. How many guards? He could only use so much of his power before it crippled him for a time. He didn't have time.

He turned, sang, and a hole opened in the wall. Trembling, he forced himself forward through pain and visions. Water sprayed from disintegrated pipes as he climbed into a white-tiled bathroom. He pulled his glasses to his neck. The bathroom door hung partially open, exposing a corner of a white wall in the entryway and a glimpse of the piano. Thomas slid behind the door and peered below the hinge.

The gray-haired guard had a military demeanor and still aimed toward the front doorway. He might have a back-up gun. However, Thomas only had five or six strides from the bathroom to the stairs where the man stood. The man's eyes flicked about, including toward the bathroom. The water and the new opening to the rain outside would surely cause some noise.

He needed someone to interrogate. Again, Thomas sang. Pain nearly buckled him as the gun vanished out of the guard's hand.

Agony flashed through him. Thomas staggered as he slammed the door out of his way and raced into the entry. Sluggish with pain and blinking to clear horrific images, he barely caught a glimpse to his right of a dark-haired, bearded man in the other stairwell. The man swiveled on the steps, reorienting toward Thomas. The man on the back stairs was still reacting with the surprise of losing his gun as Thomas raced toward him.

The bottom floor was an expansive sitting room, with glass looking into the rain. The gray-haired man started to reach toward his back. Thomas, threatened with the other man repositioning, dove over the railing toward the startled man on the back stairs.

If Thomas had hesitated, he'd have been pinned in another second. This way, he exposed himself for a moment but had a chance to take down the man in the back. He'd forced the guard in the stairwell to reposition. A lousy choice, but the only one he could manage mid-run. He might be able to sing one away, but in his state, the moment to recover would leave time for the other to finish him.

As he arced in the air, a gunshot sounded behind him. Glass shattered somewhere. Pulling his knees in, Thomas centered on the man's chest. His left arm caught the man's neck and pinned the shoulder. Thomas rode the momentum as they crashed into white-painted wood railings inset with glass panels, of all things.

The man's back snapped audibly. Wood splintered. Glass exploded.

Thomas spun over the man and narrowly missed a black stove when he slammed to the floor. Sluggish, with joints screaming, he rolled over, trying to hurry.

The third gunman would be coming up from the stairwell, at least that's what Thomas would do. How many? He knew his limits. The pain from using his ability would eventually cripple him.

He managed a lunging crawl over to the gray-haired

man's body and shoved it to its side. The man's suit had already rumpled up. The Sig pulled easily, tucked between the man's back and belt. A P365 with no safety was a bad gun for a hidden backup.

Thomas rolled to his knees, orienting toward a black speaker that rose beside the stairs. Sitting and kicking with his boots, he shuffled back toward the wood-burning stove.

Dark hair bobbed near the top of the speaker.

Thomas fired three shots in a triangle. Glass shattered, and the flat speaker tottered.

A shot returned, twanging off the iron at his shoulder. Below him, somewhere deep in the house, he thought he heard a howl. He returned three bullets. Jumping to his feet, he winced and ran for the stairs.

The bearded man stumbled near the stairwell, grasping at the railing beside it. He held his gun pressed over a dark wet spot on the right side of his gray suit. Wide eyed, he shifted to point his gun toward Thomas.

Thomas put a bullet in the guard's head.

He paused only a moment before forcing himself to the stairs. He tucked the Sig in his back with a grimace and grabbed the man's gun as he peered over the stairwell. The man had only fired two shots.

Thomas aimed the gun down the stairwell and moved carefully to the first step. His fingers burned as though the skin had been removed. Every nerve chafed at his clothes. Each joint ground and screeched with movement. He'd make a mistake soon, not react quickly enough, but he couldn't stop now.

Two steps down the stairwell, and a howl screamed from deeper below. *Haddie.* Thomas leaped down the remaining stairs and nearly stumbled to the floor of a wide hallway. Through one door, he could see a bedroom and windows looking out to gray rain and deck chairs. A second room to his right had a mirrored wall; it distorted an exercise bike so that it looked like it angled up.

Thomas took a step to the right to get a better view. The bike sat on a platform that hinged upward, exposing a dimly lit room below. His pulse rushed in his ears. Haddie was there. Any last guards would be with her. He had to get in and attack before they could react. Exhausted and trembling with pain, he might not have it in him. He didn't have many choices.

They would be focused on the entrance, and he had no idea what he was dropping into. Quietly stepping to the doorway, he could make out a curved wall and a pillar through the access in the floor. He swallowed and forced a deep breath. Leaping toward the side of the room, but away from the opening, Thomas spun in the air and sang.

The floor vanished in an oblong patch under his boots and he dropped into the basement as a fluorescent light sputtered into darkness on the ceiling beside him. It was a longer drop to the floor than he guessed.

Haddie had been strapped into an archaic chair that belonged in a medieval dungeon. Her wide eyes shifted with her head, following his fall. They'd strapped her to a wooden neck rest with fat white zip ties.

The nightmares flashed, disorienting him and superimposing over the dungeon scene. Carved stone and a man in a buttoned shirt blended with a screaming warrior who slowly lost his arm — a wooden spear clattering to the ground.

Thomas crashed onto the floor, his joints refusing to hold him. He slapped onto his side, and the gun skittered across stone. He caught the scent of burning human flesh — he'd smelled it too many times to ever forget.

The lone man who had been waiting for him seemed surprised. Without a gun, but open hands raised toward Thomas, his eyes flickered up at the hole to the gym above. Purpura marked his face.

Thomas had never met another like himself, or even imagined another.

Sunlight poured from the man's palms. Thomas clenched his eyes as unimaginable heat burned skin and pants. He smelled his skin and hair burn. Light blinded him through closed lids. Thomas screamed, then sang. The light outside his lids blipped into darkness, leaving only the bright memory.

CHAPTER 43

THE BLINDING LIGHT WAS GONE. Haddie shrieked, "Dad!"

Her dad lay on the floor, singed boots and pants steaming in ghostly tendrils. Harold Holmes had flared like the sun. Light had streamed from his hands, focused on Dad but hot enough that her own burns cringed. The gaping hole in the ceiling had damaged the light beside it, but the one over her shone, dim compared to what had come from Harold Holmes. The man and his light had simply disappeared. She'd heard both their songs. Her father had screamed, and a bell had rung.

Dad's hand twitched, and she sobbed. Tears poured down her face. Choking, she struggled against her bonds and gasped at the pain from her wrists. This couldn't be happening. Dad wasn't moving, though she thought she saw breaths — a slight movement of his chest. His usually lightly tanned skin looked sunburned. She felt sunburned.

"Dad?"

If he could just get up and get her out of this chair, then she could help him. Were any of the guards still in the house, or alive? She'd heard the gunshots and known Dad was there. *Rescuing me.* Harold Holmes had not been able to stop her from yelling. Not while waiting to ambush her dad.

The gun Dad had dropped rested on the floor just a step away from her. She had practiced getting out of zip ties in high school. Nothing applied to her current situation. Nobody knew they were here. The police, maybe. Would neighbors have heard the shots? No, it had been a long drive up the hill. Maybe some cleaning lady would come by?

"Dad?" she yelled, hoping he was just dazed. He'd fallen right through the floor. What if he were dying? Someone had to help. She couldn't have dragged him to his death and die herself now that he'd rescued her. Detective Cooper, he might come back.

"Ugmh." Dad made a slight grunt.

She could see his face. His lips moved, but his eyes remained closed. The long hunting knife hung in its sheath at his hip. If he could just get up and get a couple of her restraints free, she could cut the rest. Haddie looked down at her wrists and tried to flex her fingers. The pain nearly made her retch again. "Dad," she sobbed.

A ghostly figure flickered over her dad. She wouldn't have seen it were it not for the darkness behind him. How long had it been there? A mist of red and purple hovered and whorled in a frozen stance, leaning down with hands outstretched as if speaking to Dad. Haddie swallowed, eyebrows raising. *What? Who?* It didn't move, just ebbed, raining down to the floor, fading, and reconstructing in waves. Her mind couldn't grasp one more thing. *Have I gone insane?*

"Dad."

The figure didn't react to her voice. Haddie's tears

started down her cheeks. She'd dismissed her dad when he tried to tell her the truth. It was all so impossible, but how could Harold Holmes and Dad do the things they did? Now some ghost, who did look a bit like Harold Holmes, stood there. She could do nothing, trapped in her chair. It was too much. She just wanted to leave, to forget all this.

"Dad, please."

"Mmh." He sighed as if in response. His eyelids moved but didn't open.

The ghost remained. Never actually moving, it stood locked in a pose, leaning with hands reaching toward her dad. A cohesive mist that fluctuated and ebbed like a hologram. It looked almost like Harold Holmes, reappearing from wherever Dad had sent the man. That thought terrified her. She would never forget his face, or the pain. They needed to escape.

"Dad!" Haddie yelled.

His eyelids flickered and she saw a blink of moisture. The ghost never moved. Whatever it was, it didn't hear her, or didn't care. It focused on Dad.

"Dad. We need to leave. Get up. Cut me out of this chair. I'll get us out." She looked at the stairway, over a dozen steep steps. How would she get him out? If he could get to her chair, then she could help him climb the stairs.

"Hmm?" Dad blinked. Opening his eyes, his gaze floated around the room to land on her. His voice came out slow, dry, and rasping. "Haddie?" He didn't seem to notice the ghost.

Haddie took a sharp breath. "Can you get up?"

What if he'd broken a leg in that fall? It hadn't looked as though he could get up when Harold Holmes attacked. Now he didn't respond, and his eyes closed again. The air smelled foul, even above the scent of burnt flesh. She still tasted blood. What if he had a concussion? He needed to stay awake.

"Dad!" She spoke sharply, still uncomfortable with yelling. Surely, if any of the guards could, they would have been here by now. He didn't move. "Dad," she hissed.

"Hello?" A man's voice replied from somewhere in the house above. The voice had an accent to it. Unmistakable, but nothing she could identify.

Her heart raced and she froze, her eyes glancing between the open hole her dad had jumped through and the stairs. Who? If it was one of the guards, then they would have just come down or looked in.

Footsteps crossed the room, pausing. "Hello? Brother?" He dragged the Rs a little.

Brother? Holmes had said he had family issues. It sounded like he had planned on killing someone. Why? Did this help them? Whoever it was would find them in a moment anyway. *Don't I want that?*

Dad stirred, moving a hand, his eyes blinking. "Hmm." The ghost remained. It looked like Harold Holmes.

"Dad," Haddie whispered, moving her head back and forth against the bonds. If he could just get up, get her free, get the gun . . .

A head looked down from the top of the stairs. It took a moment for the face to come into focus. Harold Holmes stood above them. "What has my brother been up to?"

Haddie choked. Harold Holmes had a twin brother? The accent surely wasn't British. Eastern European? Russian?

The brother peered around from the top of the stairs and then started down. He wore a black suit, shiny black shoes, a white shirt, and a black tie. He was a twin to Harold Holmes with shorter hair, less suave and almost military. He walked around her dad, paused to look at the gun, and came over to study her dispassionately. Uninterested in her, he returned to Dad, walking through the ghost, seeming to not see it. Was she hallucinating?

Dad turned his head, and his fingers trembled, touching the stone. "Who?" he croaked.

The brother stroked his chin and pulled at his lip. Purpura splotched his fingers and cheeks. He had the same ability as Harold Holmes and her dad. He shrugged. "I've seen the bodies upstairs. I assume you killed them?" He jerked his head in her direction but continued speaking to Dad. "Perhaps you came to rescue her? Then where is my brother Harold?"

Dad blinked slowly. His lips moved but he couldn't seem to lift his head. He had to be hurt — a concussion or something. She'd seen him shake off dropping his bike without a limp, pick it up, and keep going. This was different.

The brother leaned in, sending the ghostly vapor swirling. "Did you kill my brother?" He laughed. "Not that I would mind; he did try to kill me on the way here, after all." He gestured around the carved-out basement. "Where is the body, though?"

He turned to study Haddie. "Maybe you know?"

She sucked short breaths as he approached. This brother seemed as callous and indifferent to their plight as Harold Holmes had been intent upon creating it. There was no help here. She had never liked Detective Cooper, but she could only hope he would return.

The brother examined the burns on her wrists, even pushing up the burnt sleeve of her sweatshirt to inspect Harold's work. "He is — maybe was — so much better at this than I am. Of course, he was willing to practice it more." He rested his hand on her right wrist. "Where is my brother?"

Haddie cried out. "Gone. Gone." The pain made her dizzy. *Stop, please, stop.* They were both so cruel.

The brother released her and walked over to poke at the gun with the shiny toe of his shoe. Ash dusted the soles. "He's caused quite a mess. Brought us attention that we do not need. Far too ambitious."

The ghost of Harold Holmes, or his brother, had returned to her dad. His fingers tense against the ground, Dad tried to push himself up so he could turn his head and watch her. Licking his lips, he spoke. "I killed him."

The brother nodded, returning to stand in the ghost, sending whorls of mist around the two men. "Where is he? Did I miss his body somewhere?"

Dad tried to speak, grunting before his head collapsed against the stone again. His eyes closed, and he seemed to take ragged breaths. Was he dying?

The brother stood up sharply. "It hardly matters." He waved at the basement, pausing at the hole in the ceiling, before turning back to her dad. "I'm going to have to clean all this up, starting with you."

He leaned down into the ghost, taking its position, and stretched out his hands. "I'm not nearly as skilled as my brother. It seems I should practice."

CHAPTER 44

Haddie yanked against her restraints. "No!"

The brother of Harold Holmes aimed his palms at Dad. A glow began forming around his body, strongest along exposed skin. Then tongues of flame emanated from his hand with the brilliance of sunlight, growing incandescent and wiping all shadows from the room.

Wincing, Dad brought up a weak, gloved hand as if to cover his face, but fingertips barely reached his chin. He was too weak. He couldn't protect himself now, let alone her. A groan escaped from his lips, but no ringing bell, and the brother's light grew more intense.

Haddie shrieked. Her voice split, at once shrill and raspy with fear and anger, and a second tone, like a tuning fork rung off a crystal glass, echoed in the air. Her fingers arched off the wood and her nerves burned across her skin. Joints groaned without moving and felt as though they'd been twisted.

The brother and his light were pushed away, back, toward some other time. In the moment, in front of her dad, they no longer existed. The twin who had tortured Dad disappeared.

A memory swelled up, but not her own. The basement faded and became the front of the building hazed in rain. The same entrance they'd brought her in. The dirty blond man fired from the open doorway. Pain. The man disappeared, leaving only the light from the open door.

The image reformed, and a dingy white wall took its place. A stack of old tires leaned against worn and peeling paint. She saw all this through an open blue door with rusted edges, a worn knob in a large hand that was not her own.

A young girl with long black hair stood in a blue dress with familiar yellow flowers. The girl watched a woman, her mother, gagging in a man's arms. The woman had long black hair like her daughter's. A jagged red line cut across her throat, the man's knife still hung there. Her hands clutched a dark brown purse against her stomach; the straps hung down to her thighs.

The eyes of Haddie's mother, dark and brown, pleaded.

The man's face was wild, his hair stuck in the air as if grease hung it there. He groped for the purse with his other hand, while the knife bit deeper into her throat. Haddie's mother sagged, and the man reached the bag. As he grabbed the edge, fingers digging deep into brown leather, he pushed her toward the little girl — toward Haddie. She knew this memory, a different version of it. One she'd never remembered, until this moment.

She saw it from a different view, her dad's, coming out of the bathroom. He bellowed, and the air rang, and the dingy man with her mother's purse vanished.

Haddie gagged, the sight of her mother, falling with her cut throat, playing out as the basement came back into focus. She'd always been uncomfortable about her mother's death, never dug too deep. Because she'd known, all along.

Her father had been too late. She'd felt his emotions in the memory. A self-loathing at losing his wife. The fear of what his daughter would think of him, knowing that he'd killed her mother's attacker. She couldn't remember her own feelings; they'd been buried long ago.

Dad mumbled on the stone floor. His eyes flickered, but he couldn't open them. His face had been turned bright red from the brother's heat. The smell of burned flesh and hair filled the room. Haddie had to get to him.

Her flesh still crawled as if the skin and nerves tried to peel off. *What am I?* She'd killed the brother. The thought brought quick ragged breaths. She could see a purple bruise on her right index finger, another inside the curve of her thumb. Had she always been like this?

The ghost was gone. It had been an image of the last position of the brother, frozen in that moment when she had sent him away. Was that it? Had she blown him back into time? She sobbed, gritted her teeth, and struggled against the zip tie that bound her left forearm. Pain blossomed anew in her wrist, but it only competed against the crawling and peeling of her nerves.

"Dad!" she yelled.

He didn't move. She couldn't even tell if he breathed.

They needed to escape, to make this all end. Nothing else mattered. Who she was — who they were — she couldn't think about. Panting, she closed her eyes. *I'm getting hysterical.* Haddie took a deep breath. *Focus.* The only need she had was to be free of these bonds. She blinked. If she could make a man disappear, or fade into the past, then how hard would small strips of plastic be? Swallowing, she forced out the thoughts of the pain that reigned across her skin.

Thinking of her bonds, detailing each one out in her mind, Haddie shrieked.

The air rang around her. The chair below her disappeared.

The ties were gone, and she crashed to the floor. Waves of burning pain rippled across her face and arms and found every corner of her body. Her knees and shoulders were rusted embers of dull aches.

A memory came. A dark room and a man with pale white skin, stabbing at a body. Midswing of a long, curved knife, he disappeared. She felt sorry and grief for the young man he'd left with bleeding wounds in his chest and stomach. Then, a sudden gunfire coming out of a wall of green leaves, a jungle with thick vines and endless trees. Silence and relief. The basement returned around her. Above, the florescent light still shone.

She'd done it. Her body screamed in pain, and her joints felt like rusted bolts while a million needles pierced her skin. She pressed a palm down at her side to sit up and gasped. The burnt skin cracked along her wrist and exposed red, wet flesh beneath. She'd have to get to a hospital.

Rolling to her side, she positioned her elbows to take her weight. Her hair rolled over her shoulder into the ash. Stark white strands. At first, even as she shifted and it moved with her, it seemed it must be someone else's. Shaking her head, it dropped down fully. *White*. Numb, she rose onto her knees and began shuffling toward her dad despite the ache in her hips and joints.

Dad's eyes opened as she shifted a knee against his hand. "Haddie." A gloved finger reached out and touched her knee. His voice sounded dry. "My phone. Call Biff."

"You're okay?" She swallowed against a thick throat. "I thought maybe you had a concussion or broke a leg. Your face." Sunburned skin peeled; he had blisters on his chin, and through it she could see the purpura.

"I'll heal. I always do." His finger rubbed against her red jeans. "You —" He didn't finish. Surely he had seen what she'd done.

Haddie swallowed. "Your phone."

He still lay on his side. During the brother's attack, he'd drawn up his knees slightly. He kept his phone in his right jacket pocket. *Under him.* She cringed at the thought of trying to slide her hand under his body, scraping her burnt wrists against stone.

"Can you roll onto your back?" she asked.

He closed his eyes, took a deep breath, and shifted. A groan escaped as he tilted and straightened his legs. He had a wet hole in his pants on his left thigh.

She remembered the image she'd had of the man firing from the doorway. These were his memories. "You've been shot." A glimpse of her mother sent a shiver through her. They would have so much to talk about if they got out of this alive.

He didn't answer. Eyes wide, he gasped and moved his arm to position his fingers into his jacket pocket. He pulled out a black phone and laid it beside him. The screen was shattered.

Haddie winced, extending her hand and pressing the button on the side. Distorted purples and blues flickered across the screen. She'd have to go upstairs. "It's broken. I need to go look for another phone." Part of her apprehension came from the stairs, the other part from being away from Dad.

He nodded. "Okay." His eyes closed. "Going to rest."

Forcing herself to her feet threatened to send her tumbling, but she stood. Her body, both skin and bones, ached. She couldn't bring herself to touch the railing; her wrists screamed at the thought. One careful footstep at a time, she made her way up, not feeling safe until her shoulders crested the floor. It seemed to take forever to get all the way up two flights of stairs.

Wind and rain whistled through the house, leaving an eerie, abandoned sense to it. A window high near the ceiling had been shot, letting rain splash down and mist the polished wood floor. The front door stood open, and a window next to it had been shattered.

The bearded man lay at the top of the stairs, blood pooling around his head, thinning and spreading with the rain. A bullet had pierced his cheek just under his left eye; otherwise, he looked peaceful. Stepping through his puddle, Haddie hoped he kept his phone in his jacket. Dad had shot the man twice, once in the chest, then the head. Execution style. *Focus.* Rather than kneel, she forced her hips and knees to bend and crouch, grimacing as she poked with stiff fingers across the front of his jacket. *I really don't want to go digging in a dead man's pants.*

Her phone rang downstairs, where she'd first been dropped into the red chair. She almost slipped as she jerked up. Shuffling her feet to wipe off the blood, she made for the stairs.

The gray-haired man lay by the stove. Two dead men. Dad had killed them. She couldn't put any thought through her mind without dredging up the other impossibilities.

Focus. The railing had been demolished, leaving glass shards on the step for her to avoid. Her phone sat on the zebra-striped couch. She hurried without slipping or falling to see the caller ID.

Liz. She couldn't know about this. She'd be frantic by now.

Leaning over, Haddie answered the call with a stiff finger, leaving the phone on the zebra stripes and putting the call on speaker. "Hey." Her tone an attempt at false calm, she swallowed, suddenly wanting to cry again.

Liz swore. "What is going on? Everyone is looking for you. What happened? Are you okay?"

White hair slid over Haddie's shoulder, as if mocking her. "I'm fine. Hanging with Dad up in the mountains." She raised her eyebrows and took a breath. "Clearing up some personal things. Can I call you back tomorrow?"

"Are you kidding? That's it?" Liz sounded angry. "All day, no answer. Your Dad was looking for you. And you want me to believe you're having a damned picnic?"

"Yeah, it's complicated." Haddie regretted answering the phone, but Liz would have been nuts. "But please, don't worry. I'm great. We're finally working through some family issues."

"Haddie?" Liz pleaded.

"Please, Liz. Give me a day."

Liz sniffled. "Okay. You're with your dad for tonight?"

Haddie took a deep breath and picked up the phone by its edges, wincing at the fire in her wrists. "Yes. I'll call tomorrow."

"Okay." Liz didn't drop the connection.

"Bye, Liz." Haddie poked the phone with her left hand to hang up and headed for the stairs.

She had no idea what she was supposed to tell Biff. Bring the tow truck for Dad's bike, two body bags, and a mop? Now that an escape seemed possible, she didn't want Detective Cooper dropping by. Dad had killed two men. No matter the circumstances, which no one would believe, he'd be in jail. Because of her. She had no experience in this, and it bothered her that she thought her dad might. She didn't know what to think of him. So much had changed over the past few days, more than she could absorb.

When she finally made it to Harold Holmes' secret stairs, Dad's eyes were open. Grunting, he shifted to sit up as she started down the stairs. She finally understood why he had so much trouble with his joints. Hers felt the bolts had been overtightened and took extra force just to move.

"Let me call Biff," he said. His face looked horrible, peeling, burnt, and discolored.

"Planned on it." Haddie descended carefully.

"We'll need to get somewhere where they can look at your hands. I don't know if you'll . . ." He trailed off. "I heal quickly. Maybe you will too."

Haddie blinked and stumbled, stopping just short of falling to her knees. Was she now going to stop aging as well? *This is too much.*

He saw her expression. "Don't worry about all this right now. Baby steps. We'll deal with the rest as we need to." Dad put out his hand for her phone. He pulled off a glove and pressed the button. There were no purple marks; his entire hand was purple. "Passcode?"

CHAPTER 45

HADDIE WAITED, nervous and fighting tears, as Dad climbed up the stairs. He placed each footstep carefully, holding onto the railings with both gloved hands.

"Biff will get my bike on the truck and meet us outside. He won't come in."

It had taken the last quarter of an hour to get her dad to stand. He'd been shot, and he said that his joints weren't working properly. She could believe it. Each step he took seemed excruciating. Her own joints burned, but her wrists were in the worst pain. Harold Holmes had seared the tops, so that moving her fingers stretched and ripped burnt skin. She couldn't stand looking at it.

"What did you touch?" he asked.

"What?" She feared he would stumble all the way back down. If Biff came in, he could help Dad. "I didn't touch anything."

"Think carefully, Haddie. If you have left one fingerprint here, we need a different story."

She moved her arm and froze at the pain. "I was bound when I came in, all the way down to the basement, so nothing." Her hands had been tied to the chair; she'd gripped it. "The chair."

"No longer a problem." He grunted and paused, three steps from the top, his shoulders already floor level to the gym.

Suddenly, she had a moment of regret for how she'd treated Dad. A spoiled child. He'd been telling her the truth. The truth she'd demanded. How could she expect to understand it — until now?

"Did you touch anything just now, getting the phone?"

Haddie shook her head. "I pushed on the dead guy's jacket. I couldn't bear using my hands on the railings. Then, my phone."

Dad made it to the top and stepped beside her. "We're going to have to make your boots disappear." He pointed to a partial bloody boot print on the black mat beside the stairs.

She led him to the next stairs up to the foyer. Her own legs had gained some stability, but he looked ready to drop. "Do you want to hold onto my shoulder?"

He shook his head. "Railing is sturdier. You're not in good shape." Turning up at the opening, rain misted his face. "That's good."

"What?" she asked.

"Weather and animals might disturb the scene enough, if no one comes up to check on the residence for a couple days. We can hope."

Had he done this kind of thing before? Kill people and leave the crime scene? Now that they were close to escaping, she felt guilty. But why should she? Harold Holmes caused all of this. They would think he just disappeared after some shoot-out in his house; that would be good. *Except for Mel.* Haddie's chest tightened. She — Dad — had wiped away the evidence of the actual murderer. There was nothing to prove Mel's innocence.

"Where's your car?" Dad climbed the last step to the foyer.

Haddie swallowed. "I heard them," she said, nodding toward the body on the floor, "making plans to have the car moved to a rest stop up north."

He took a breath and nodded. "That would make sense. Somewhere on I-5. It'd take at least twenty-four hours before it got called in."

She turned to face the open door with him. Wind blew in, but the rain came from the shattered window above. The downpour had turned to a drizzle outside. No Biff. Two black Explorers, the red Cayman, and Dad's Shovelhead sat on the pavers.

Shaking, Dad pulled out her phone and started dialing. "Trig, I need a favor. Got a blue RAV4, license plate —" He turned to her.

"924FLN," she said.

He repeated the number. "Left up on a rest stop on I-5, somewhere north of Eugene." Dad paused as his friend responded. "She was drunk, we don't know where exactly. Take a look. If you find it, there might be keys in it. Either way, could you tuck it behind my garage? I'll owe you. Let me know what you find."

The rain misting in above had settled on her wrists, and they felt chilled. Haddie shivered. How would she explain these scars? Even sleeves wouldn't cover them.

Dad pointed toward the overhang just outside the front door. "Let's wait out there. We'll get those burns looked at first. I've got a biker up in Lowell, an EMT."

Haddie stepped outside, wanting to tuck her hands someplace warm, but the idea of placing them against anything made her nauseous. Her torn stitches didn't even hurt that bad. She wondered if a hospital would be a better plan for both of them — he'd been shot. Maybe Dad didn't want anything recorded. Hiding a crime was rather new to her.

"We'll hole up in Idaho for a day or two. We'll need a story."

"Idaho?" Haddie choked. "Rock, I need to —"

Dad shook his head. "Leave him at the vet, or have your friend take care of him. We've got to heal for a couple days. You haven't seen your face."

She raised a hand, winced, and dropped it again. His looked horrifying, purple-spotted skin already peeling. Haddie nodded. "I'll call Sam."

"Later, vet first." He nodded as Biff's white Silverado wrecker pulled up the driveway. "We'll delay talking with Detective Cooper. We went on a trip out of town. Idaho. I was concerned for your safety and got you out of here." He limped toward his bike. "We can see what comes up on the news and adjust our story if we need to. Okay?"

Numb, she nodded her head, walking alongside him.

Biff jumped out, rounding the front of his truck and went straight for the Porsche. "Just the bike?" Dark brown hair, usually combed up and out his face, was plastered to his side from the rain. He had a tightly trimmed beard that followed his chin line up to sideburns and a groomed mustache. His eyes widened as he looked at her dad. "Jeez, T, what happened?"

"Sorry, Biff. Zero questions."

Biff closed his mouth and glanced at the house. His eyes returned to his usual squint, but he just nodded and ran to Dad's bike.

Haddie followed Dad to the truck.

"Did you grab everything I asked for?" Dad asked.

"Back seat, T."

Dad opened the back door on the passenger side, pushed a black bag to the next seat, and grabbed a large first aid kit off the floor. "Get in."

Haddie stared at the opening, the steps, and the seat, then using her elbows, climbed in as her dad started pulling out ointment. He had a bullet, or at least a hole, in his leg, and he stood there in the rain. His face looked swollen, marbled beyond any natural coloring. He'd just killed four people, and she'd killed one.

"What are we?" Haddie whispered.

"I don't know," he said.

CHAPTER 46

HADDIE HANDED Biff her empty breakfast container; she'd scraped every bit of food out of it. She could've eaten twice as much. Dad seemed just as hungry.

"Thanks, Biff."

His hair had dried, and he'd brushed it so that his bangs swept high up over his forehead in his usual flourish. He winked, tossing his head with a tilt. "Of course, ready for breakfast dessert?"

Haddie raised her eyebrows and glanced across the hotel room at the other white plastic bags on the dresser. Dad had finished his meal and gone back to sleep on the other queen bed. The heater poking out of the wall between them thrummed. For a cheap hotel off I-84, it was clean and had smelled like fresh laundry when they checked in last night. Now, sausage and eggs dominated the room.

"Dessert?" she asked. Propped up with extra pillows against the wall, she'd planned on making her calls, but her stomach could handle some sweets despite the antibiotics.

Biff swaggered with her empty Styrofoam and tossed it into an already burdened waste basket. "Only the finest.

Chocolate croissants, cheese Danish, blueberry muffins, and a mix of rugelach — my personal suggestion. Don't ask how I found rugelach in Caldwell, Idaho. I got mad skills."

Haddie's mouth watered. "Chocolate croissant." She looked down at her two arms, her left bandaged up to the elbow. "And a blueberry muffin." Her wrists only twinged when she pinched thumb and forefinger, or reached back for her hair, or stretched out for the faucet.

"No rugelach?" Biff feigned shock, and perhaps indignation.

"Later." She pointed to the phone in her lap. "Maybe after my calls."

Biff placed both items on the small nightstand beside her and continued cleaning up their breakfast.

David had left a text, wondering if she still had time for coffee. She'd ghosted him yesterday, and still he acted nice. She touched a strand of white hair, and then her cheek. *Can't.*

Haddie took a long deep breath and dialed Liz.

"Hello?" Liz answered quickly, the sounds of other voices diminishing as if she walked away from people. "Are you okay, Haddie?"

"I'm fine. We're holed up in a hotel in Caldwell, Idaho for a few days. I'm healing, and Dad is keeping me safe. He sort of kidnapped me to keep me from being stupid." Haddie picked up the croissant and took a bite, dropping crumbs down the purple Mackinaw they'd bought last night. She looked hideous in it, but it was warm, and the sleeves rolled up.

Liz sighed. "Okay. Good. That's good. How long?"

Haddie looked at the purpura along her hands; her neck had been the worst. "A couple days?"

"Okay, that's great actually. Brilliant idea. I just . . .

when you didn't answer yesterday, I got worried. Then Detective Cooper's been calling. Oh. I told him I talked to you yesterday."

Haddie raised her eyebrows. She'd been ignoring his calls. Eventually, she'd have to tell him something. "I'll call him. You were first on my list — after the vet."

"How is Rock?" Liz sounded calmer.

"Doing good. They want to keep him 'til Monday. His vet will let me know then if he's ready to leave." Haddie polished off the last of the chocolate croissant and eyed the blueberry muffin. Was she supposed to be this hungry?

"If you need help with him —"

"Sam will take him, if I'm not back by then."

"Not until they find these guys." Liz's tone sharpened.

Haddie couldn't tell her the threat was over. Couldn't even hint at it. "You're right. I'll talk with Dad first."

"Good." Liz's tone relaxed.

"I was supposed to go out for coffee this weekend."

"Ooh. Tell."

"Name's David — tall — my type. But I was supposed to text him yesterday, forgot, and now it's just weird."

"Nonsense," said Liz. "He'll think you're mysterious and worth waiting for. Text him back."

Haddie reached for her hair and winced. She wouldn't be able to face him like this, to explain her face, her wrists, her hair. *I'm a mess.* No, better to let it go. She'd never see him again.

Eventually, she finished her blueberry muffin and hung up with Liz. Rock should be on the bed beside her, convalescing. She could handle being away from Eugene for a few days, but she missed Jisoo and Rock.

Biff sat near the door, balancing backward in a small,

padded chair. "Need me to see if the maids have a vacuum you can borrow?"

Haddie frowned. "What?"

He motioned to his chest and pointed at her. She had a dusting of crumbs across the purple and blue checkerboard wool. Wincing, she disturbed some with her hand. *Jerk.* Ignoring him, she blew croissant flakes off her phone.

Sam answered quickly. "Haddie." Her tone sounded desperate.

"I'm fine, Sam. Here in Idaho, hiding out. The vet is keeping Rock until Monday. Sorry I didn't call earlier. I've been tired."

Biff whispered, "And hungry."

Sam sniffled. "I was wondering. Then you didn't answer, and Detective Cooper keeps calling."

Damn him. "I'm sorry, Honey. I really am. I just need to wrap my head around everything. I'll be back soon."

"But you're okay?"

"Of course, I've got Dad and some jerk here watching over me. It'll be fine."

Biff acted hurt, offering an exaggerated pout.

"How's Jisoo?"

"He's been in everyone's food. Ignatius took it personally."

Ignatius, Sam's iguana. David liked iguanas, according to Terry. Haddie calmed Sam down before moving on.

Terry took her call with his usual joviality. His earlier texts had been probing, but short. The attacks on her and Rock hadn't been a surprise; he tended to keep up on local news.

"Idaho?" he asked. "Why not Cali?"

"Dad." She'd managed to pick off most of the blueberry

muffin crumbs. The croissant flakes tended to crumble to dust.

"What are you doing about your client?"

Haddie's chest grew heavy. She'd doomed Mel. "I've got a few days off from work."

"Yeah, of course. The boards have been lighting up on the charred stiffs. Supposedly, the FBI and NSA are all involved now, fighting a Chinese infiltrator with genetically modified abilities. But the growing conspiracy is that Shasmiel has returned. Then I like the Swiss research equipment —"

Haddie really didn't want to focus on the burns, or Mel. "Terry?"

"Yeah?"

"Other than your boards, what have you been up to?"

Terry chuckled. "Talked Chelsea into coming out for game night. Intro to D&D."

"The med student?"

He laughed. "Told her she has to be a cleric to start." A loud slurp sounded. "So, your boyfriend. D&D?"

Dad leaned up on his elbows and looked over to her. His face still looked horrifying, but the color looked lighter.

"Funny, Terry. Not boyfriend. Listen, Dad's up. I'm going to go. I'll check in with you."

"Later, Buckaroo."

Dad rolled to his side and picked up the coffee mug he'd been using to drink water. The sheets of peeling skin glossed with ointment.

Biff kicked up off his chair and headed over. He'd kept them hydrated throughout. Haddie had been drinking a jug of unsweetened tea he'd found her on one of his outings. Biff checked her mug as he grabbed her dad's. "Drink up."

Dad rubbed his hair back. "You leave a message for the detective?"

"About to."

"Check the news. See if anything comes up before you leave a message."

They'd sketched out a timeline that fit both the detective's known visit to Harold Holmes and Dad's interactions with Liz. The entire process kept Haddie holding her breath. She'd awakened during the drive last night to find they'd stopped along the Ochoco Reservoir to toss the guns in. Nearly puking from nerves, she'd had a melt down for a few miles afterward.

No news came up about any shootings in Lane County, except a domestic dispute in Florence. Haddie took a deep breath and dialed the Eugene police department. "Detective Cooper, please." She could only hope he wasn't available for the call.

The dispatcher had a pleasant, if distracted tone. "I can put you through to his voicemail. If it's important, I can get you to someone else."

Haddie sighed. "Voicemail is fine." She waited for the beep. "Detective Cooper. This is Hadhira Dawson. I got your voicemails. Sorry for the concern. I'm fine. I decided to take a trip with my dad out of town for a few days, considering everything that has been going on. I'll be back next week and make sure to check in with you then." She hung up and looked at her dad.

He nodded. "That's good. He'll call back, but won't push too hard."

Biff dropped off more water for Dad and filled her mug with tea. "So, lunch?"

Haddie absently picked out a few items. If all this food went to her hips, she'd kill Dad.

After each item, Biff countered with, "And?" Finally he left, leaving her with Dad.

Haddie took a deep breath and texted David. "Sorry, had to go out of town."

"Are you hungry?" Dad asked.

"Famished." She stared at the screen.

There hadn't been anyone she'd been interested in for a while. School had kept her too busy. *Bad timing.*

David replied, "That's cool. I'm still up for coffee whenever you are."

Haddie smiled and then looked at the bandages. "It might be a few days before I get back."

"Okay. All right if I text later?"

Haddie nodded — to herself. "Yes. Gotta go."

Dad watched her, waiting until she finished texting. "I'm starving too. Happens when I get hurt and need to heal."

She put the phone face down and stared at the bandages. "You think I'm like you now?" She didn't know exactly how she felt about not aging. Her vanity kicked up a little, though a look in the mirror would push that down.

What would David look like when he was older? *It's just coffee.*

"Maybe. We'll see how those wounds look by Monday."

Monday? "That fast?" Haddie held out her bandaged hands.

"The purpura takes three or four days for me. The worst of it, at least." He gestured at his head. "How about your, um, hair?"

Haddie looked down at the white strands draped over the purple Mackinaw. What was she going to do about it?

CHAPTER 47

HADDIE SAT at Detective Cooper's lonely desk, listening as he explained his concerns in painful, droning detail. He would get around to his question eventually . . . hopefully.

When she'd stepped into his office, she'd been surprised by the comprehensive neatness and order. He likely would have a stroke if he went into her apartment. The plain black coffee mug on the beige coaster might actually be empty, just there as a prop. He never sipped from it. The handle lined up perpendicular to his side of the desk. The cheap, faux-leather inbox had a solitary memo placed upside down. It sat in the corner so perfectly equidistant from the edges that she could imagine him leaned over it with a ruler. No, he likely had a T-square in his top drawer, next to the level.

As simple as his office seemed, he was not a simple detective. He spoke quietly and clearly. He detailed the results of his findings, both on her and Dad, and on elements connected to the Colman case, including the bizarre burnt remains found in the Ford Explorer parked outside Harold Holmes' estate in Cottage Grove. Liz had learned about the corpses yesterday, only a few minutes after an excitable Terry.

Due to the new bodies, Mel was free and back at her apartment, all charges dropped. Andrea had been with the DA on Sunday as soon as the news hit. She'd even texted Haddie then, and again this morning when Mel walked out. It was likely that Haddie still had a job, all thanks to Harold Holmes' brother leaving a pair of crisped thugs conveniently parked outside the house of the Colmans' murderer.

"We've yet to question Harold Holmes. He seems to have disappeared, and the FBI is now involved in the investigation. Some of his business arrangements are raising questions." He paused as if to gauge her reactions.

His investigation of her and her father had been thorough, legal, and frustrating. They couldn't let him know what they had actually been up against. First, he'd never believe them. Second, they'd put Dad in jail.

Cooper was like her cat, Jisoo. You'd yell at her, tell her to get off, and she would ghost off somewhere as if she cared less, then be back when you'd forgotten about her. Cooper snooped and dug through stuff he didn't belong in, except he certainly wouldn't knock pens on the floor. He droned on about some of Harold Holmes' business dealings. He wanted something from her and hoped she'd engage. The office smelled sterile, not disinfectant-masking funk, but like ozone. She glanced around the edges of the room for a purifier or ozone generator. Nothing. Really nothing.

He was getting to the point; she recognized his hand gesture and the way he tilted his right shoulder back. He should never play poker with her dad.

"Ms. Dawson, where have you been?"

Haddie rested the tip of her riding glove finger on his inbox, testing to see if the detective brought out a T-square.

"Riding with Dad. Clearing my head. Spooked about the attack." She'd had to use a jar of makeup to cover the purpura and wore a tall choker she'd found in her drawer.

"I've called, left messages. You checked in on your dog three times in the last two days but didn't go home. I got one message from you on Saturday."

She returned her hand to her lap, leaving his inbox in place, no reason to torment him. "Rock won't be allowed home 'til tomorrow."

"Do you know anything about the deaths at Harold Holmes' mansion?" With his index finger, he tapped the side of his head at the cheekbone, another tell.

"No. Why would I?" Haddie poked her glasses up her nose. Liz hadn't mentioned any warrants, so they'd cleaned up well enough.

He stared at her sunglasses; makeup couldn't fix bloodshot eyes, and eyedrops had failed. She breathed slowly and deeply, bringing back memories of yoga classes during her first year of college. She could wait him out on this.

"Interesting hair style."

"Yep." She'd considered having her hairdresser add blue or pink to the white, but there was no way to hide the purpura on her scalp. Maybe once that went away, she could do something other than stark white.

"You visited Mr. Holmes the morning of his disappearance."

"Yes." Haddie smiled.

"And —?" Finally, Cooper showed a little frustration, waving his hand from the side of his head out into the air in exasperation.

Haddie shrugged. "He didn't give me any new information on Mel's case. I thought he might have seen someone entering the victim's office on a regular basis. I was looking for Mark Colman's business partner. Seemed like a nice man, but you can never tell."

"Well, your visit, which Ms. Backhus seemed concerned about after your disappearance, is what caused me to dig into his background a little. Petty stuff early on, and one Interpol query, but it seems even they really didn't catch on to what he was into. Records show he had some financial dealings with the original victim." He wasn't giving her anything that Liz hadn't already told her. "With everything considered, and the new victims, the DA dropped the case on your client. I'm looking for the witness, the postal worker, but she disappeared too."

"Shame, it could have saved us some trouble if you'd known about Holmes and his connection to Mark Colman." *Or even looked for any other connections, before settling in on Mel without any real case to back it up.*

Cooper tilted his head, perhaps catching some of her tone. "Yes. I'm going to assume that he was behind your attempted mugging and home invasion."

You think? Detective Cooper still dug. Unsatisfied. He'd have to stay that way. She looked out his window to the blue sky.

"Harold Holmes was adopted. He has a twin brother named Dmitry Markin, still living with his father in London. We're trying to contact him now."

"Hmm, families can be complicated." Nothing Detective Cooper offered wouldn't be in the media soon. He just wanted her to engage.

"How's your dog?" He tilted his head up and furrowed his eyebrows, affecting a concerned look.

Really? "Better, thank you." She raised her gloved hand in the air questioningly. "Is that about it? I'm behind on some classwork." Failing would be more like it if she didn't seriously buckle down.

He took a deep breath and leaned forward. "All good at the firm?"

Get on with it. "Great. They gave me a week off to get caught up at school."

The sunglasses really bothered him. She tried not to smile. Whatever patience he'd brought to this inquisition was fading.

"Have you talked with Special Agent Wilkins?"

"Who's that?" Haddie asked. Liz had been quite surprised at the FBI's interest in Harold Holmes and the burnt bodies. The agent had not approached Haddie yet.

Cooper's lips tightened. "What aren't you telling me?"

That I've done nothing but sleep and eat for the past two days. That I've got strange, ancestral powers out of nightmares. That I killed a man. Haddie shrugged, leaned forward, and rested her arm on his inbox until it shifted. "Bought Rock a new chew toy as kind of a get-well gift." She resisted looking over the rim of her sunglasses. "Are we done?"

Cooper frowned, then gestured toward the door. "Keep out of trouble and off my radar, Ms. Dawson. Stay inside the lines."

CHAPTER 48

Haddie sat on the fat blue couch in Dad's office. The smell of grease and gas coated the air. The last remnants of the sunset played on the oak tree outside his window. As she held her phone, she examined the healed edges of her burn.

Rock whined, stuck in his cone, trying to get comfortable leaning his head on her leg.

She reached in and rubbed under his chin. "Don't worry, Momma's gonna take care of you."

Dad's face had become almost recognizable. They both healed quickly. She couldn't grasp all the implications. It was still too much.

"What are we, Dad? What were they?" she asked, scrolling through the news reports on the murders at the Harold Holmes estate.

He leaned back in his chair, boots on his desk beside a bottle of aquavit. "I don't know." He tossed back a shot. "Other than me, I never thought there was anyone else." He pointed at her with the empty shot glass. "Or that there ever would be anyone else."

She paused, looking up from her phone. "I think I know what we do."

He looked over and nodded, as if for her to continue.

Haddie still hadn't worked through all her feelings. However, she didn't feel threatened or apprehensive, waiting for the next attack. "I told you about the ghost." She touched her white hair, flowing over the brown leather jacket. "I think it was Harold Holmes' brother, parts of him at least. I think we push people, spread them out through time."

"Like their molecules?" He grimaced. "Gruesome."

She cringed. She'd been the one to make the brother disappear. "What if they did a swab of the area and a DNA test? Has anything like that been done?"

Dad shrugged. "Forensics haven't been that developed until lately. It hasn't been an issue for me."

"What do you know about . . . our abilities?"

"Not much. I came into it by accident." He frowned, as if remembering something. "I didn't even know it was me the first time. It happened again, and I was afraid of it. I eventually learned that intent was important."

"Intent?" she asked.

"What I intend to disappear, I focus on. Helps it work properly, without taking other things with it."

She'd been working on the zip ties, but the entire chair had disappeared. Could she have mistakenly affected the floor, her arms, or even her dad? Haddie shivered.

"The other thing I've learned," Dad said, studying his shot glass, "is that mass causes the most damage." He gestured the drink toward his chest. "To me."

That made sense in her moving-molecule theory. She sighed and returned to her phone. They'd planned on a couple of days of rest. The college had taken the attack on her into account, giving her arm time to heal. She glanced from her screen to the bright red scars on the back of her hand. Dad thought they might go away. "So, what can kill us? Beheading?"

He downed his aquavit. "Don't know, haven't tried that."

A better question would be what he'd survived. He'd lived for a very long time. That might be a longer conversation.

Her phone buzzed. She had text from David.

"How's it going?"

"Okay. Hanging out with my dad."

David typed, "I'm thinking we should skip coffee."

Haddie flushed and stared at the screen.

He started off with winking emoji. "Move right to dinner? Too much?"

She snorted. "Maybe." She let the text sit for a moment. "I like Thai."

David sent a beaming emoji. "Tell me when and where."

"Soon. Gotta go."

Still smiling, she searched for more about Harold Holmes on the news. Haddie frowned at the image that she'd navigated to, the burnt corpses that Dmitry Markin had left in the Ford Explorer. One, burned but whole in the back seat, with a charred face and white teeth. The second, blackened body parts crumbled into the passenger seat and floor. They were likely the two men who had been tasked with killing Dad and the brother. "Harold Holmes and his brother . . . they were different from us – at least they had different powers."

Dad poured another shot. "I noticed."

Someday, somewhere, there had to be a clue. *What am I? What are we?*

<<<< End >>>>

Penumbra - Book One in the AngelSong Series is to be released in the winter of 2022 followed by each book in the series. Each novel is scheduled to come out on a monthly basis.

Red Tempest - Book Two

Coerced - Book Three

Demons' Lair - Book Four

Infrared - Book Five. (End of the AngelSong Series)

All books in the series have been written and at the time of this writing are waiting on edits.

Please join my mailing list if you'd like to be kept up to date on this series and the upcoming Khimmer Chronicles series.

ACKNOWLEDGMENTS

A large part of my ability to follow through with publishing this book is attributed to April, my wife. Without her listening to my ramblings and concerns, I might not have continued forward until we reached this book. She has also provided developmental, copy, and proof edits at points. She is not one to mince words and sometimes they stung, but they always brought me to a better place.

If you've reached the end, then Robyn Huss, my editor, is the one you need to thank for that. She has taken some of my worst writing and made it my best. The laws that govern the English language are beyond my retention and I constantly slip into old, bad habits until she points them out to me, once again.

Brandon Sanderson with his YouTube BYU class, David Farland at Apex Writers, Jody Nye at DragonCon, and other masters of the craft have been my mentors wherever I could glean a piece of advice from them.

My writing groups from JordanCon, DragonCon, and Apex are irreplaceable in making sure I keep on track.

Thank you.